"Tarantino meets Hiaasen on the wrong side of Honolulu in *Careless Love*, a high-spirited, high-octane thrill ride from Steve Zettler."
JON CLINCH, AUTHOR OF *FINN* AND *MARLEY*

"Zettler's story is sweeping, yes—yet he crafts it with such intimacy that I devoured, endured, delighted, suffered all his characters' beauty and ugliness with each word."
CHRISTOPHER CHAMBERS, AUTHOR OF *SCAVENGER*, AND
BLACK PANTHER: TALES OF WAKANDA

"Rough and profane with a big heart, this is a love story like no other—and a harrowing reflection on the Vietnam War and those still living with its consequences."
JASON REKULAK, AUTHOR OF *THE IMPOSSIBLE FORTRESS*

"*Careless Love* is a powerful, can't put-it-down novel that will bring tears to even the most callous reader's eyes. Steve Zettler tells the gripping tale of a young artist whose dying mother drops a bombshell: the artist's father was not who she'd said he was. What follows is a relentless search to learn about the true father by traveling to the Hawaiian resort where the artist's parents first met and uncovering, bit by bit, the heart-wrenching, bittersweet details of their deep, ill-fated love. Vividly written, *Careless Love* depicts a passionate couple struggling to overcome scars of the past, endure betrayals and violence, and run away in time to escape tragic fate. Careless Love is a zinger of a tale that will stay with readers long after they've finished the last line."
MERRY JONES, AWARD WINNING AUTHOR OF *CHILD'S PLAY* AND
THE WOMAN IN THE CUPBOARD

"Steve Zettler's *Careless Love* illuminates the lives of others to understand the lies they tell themselves. To know the truth of another is to navigate the darkness of lies and untruths but we yearn as voyeurs to live vicariously and viciously through knowing who someone else is."
ADAM BYATT, AUTHOR OF *MOUNT PLEASANT*

About the Author

Steve Zettler is a professional writer, actor, and photographer. He is the author of the international thrillers *The Second Man, Double Identity,* and *Ronin.* He is also the coauthor of the *Nero Blanc Mystery Series.* He has worked extensively as an actor in New York and in regional theaters, and created a memorable role in a Pulitzer Prize winning play. He has also worked on countless television shows and many feature films.

More information is available at
www.stevezettler.com

steve
zettler

Cover design by Jessica Bell
Cover images by
Interior design by Amie McCracken

A catalogue record for this book is available from the National Library of Australia

For Cordelia Dietrich Zanger

"Only the dead have seen the end of war."
Plato

Grace

At her memorial service, I wanted to believe my mother's story had something to do with me, that I was in some way a player, that I factored into her bygone scenario—the life that was hers before I was born. A little crazy, a little self-centered, I'll admit.

"Jesus, get a grip, will you?" Frances had said to me more than once.

At the time of her death, my mother was approaching her seventies, a vibrant woman, and much too young to have left me an orphan. At my age I never suspected the word "orphan" would apply, but it does. There is a certain vacuum that invades your spirit when both of your parents have evaporated. I was angry with her and the world, feeling totally deserted, and at her service I cried only for myself. Not one tear was shed for her. That much is clear to me now, and it has been a cause for a good deal of personal discomfort. I couldn't for the life of me get used to the word; orphan. How could she have done this to me? Just left. It seemed so unfair.

Then for some unanticipated reason on a thick morning in mid-August, I stared into my bathroom mirror with a changed perspective—one that wasn't nearly so egocentric.

It's hard to explain but I felt she was there, gazing at me through the glass and also telling me to get a grip, figure it out, grow up. I saw her, that much I know. But I saw my mother as a winsome young woman. I was finally able to stand at a distance and see things from her viewpoint. Almost instantly I had a craving to know her in her younger days. I didn't bother to dress; I went straight to my studio, took out a new canvas and painted the image that had invaded my mind. It took nearly a week and when I finished I sat on my battered acrylic-and-oil-stained studio couch with my dog and studied her for hours. I realized that in all likelihood she had spent her entire life feeling herself robbed. And in reality, at the time of my conception, my mother and all of the men and women that I would eventually come to know were much different people, living in a different era. How could her mind, their minds, have been concerned with the psyche of someone yet to be born?

I'll go back. A few weeks before she died my mother decided the time was right to tell me the truth about my father. I can't say for sure what brought this on, but I can only guess she'd come to the realization that death was approaching and so felt she had a certain obligation, if nothing else, to set the record straight. I'll admit, at times her frankness would shock me—using words and phrases that stunned me to silence. She was kind, loving, fair, generous and honest, so naturally I was a bit surprised to learn that there was an entire episode of her life about which I knew nothing. I now understand that she would speak of the events more for herself than for me, which ultimately is how it should be.

She began by informing me that the man she had divorced when I was not quite a year old; the man who had taken me, despite the collapse of his marriage, to Disneyland on an annual basis; the man who took me to Athens and

Istanbul after my high school graduation; the man who took me to the Getty and Los Angeles County Museum on more occasions than I can count; the maniacal baseball fan who treated me to countless Dodgers games, at least ten a year, including every game of the 1988 World Series; the man who, quite literally, held me up as yet another one of his achievements; the man who paid for my entire education; and the man whose ashes my mother and I had placed in a vault at Forest Lawn Cemetery twelve years ago, was in fact, not my father at all. I'd like to say that this revelation left me speechless. It should have, but it didn't.

"Get out of here. Not Nick? What the hell are you talking about? That's not possible."

My mother, Grace was her name, always had what some would call a flare for the dramatic, and at first I wasn't certain whether this bit of business was fact or fiction. God knows she loved to surprise people, and I was often her favorite target. Like many of her friends, I had always considered my mother a very strong person, certainly someone I, as well as everyone she encountered well beyond her friend-ships, admired. Though I never once stopped to examine from where this strength might have come. And to specu-late that there was once an age when she was possibly a less strong, less confident individual seemed anathema. But clearly that time and place had existed. She was an abused woman who had broken the cycle of abuse with, as she put it three days before her death, "more than a little help from a friend."

That friend was Sally Fulton, our neighbor and the mother of Frances. Frances was born just a few months after me and we've shared virtually every thought since the 1980s. We went to grade school and high school together. When we were thirteen we believed we had invented oral sex and spent several days trying to figure out a way to trademark it. It was Grace, of all people, who found us out and informed us that people had been doing it since the beginning of time. It was nothing new. She then sat us down and gave us a "birds and bees" lesson that was far more detailed than many pornographic movies. And later it would be Frances who helped me forge my way through my mother's dying days and set me out on a life-modifying odyssey.

It seems tragic that so often we wait too long after they are gone to analyze the lives of those we have loved. But in the end, it was this love that compelled me to examine Grace's life more closely. These roads aren't always that easy to traverse. They can be like muddy paths after a drenching jungle rain, and quite often one wishes they had never started the journey in the first place.

My father's name was Nick. And like many kids in Southern California, I grew up calling my parents just that: Grace and Nick. The one thing that still seems strange about all of this is that if I were to be called upon to tally up the number of times people told me how much I resembled Nick it would be well into the hundreds. "There's no doubt about whose kid you are," seemed a constant refrain in my youth. Why these Hollywood types think that's an original line I'll never know. I've heard it so often I could choke.

At any rate, if this man I grew up with, on selected weekends and school vacations, wasn't my birth father at all, I honestly believe he was just as clueless to the reality of the situation as I had been and therefore died believing in his heart and mind that he had sired a child. And why not? I was born, according to Grace, nearly two months premature in 1980, so all mathematical calculations, with regard to any possible fertilization date, are out the window. However it turns out there are no hospital records to back up this claim of hers, and Nick evidently didn't ask any questions. I can only wonder if it was simply because he was afraid of what answers he might discover—the answers I would discover. At the time of his death, he had been nominated four times for a Best Director Academy Award and had won twice. He was wealthy, he lived in a make-believe world, and anything he wanted to make happen, happened. His creativity was endless. Reality was what he chose it to be. If he didn't like what he saw he stepped into his own world of fiction and closed the door.

Despite the charming and rugged man's-man image, Nick Rolston presented to his public, along with the testosterone infused films he made, and all of the generosity he ladled in my direction, he was not an easy person to live with. He was a classic narcissist and misogynist, and if I could recognize this, my mother must have known it far better. And at the time, I'm sure that my parents' divorce came as no surprise to any of their close friends. Being only a year old, Frances and I were far too young to remember a moment of it. Though we sure talked it to death as teenagers. We were no longer teenagers—that hasn't stopped us from talking.

"You have to figure this out. You can't let it drop after one staggering, mind-blowing statement from Grace. You need to get her to open up about this; it's the only way you maintain your sanity. Which, by the way, has always been somewhat questionable. I hate to be even more blunt, but time's running out on you."

"I'll think about it."

"Fuck thinking about it. Jesus. There's some guy out there walking around who's your father—your real father. You don't want to know who the hell he is? You don't want to, I don't know, maybe, say, meet him? Have a friggin' conversation? Get his name, for Christ's sake?"

Frances was right; she generally is. I had a lot to learn.

"You're all set, Grace," Sally had said. "I'm driving you to
LAX tomorrow morning. Pack enough for a week. Don't forget
a bathing suit."

It was a sweltering Tuesday in mid-August 1979. After
carrying on a not so clandestine affair for over a month Nick
had finally asked her for a divorce the previous Friday. And
Grace, who was known to have the ability to turn the most
dismal of occasions into a rodeo simply by walking into a
room, had been stunned into absolute silence. Even Sally
was astounded by her reaction.

"Come on. He's a shit, and you know it. Sorry, but he is.
We all know it. You had to see the handwriting. Snap out of
it. Don't tell me you didn't know this was coming."

Grace said nothing.

"Well, there's no turning back now. I've set everything
up. The Pickering Club is the perfect place to find a new
perspective on life. You'll like it. No one will bother you.
Nobody bothers anyone in Hawaii. That's why God put it
there, out in the middle of nowhere. You'll have a full week
to think. More if you want it; just call me. You need to get
the hell out of the Palisades right now and be alone. Nick
may be gone, but he'll walk through that door any time he
fucking feels like it, even if it's just to piss on the bushes,
and you know it." Sally studied Grace for a full minute. She
wasn't happy with what she saw. "Okay, fine, don't talk, but
I'm taking you to the airport tomorrow, like it or not. Even
if have to put you in handcuffs and strap you to the plane's
seat. The club is expecting you. There will be a car waiting
for you in Oahu."

My mother never remembered a word of that particular
conversation. I had to get it all from Sally. Nonetheless,
Grace did acquiesce. She told me that by the time her mind

became somewhat focused on her surroundings she was sitting in the LAX-TWA lounge, chain smoking cigarettes and pressing the wrinkles out of a first-class plane ticket—destination, Honolulu.

"Wait. Hold on a second. You smoked?"

"Back then, yes. I guess I never told you that either. Sorry. I smoked like a fiend."

"Christ. You think you know someone."

"I can't believe I put Sally through all of that. I was a basket case. I didn't know where to turn, and she pointed me in the right direction." Grace was quiet for a while, and then added, "Are you certain you want to dive into all this? It's not pretty."

"Are you? That's the question. I'm sure I could go to Hawaii and piece it all together on my own."

"You should do that anyway. You'll feel better about yourself."

**

As my mother chose to remember it, it began like this: a question, *What happened to your finger?* had floated into her head, and so it was, in fact, what drifted from her mouth. Very little thought was involved. But that could be Grace at times; it made sense to me. I'd seen her do it time and time again—she always spoke her mind. By her own admission, she seemed to give those words little weight and no discernible emotion, letting them fall into the warm Hawaiian night air with a good deal of indifference. They meant nothing to her at the moment, and if she had given them any serious consideration she would have most likely said something else, or perhaps nothing at all, and just passed him by.

"What happened to your finger?"

These were the first utterances of any real significance my mother had offered for quite some time, and only faintly significant at that. But I learned they would, in the years to follow, cling to her inner soul and remain dreamlike until the day she died. "What happened to your finger?" They were the very first words she'd spoken to him, and she would never regret what some might call her complete lack of tact.

Grace Rolston had been silent, had not said anything for over a week. Correction, she had not been totally silent—clearly she had spoken a few words to our neighbor, Sally. There must have been a response to the ground attendant when the woman had asked, "How many bags will you be checking?"

"Just this one."

And then the reply to the olive-skinned young woman at the Pickering Club reception desk after arriving in Honolulu: "Grace Rolston. You should have me down for a week. Sally Fulton arranged it all." And a few hours later to the round and eternally smiling dining room waiter, "I'll have the lamb, medium-rare... If you can swing it?"

"Yes, ma'am."

But that was it. The previous week had been nothing more than a series of nods and headshakes designed to communicate the words, yes and no. And a not-always-polite shrug that was intended to mean maybe. These headshakes and shrugs had for the most part been accompanied by a pleasant-enough smile when she could muster it, but even the casual observer should have been able to see that my mother was in some kind of serious turmoil. I've learned that at the time Grace was not so good at playacting. Camouflaging turmoil would not have been in her bag of tricks, however she was astute enough to conclude that these casual Southern California observers, all with pleasant enough smiles of their own, couldn't care less if she was in any kind of turmoil, pain, or upheaval. Her husband had just walked out on her, so what?

It was the realization that not a soul had a speck of interest in her plight that convinced her she'd made the right decision when she'd opted to tuck that .38 caliber revolver into the corner of her suitcase under the crimson two-piece bathing suit from Lucie's on Rodeo Drive—just in case the days and nights in Hawaii became more of the same; just in case no answers could be found even though Sally, the one person who had shown a modicum of interest, promised on her soul that there would be answers in Hawaii, if she gave it time. Seeing was believing as far as Grace was concerned.

Answers? she thought. *There are no answers.* My mother freely admitted to me that she had no intention of ever returning from Hawaii alive. Suicide was very much on her mind that August.

"I want you to have it. There is no need to be afraid of a gun. Everyone has one now, which is a good thing. It's loaded, so be careful. I've set up some lessons for you at a range out in Topanga. It's for your own protection. It's yours. Hide it somewhere in the house. Somewhere you'll be able to find it easily, of course. And please, for Christ's sake, don't lose it. That's all I need is LAPD connecting me to some drive-by in Crenshaw."

It wasn't Sally who'd said that. Sally wouldn't knock anyone in that manner. It was Nick who'd said it. *Probably five years ago? When he gave me the gun? At least five,* Grace reflected as she pushed a half-eaten, once-frozen, chocolate éclair across the pink linen tablecloth and past the sweating glass of ice water towards a white carnation in a pink porcelain vase. Nick had given her the pistol for protection. *Right. Protection.* It had been five years before this little jaunt to Oahu, to be sure. I found the yellowed receipt next to her will, though apparently my mother dropped the pistol off the Catalina ferry into the Pacific Ocean shortly after I was born. She told me it was Nick's use of the word, *own,* as in *own protection,* that had always made her laugh.

"My own protection, Nick? Don't you mean this castle's protection? This monument to your achievement? Your corner of California that I stand guard over night after night while you run around the globe? God forbid someone would steal one of your precious pieces of art."

"Think what you like, baby, but I don't feel comfortable with you being here alone, 'night after night,' as you say. This town has more nuts than The Big Apple. You need to be protected, that's all. All women do. That's where it's at. Look what happened up in the hills the other week? The weirdoes? That's all I need is a dead wife... or that kind of publicity."

I need to be protected? Hah, there's another laugh.

Though the fact was, she had been protected by Nick from the day she'd met him. He'd gathered her up like a stray cat and handed her an existence that should have been altogether out of reach. Her hair was pampered by a salon in Beverly Hills, *thank you, Nick.* The dark teal dress she was wearing that evening had cost eighteen hundred dollars, *thank you, Nick.* Her makeup was supplied by studio professionals, *thank you, Nick.* Her home, her tennis lessons, her car, her appearance, all of it handed to her by Nick. And now that she was in Hawaii to create some space between herself and Nick, she was being *protected* by Sally Fulton.

"I don't know how to put it, other than I was just then swallowed up in a wave of depression. I woke up to the fact that I wasn't a real person any longer. I owned nothing. I had no roots to fall back on. No family. Anything I ever cared about was fading away right before my eyes."

Those violet eyes of hers scanned the formal dining room of the Pickering Club. It was an ocean of pink. Eighteen tables covered in pink linen. The white flowers in their pink vases. Pink-on-pink wallpaper, and painted pink woodwork. Waiters and busboys in starched pink Eisenhower jackets with matching pink shorts, with pink grosgrain ribbon stitched to the seams, and pink knee-socks with white loafers. The only relief in color came from lushly green and leafy potted palms that had been scattered near the doorways. But the yellow glow dancing from the candles, chandeliers, and wall sconces cast the plants in a shade of green that more resembled World War II serge uniforms. Padded pink Naugahyde covered the swinging doors that led to the vast kitchen, and both the *in* and *out* doors swung lazily as the wait staff cleared the last of the tables and prepared them for dawn's breakfast service. She said she felt that her body, her auburn hair, and her teal dress clashed with everything on the island of Oahu.

Just one couple remained from their ritual evening meal. They were perched at a table near the kitchen doors and they sat stonily, smoking filtered cigarettes, drinking house brandy, and not speaking to one another. They appeared to be in their fifties and kept their eyes fixed on Grace for the most part, finding nothing else of interest in the room at that late hour, no doubt.

Grace glanced down at the diamond-and-ruby-inlaid platinum watch that hung from her slender left wrist. Nick had given it to her one Christmas Eve. *What was it? Eight years ago? Who knows? And who really cares at this point?* It had arrived by way of overnight courier from Cartier in Paris with a note saying, "I'll be in L.A. by New Year's, promise. Sorry about this, baby. Hate to miss out on Christmas, but I'm bringing home the bacon. Nick." The note, not in Nick's handwriting but that of a Cartier sales clerk, still folded and kept wedged in the gray velvet box in which the watch had arrived. The dial on the watch now showed nearly a quarter to twelve; almost three in the morning in L.A. But Grace felt no jet lag, only a weariness, and a cigarette seemed the next logical step. She slid the heavy rattan chair backwards, stood, and worked her way through the forest of pink and palms and out onto Pickering Club's wide wooden veranda. The older couple's eyes followed her every step of the way, as though by leaving she had insulted them in some fashion.

It wasn't that club members were forbidden to smoke in the dining room in 1979, the pair in the corner had been puffing away all night; she just needed to distance herself from their stares. If she had rented a car she would have driven to a deserted beach—somewhere dark, stopping to buy cigarettes along the way perhaps.

The fact that Grace had no cigarettes, the fact that she had failed to bring any to Hawaii in the first place, in no way impeded her slow but determined trek to the veranda. Things would have to work out. Except for this damn marriage of hers, things generally did work out for Grace. She was that kind of a woman. She was lucky. She was lucky to have traveled this far in life without going off the deep end, she would tell me. It's just that no one had ever bothered to point out how lucky she was, so her belief was weak in August of 1979. At this juncture, a sense of despondency and hopelessness clung to her like a tick, so *lucky* wasn't occupying much space in her mind.

She spotted him instantly. *Too young and good-looking for this place*, she thought, *I wonder what his problem is? He's got to have one. Everyone has a problem these days.* His hands rested on the veranda's brightly-painted wood railing, his gaze was fixed on some nonexistent object far off on the moonlit horizon. Perhaps it was that date palm that held his attention, most likely it was nothing. *Right, he's the type that looks at nothing. Looks at nothing for so long he thinks he sees something where nothing is, and nothing ever will be. Not in our lifetime.* There was an aspect that was unfocused about him. *A dreamer maybe? Who else focuses on nothing?* But he was a smoker, Grace was sure of it. He had the look: dark deep-set eyes, lines at the corners well before his time; scotch and cigarettes all the way, no doubt about it. *Okay, maybe not scotch, maybe… Hell, I don't know. Who gives a damn as long as he has an extra cigarette?* Mid-thirties, she guessed, dark brown hair that fell over the tops of his ears; an expensive cut, and just long enough in the back to touch the collar of his dinner jacket. *Had to be cut by a New York barber; L.A. salons never do hair like that. Why is he alone? Gotta have a problem, or a disenchanted wife in at the bar sobbing. That's probably more like it.*

Grace approached him silently from behind, but then halted. She stood in his shadow for what seemed an eternity—as if some child, some young girl, maybe even herself at twelve, had stepped up and erased the blackboard that was her mind; leaving it nothing more than a grayish slate, streaked with blurry shades of green and blue pastel chalk. She thought, *I really don't want to go any further. I want it to be over. Asking strange men for cigarettes? This must be the bottom. The abyss that's nothing but black smoke; smoke that closes in on you until there is no more oxygen. Then Lucifer greeting you as a long-lost cousin, promising to be kind, gentle.*

And that's when, "What happened to your finger?" floated from her mouth.

He turned slowly, looked down at his left hand, and then looked at Grace. There was an odd smile; a smile that made her think, *Maybe he doesn't even know his finger's missing. Maybe he thinks everyone in the world only has a thumb and three fingers on their left hand? Maybe he doesn't speak English? Maybe I should go back inside? Hide? Retreat? Run?*

He said, "I lost it." And then after the smallest pause added, "To be more precise, someone stole it."

"Stole it?" she asked.

"It's a long story."

"How does someone *steal* your finger?"

"It's a long story."

"It must be... You don't happen to have a cigarette, do you?"

"I quit about three years ago."

"Shit. I should have known. Everyone has. What's the world coming to?" She smiled at him and felt a strange sensation in her jaw, as if she were using muscles she didn't know she owned, as if English had become a lost language to her and she should be speaking in Portuguese or French. "Why did you do that? You should be more prepared for people like me to drift into your life with no warning. So did I... Quit, I mean. More recently, though. You seem to be having greater success than me."

Am I flirting with this guy? I should have my head examined. She glanced off to her left, then tried her right, wanting to run away. The veranda was empty. Shadows from the rustling palms danced across the open space and the flickering made it appear as if they were actors in a silent movie. He mistook her movements, believing she was still searching for someone with a cigarette.

"Forget it," he said. "It's just me out here. We seem to be among the few guests content to finish dinner at eleven-thirty. Except for those two old-timers by the kitchen door, the rest of them have all doddered off."

Grace laughed. The sound seemed odd to her, almost new. It had a ring of sincerity, which surprised her. "They were giving me the creeps. Did you get a good look at them? Do you think they were mutes? I never saw their lips move. Not once. I guess they could have been stuffed. You know, mannequins, just dropped there by management to give the place a feeling of animation?" She was quiet for only a few seconds. "'Doddered.' Now that's an excellent word. You and I must be it... I mean, *it*, as far as people under the age of forty go. Do you think any of these fogies check in much below fifty-five, sixty?"

"A couple of the busboys are fairly young."

"Hah. They don't count; they work here. Busboys are always young. That's why they're called boys. Sooner or later, they graduate to waiter and no one ever calls them boys again. It's a restaurant thing. I speak from experience. A tragic story, really. Did you know about any of this before you came? The age barrier? All that friggin' pink? Jesus, I've never seen that much pink before in my life."

"I've been here before."

"You're kidding? You've got to be kidding me? Why on earth did you ever come back?"

"It's a long story."

"You're full of long stories, aren't you?" Grace leaned on the railing next to him, almost close enough to touch. She tossed her head to her left, and then right, and her long dark auburn hair blew away from her bare shoulders in the slight breeze, leaving it trailing straight down her back and halfway to her waist. *Yes, I am flirting with this guy and I don't care who cares; I really don't.* "She didn't prepare me for this."

"She?"

"The person who suggested I come here. My neighbor. The person who arranged this stay for me. I mean my room at the club. I'm here on a friend's membership. Believe me, I don't belong. To the club, that is. She didn't tell me everyone would look like my grandfather."

"Maybe she was trying to protect you."

Grace looked at him from the corner of her eye, without turning her head. "What the hell does that mean?" *Protect me? Has this guy been reading my mind? This is nutso.*

"Nothing, really. It's just that it's pretty hard to get into trouble out here. That's why certain people, certain people our age, are told to come... By the older people that is. People who believe they need to protect other people. Protect us. People like us. People they think are in trouble. People that may need to be talked off a ledge. It wouldn't be the first time."

A stiff breeze kicked up. It lifted her hair and swept it across her face. She shook her head once more and leaned back over the railing. And again her long mane fell off her shoulders and dangled to her waist behind her. He laughed.

"What's so funny?"

"No, no, I was only thinking how ridiculous that all sounded. I'm sorry, don't pay any attention to me. I just haven't talked to anyone all day. I'm rambling. That can happen here. Opportunities for meaningful conversations are limited to the bartenders. Anyway, you can't get much more buffered than life at the Pickering Club."

"I'm going to let you in on a little secret... I can get into trouble anywhere. Don't tempt me. This place could use some fireworks."

"No argument from me."

"All I want is a cigarette. And I sure as hell don't need to be *protected*. And I am not in trouble. And I'm not out on a ledge, so there. Not yet, anyway. Maybe you are, but I'm not... *Are* you in trouble? On a ledge?"

He laughed again and looked down over the railing. The drop was about thirty feet into a bed of leafy philodendron.

"Don't do it. You'll ruin the tux, you'll live through it, and feel like shit in the morning... You didn't answer the question. Are you on a ledge? You're not running from the law, are you? Are you a cat burglar? You kinda look like one. Got that Gary Cooper thing going for you. Wouldn't that spice things up? Screw the fireworks. I have some very nice jewelry. Take this watch, for instance. It's from Cartier. The Paris store."

Whether he had a response or not, nothing came. He didn't even smile; nothing like the casual observers of Los Angeles. They would have laughed out of politeness. They would have picked up on her facetious demeanor and laughed, even though they had no idea what the hell she was talking about.

"Do you feel like helping me locate a cigarette?" she said at last. "I mean, since you've been here before you might have a better idea where to start. The place is deserted, and I'm not going anywhere near those crones in the dining room. I've seen *Rosemary's Baby*. Next thing you know I'll be giving birth to something with hooves."

Now he laughed. "If I was a nice guy, I'd say no and do my bit to help you quit."

"But I don't need to be protected, remember? Least of all by a..." She stopped, regrouped her thoughts. "Besides, you're not a nice guy, I can tell by looking at you."

"Really? How's that?"

"Nice guys don't lose their fingers. People don't just lose fingers by minding their own business."

"I told you... It was stolen."

"I want to hear about that."

"Maybe we should get you a cigarette first."

Ronnie

"We'll try the kitchen. The club no longer has a cigarette machine." He slid his hands into the pockets
of his black trousers as they moved toward the Pickering
Club dining room. "I think the new manager's Swedish. He
had the machine tossed out. I gather he's a health nut. He
certainly looks healthy enough."

"And you still came back?" Grace said, forcing a smile. "You
must be a sucker for punishment. I would have definitely
taken the fact that there was no longer a cigarette machine
on the premises as an omen. Even hospitals have cigarette
machines in the waiting room. You can't watch people die
without having a cigarette every now and then, even if you
don't smoke. It makes you feel as if you're participating in
the death process in some small way... Okay, the kitchen.
I should have thought of that myself. I used to work in a
restaurant. There's always a cigarette in the kitchen; usually
in the cook's mouth dangling over someone's dinner order."

They strolled together across the veranda—again close,
but not touching. He would later tell her that he'd felt
he'd known her far too well already, as though he'd slept
with her in a past life many times. That his mind had been
chewing over the fact that she was wearing both a wedding

and engagement ring—evidence he had consciously looked for the moment he saw her. And he had smiled at himself, undeniably disappointed to see the rings, already jealous of the man who had put them on her finger.

He reached forward and opened the dining room door for her, and the gauzy pink curtains were sucked out into the humid night like waves of golden-red tissue paper. They were momentarily blinded by the sheer fabric sweeping across their faces.

"What kind of restaurant?" he asked as they pushed the curtains from their eyes. It was a sincere question, not just something to make conversation. She didn't see it as small-talk; he seemed to have an actual interest. The tone was one she hadn't heard in years, perhaps never.

Still, Grace found herself wanting to lie. She told me that the truth, at this point in her life, seemed jarring to her senses. *I've come too far. I've escaped, haven't I?* She'd gone beyond serving cheeseburgers and beers in a dive in Long Beach, beyond living at home and all the ruination that went with it. She had no desire to look back, to be reminded of that life, of the abusive people that had once crawled into and out of her bed. And the pain—all the pain, emotional and physical—that went with it. Then as quickly as the veil began to close before her, she said another emotion swept through her brain, and a voice said, *Don't lie to this man. Don't do it. Don't go there. Bring an end to the lies, Grace. You're getting a second chance. Grab it.* And the young girl returned to write something on the blackboard, and Grace's eyes scanned the words and her lips moved and she read the words aloud. "It was an Irish pub in Long Beach."

"Long Beach, New York? You live in New York?"

"California."

"Ah... Because I live in New York."

Grace refrained from replying, *Really? With that haircut and accent? What a surprise.*

The dining room of the Pickering Club was nearly dark. The candles on the tables had been extinguished. The couple in the corner had vanished, but their table was not yet cleared of empty coffee cups, dessert plates, and brandy and water glasses. The chandeliers had been dimmed to a low amber glow allowing a soft bluish light to filter in through the French doors on the south side. He walked between the tables toward the kitchen with the ease of a dancer or a wine steward who'd worked the room for decades. Grace followed, thinking she should take his hand as if he was guiding her through a dense thicket with a thorny underbrush, albeit pink. There was a feeling in her that she would be lost without him, and she stayed close on his heels. The faint clatter of colliding pots, dishes, and glasses could be heard from the opposite side of the padded swinging doors, along with the soft murmur of Hawaiian voices.

"I think we're in luck," he said, and pushed against the entryway. Grace thought it curious that he had no compunction about walking straight into the kitchen of a private restaurant.

A flood of garish green fluorescent light cascaded from the kitchen and into the dining room, attacking them and washing out the features of their faces, giving their skin a flat appearance, as if they were wearing pale jade ceramic face-masks. The harsh illumination stung their eyes. They both squinted, and then turned toward each other before lifting their eyelids. He smiled and so did Grace. She flared her nostrils. The kitchen smelled vaguely of the Opakapaka that had been the dinner special.

"You're sure you want to do this?" he asked.

"You make it sound as if we just entered through the gates

of hell and there's no turning back. Which, I might point out, you did without giving it a second thought. You seemed like you owned the place. Anyway, all I want is one cigarette. One lousy cigarette. That's it. Then I'm really quitting. For good. I can guarantee that. I'll never have another."

"Moving on, then?"

"Yes. That's exactly it. I'm moving on."

He twitched his shoulders slightly. Grace interpreted the movement as a shrug. She lowered her brow as her violet eyes scanned the kitchen. There were six large gas ranges with overhead broilers along the far wall. A huge gray-black exhaust hood hung above them. A long stainless steel steam table spread out in front of the ranges with a pickup wait station at the end farthest from the dining room door. Beyond the ranges was an area for washing pots, and beyond that sat a large stainless steel commercial dishwasher. The kitchen walls were painted a light shade of institutional pea green. A dark-skinned Hawaiian scrubbed away at the pot sink and others were finishing up the last of the dinner dishes, silverware and glasses, and laughing with one of the busboys. None of them seemed to notice that their space had been invaded by a couple of light-skinned Haoles.

"Do you think they speak English?" Grace asked softly.

He laughed. "This is Hawaii. White people have been making their lives miserable since the 1700s... The Pearl Harbor Navy Base? Not too far from here. World War II? The Army barracks? Didn't you ever read *From Here to Eternity?* See the movie? Burt Lancaster? Frank Sinatra? Montgomery Clift? How about Captain Cook? They're having their twentieth anniversary of statehood in a week? Believe it or not, that makes them Americans. My money says these guys speak better English than I do."

"Thank you for the history lesson, Kahuna, but there was

nothing there I didn't know… Who hasn't seen *From Here to Eternity?* After *Rosemary's Baby* it's my favorite movie. You forgot to mention Donna Reed and Ernest Borgnine. Look, I don't want to sound like a racist, because I'm not, but in Southern California, not everyone with brownish skin tones speaks English all that well. I just forgot where I was, that's all." Grace took a deep breath and sighed slightly. "I say the guy washing out the pot sink is our best bet. That's how it worked at O'Rourke's in Long Beach. All the pot washers smoked. It probably was the first question on the job application."

"I gather some of the waitresses smoked as well."

"Very funny, but a good point. Actually the entire crew at O'Rourke's smoked. But that was back in '68. Everyone smoked *something* in '68. Even Nih—" Grace stopped herself short. *Was I going to say, 'Even Nick'?* The last thing she wanted to talk about was her husband. It's why she'd come to Hawaii in the first place, wasn't it? To put distance between herself and Nick. "Real distance," as Sally put it. The kind of distance Nick could never cover in his lifetime. *Nick*, she thought, *Jesus, how could one person make another person's life so miserable?*

"Are you okay?"

Grace smiled at him. "Peachy."

"You don't look *peachy*. *Peachy* is not a word I would have used. You look more like someone just slapped you across the face."

"Thanks. I'll look better after a cigarette. Do you mind asking for it?"

"I shouldn't, but I will."

"Yeah, yeah…"

He crossed the kitchen, but Grace followed him only half way, stopping next to a broad wooden butcher-block table.

The edges were scarred with slashes and gashes and there was a small gully in the center of the aged wood carved out by the many meat knives and cleavers that had assaulted it throughout decades of use. She ran her hand over the rough yet oily surface, visualizing the pork, beef, and lamb blood that had seeped into the heart of the wood. Again, she thought back to her days as an O'Rourke's waitress, her days before Nick. Things had seemed so simple then—not very pleasant, but at least simple. Then Nick had walked in the door and her life forever changed. Changed for the better, sure, after all was said and done. But she wasn't feeling any of that at this point in time.

"Excuse me," he said to the Hawaiian at the pot sink.

The man looked up from his work. "Yes?"

"Ronnie? This is what bartenders do with their time off? Wash pots?"

"It's a long story."

He turned and looked at Grace who was smiling. "I suppose I deserved that."

"Kind of a late night for you isn't it, Mr. Corbet?"

"Yeah, well, for you too, I guess?"

"Daytime pot washer didn't show up, so I stepped in. Flakey dude. Been out for almost a week now. He's got a problem of some sort. I've never seen a pot washer without a problem. Skinny little Haole hippie, this one. Spacey. Not sure why Mr. Pressten ever put him on, unless he was looking to..." Ronnie took a moment to consider what he was about to say. "Never mind... But what the hey? Everyone's got a problem these days—ever notice that?"

"Not really."

"Sure. Look around, Mr. Corbet, just look around you. Problems, that's all you're gonna see. You're a lucky man if you believe they only belong to other people. Trust me, they're contagious. They'll infect you if you let them. Anyway, things got switched up here in the kitchen. Don't ask... I'm picking up some O.T. Why not? Baby needs shoes, right? Isn't that how it goes? But the thing is: the kitchen's closed. Chef's gone home, short order cook ducked out as well. Gave me a few bucks to clean the grill for him. Sorry. Not a thing to eat. There's a jar of hot red peppers, that's it. But they're always out because nobody has the stones to eat them. Sorry, I forgot about the lady. Anyway, they locked the walk-in fridge before they scooted, like we're going to swipe a steak or something. See, that's what I mean by problems: the left hand doesn't trust the right anymore. Brothers steal from brothers. I've seen it happen."

"No, I wasn't looking for food, I was wondering if you might have a cigarette you could spare?"

"Just one?"

"That should hold us."

"It wouldn't hold me. They're Luckies. I'm not sure the lady's gonna go for them."

"How do you know it's for the lady?"

"Good point."

Ronnie held up his wet hands and leaned his chest away from the pot sink. He glanced down at the breast pocket of his flowered shirt, which was nestled under the bib of his black rubberized work apron. The move exposed an open pack of cigarettes. He smiled and said, "Go ahead and take a couple. I have a carton back behind the bar."

Corbet shook his head. "One will do us, but thanks for the offer." He removed a pack of Lucky Strikes from Ronnie's shirt, shook out a cigarette, and returned the pack. "Thank you, Ronnie."

"Not to worry."

"You may have helped save someone's life."

"Yours or hers?"

He only smiled, crossed over to Grace, and said, "No filter."

"Beggars can't be choosers." She then waved to the bartender, and though he wore nothing on his head, he made an amiable gesture that resembled a 1950s style hat-tip.

"So much for me being cagey. I didn't want to let on it was for you."

"Why not?"

"It didn't seem... It's just me."

"And who said chivalry was dead?"

As they walked through the dining room, Grace lifted a book of matches from one of the tables, and after they found themselves back on the veranda, at the exact spot where they'd met, she said, "I'll trade you. You give me the cigarette and I'll give you the matches. That way you can do the gentlemanly thing and light it for me."

He did as she asked. Grace sucked the thick smoke into her lungs and said, "Christ, I needed that," as she exhaled. "Want a drag?"

He shook his head and said, "Even, who?"

"Pardon me?"

"Even, who? Back in the kitchen you said, 'Everyone smoked something in '68. Even Nih—' Then you stopped yourself mid-word and maintained you were 'Peachy,' which I didn't believe for a second. Remember? I said you looked like you just got slapped in the face. So, even who?"

After giving it some thought Grace reached up, seductively placed her hand on his neck, and pulled his ear down to her mouth. She then whispered in a very husky voice, "Even... You. *You* smoked in '68. You admitted it. You said you'd only quit three years ago."

When she released him, he said, "And, I don't believe that for a second either."

"No. But it seemed a lot more polite than saying, 'None of your fucking business,' didn't it?"

He laughed. "Good point. How long has it been since you quit?"

"This morning. I left my cigarettes in the airport lounge in L.A. Even asked for a nonsmoking seat on the plane so I wouldn't be tempted to bum one off of any of my fellow passengers. I thought I had it licked. The timing seemed right. Actually, it still does. I'll be fine after this one."

Corbet glanced at his watch. "Well, given the time difference you've managed to last over twelve hours. That's very commendable."

"Commendable?" And she laughed. It sounded more like a bit of a choke, which embarrassed her to a certain extent. "Thanks."

Grace inhaled deeply once more and let the smoke slowly drift from her nostrils and mouth. She pulled a small piece of brown tobacco from the tip of her tongue and flicked it over the railing and into the night air.

"Yep, that's me all right, a very commendable person." She took another drag. "Do you have a name? Other than Mr. Corbet? Which happens to be what I heard the pot washer call you, in case you think I have some unique mental abilities."

"Lee."

"Lee, huh?"

"Yep. And you?"

"Grace."

"Grace? That's your name, Grace?"

"Something wrong with it?"

"No. I just figured you for a more Southern California name; you know, one that ended in a 'Y,' or 'I-E.' Debbie or Sherry, maybe... Barbie?"

She again choked slightly on the smoke. "Please. Don't make me laugh. I want to enjoy this cigarette. It may be my last."

"If you're planning to quit, I'd guess it is your last. Or is it more like a firing squad at dawn?"

"Firing squad," she said dreamily, and not as an answer to his question. Grace took three more drags from the cigarette before she spoke again. "Is it true that only one soldier on a firing squad has the real bullet and everyone else has blanks? That way none of them know who fired the fatal shot?"

"Have you ever fired a gun?"

"No... Not yet, anyway. I was supposed to go to a range once, but... Never mind. No."

"When you do, if you do, you'll be the first one to know if the gun has blanks or real bullets in it. Real bullets give you a very nice kick, blanks don't."

"I see. A nice kick, like Cole Porter's champagne. Well, to everyone other than Cole Porter, that is."

"Right. But a hell of a lot quicker. And you don't wake up with a hangover... You don't wake up at all. Depending, of course, on which direction the gun is pointed."

"Isn't it ironic that you would also consider that there are in fact two directions in which a gun can be pointed? Rhetorical question, no need to answer, but it's something you might want to look into."

"I suppose everyone's considered blowing their brains out at one point or another. Human nature."

"Even you?"

"Even me... More than once."

She stepped back a few feet and looked him up and down. She smiled at him and said, "So I don't look like a Grace? Well, you don't look like a Lee. You look more like a Dick."

"Thanks."

Grace spun around and faced the building, turning her back on him. She felt the warm blood rushing to her face, and she quickly folded her arms over her chest, feeling unhinged. Her face was hot and her body was now cold. She was immediately aware of her stiffened breasts straining against the silk of her thin dress.

"I can't believe I said that. I'm sorry, I really am. All I meant was that you look like someone who doesn't take a lot of crap from people. Believe me, it was a compliment. In other words, I expected you to have a name with a harder edge, that's all. Jack, Frank, Rick, Hank—you know, something that ends in K. I have nothing against Lee... I have nothing against Dick for that matter." Grace brought the cigarette to her lips and once again inhaled deeply. "Say something, will you? I think it's well beyond the time for me to shut the hell up."

He once told her that the temptation to approach her from behind at that moment and place his hands on her bare shoulders and pull her close was almost too much for him, he found her that attractive. But he reluctantly held back. *Hell, she's married. A disenfranchised husband's probably sitting out at the bar right now crying into his beer.*

"Well, you weren't all that far off," he said at last.

"Meaning?"

"It's Peter. It's Peter Lee Corbet. And if you want to be real picky about it, my father and mother are French. The birth certificate reads Pierre, and the last name would be pronounced *Cor-bay* if you're in France."

"Peter doesn't end in a K."

"No, I guess you're right. My mind must have gone to something else."

Grace walked to a nearby deck chair, bent at the waist,

and crushed the Lucky Strike into an ashtray that sat on a small wrought iron table next to the chair. "That's it. I've quit. It's the new me." She turned to face him. "So, who stole your finger, Peter Lee Corbet?"

He leaned back against the railing and smiled at her. "That can wait. Ancient history, really. Not worth... What I mean is, I don't really like to... Look, we're both here for a week, right?"

"You may be. I'm not convinced I'm going to last that long."

"Really?"

"Really."

Mitch

I found the real players in this odyssey not overly difficult to track down. Only in their sixties and seventies, most of them are still alive and well, living in Honolulu, Ronnie being a perfect example. In 1979, he was the beach-side bartender filling in as pot washer. In twenty-two years, he would be elevated to the general manager of the Pickering Club, a position he still holds to this day.

After her death I took my mother's advice and traveled to Hawaii. Three trips in all, and Ronnie never failed to greet me like a long-lost relative. He was instrumental in helping me fill in some of the gaps in Grace's story. Nothing gets by the bartenders; they have memories like elephants. They don't forget names, they don't forget faces, and they like to talk. At any rate, the people I would eventually meet offered up the missing pieces and often unsavory details with far more enthusiasm than I ever expected or required, or for that matter, cared to hear about in some instances. It seems to me that Baby Boomers take a certain amount of plea-sure in being blunt. I've yet to be convinced it's a good thing. Nonetheless, there were these three days in 1979—three days that had left an everlasting imprint on their minds. Memories they would take to their own graves and at times give them grotesque nightmares, cold sweats, and sobbing fits. All of them had been left shaken to their core, knowing it was a tragedy that could have well been avoided. Each and every one of them had been left with an unfading scar.

"Raymond Slack."

In her last days, my mother must have uttered this name a half-dozen times. It was never vocalized within a complete sentence, only the name alone. And when she spoke this name her face became so tormented and contorted I almost believed she was having a seizure. Regrettably, by the time she mentioned Raymond Slack she was medicated to a point that she was unable to explain who he was or how he fit into her life. It was the first I'd heard the name; the drugs seemed to be functioning as an exorcism of sorts. The name escaped her mouth as volcanic ash. Because Grace's final cohesive thoughts were focused on Lee Corbet, I was left to assume Raymond Slack somehow played into her extended week in Hawaii. I would learn that she met Raymond Slack only once. They never spoke to one another.

When I first arrived on Oahu, I opted to make Raymond Slack my starting point, thinking he had little or nothing to do with Lee Corbet. Therefore, once I got the facts straight, he could be removed from my list of people to track down. I had checked into the Pickering Club in the late afternoon. As with Grace, Sally Fulton had arranged everything for me. She provided Ronnie with what must have been a full dossier on me. He greeted me like family. He was clearly very fond of Sally Fulton. There was very little I told him that he didn't know already. He's now in his sixties, but I can't imagine he looks much different than he did when he was washing pots and approached by Grace and Lee those many years ago. He likes to tease, he likes to laugh, but when conversation came to Grace and Lee a serious side surfaced.

"I can give you the same bungalow your mother stayed in if you like. But there are others available if that would be difficult for you."

"No, I think I need to walk in her steps if I want to make any sense of it all. Her bungalow would be fine."

As he escorted me to the room, he cleared his throat for no apparent reason, which made me believe he wasn't enthusiastic about what he was planning to say. "Now about Raymond Slack..."

"Yes?"

"I could give you a lot of second-hand information and opinions; I never met him, but I think you need to go to the source."

"The source?"

"Yes. The Honolulu Police Department. You'll want to talk to a Lieutenant Ho. He's a friend of mine. He handled the investigation. He's probably gone for the day, but I'll give him a call and set you up with an appointment for tomorrow. Okay?"

"The police?"

"This is it, bungalow seven... You need to talk to Lieutenant Ho."

Even though I had never been to Hawaii, the bungalow was pretty much what I expected: king-size bed, overhead fan turning lazily, straw rugs, and rattan furniture with red and orange hibiscus-printed cushions. I walked every inch of the room, bathroom, and patio trying to visualize Grace, but nothing stirred any emotion. It was as if she had never been there. Despite the heat, the room felt cold to me. I had come to know that rooms lit up when Grace walked into them and perhaps that was the issue: the windows were covered with heavy drapes and opening them had little effect. There was no real light. The palms and lush gardens kept the sun at bay. The bungalow was still dark. Only the small patio received direct sunlight.

Taking a shower that evening, I stood under the water for a half an hour. I hadn't gone to Hawaii to paint, but I found myself missing every aspect of it. I cursed myself for only bringing a sketchbook. I missed the stickiness of acrylic, the smell of oil, even cleaning brushes. Despite being jet-lagged, I didn't get much in the way of sleep that night. I can't say I had unpleasant dreams; I can't say I had any dreams at all. It was just that my eyes refused to close. I yearned to do something with them, so I sketched an empty room in charcoal.

**

It turns out the Honolulu Police Department has a fairly extensive file on Raymond Slack. Lieutenant Archie Ho remembered him very clearly. Raymond has a "rap sheet." He is no longer alive and all of his unpleasant history is now a matter of public record. He had several charges of aggravated assault, he spent innumerable nights in different city "drunk tanks," three convictions for driving under the influence, a driving without a valid license charge, endless citations for disorderly conduct, one charge of witness intimidation, and one charge of aggravated manslaughter. Other than the various Honolulu "drunk tanks," Lieutenant Ho said he never spent a single night in a Hawaiian correctional facility.

"It's not like I didn't go after him. Witnesses wouldn't testify."

My background is not that of an investigator. It would never suit me as a career —it's exhausting. In my case, not so much physically exhausting, but certainly mentally. I'm guessing that someone with more experience in this sort of thing, someone less emotionally involved, could have rooted out the truth within a few weeks. However, it was all too personal for me to hand over to a professional. I needed to meet and know the people involved. It makes no sense, but I needed to know Lee Corbet as a person, as my father.

It took me nearly a year to piece together the events that led up to Raymond Slack's death. He was not a likable person, to say the least. It seems that in the course of his life, he left little in his wake apart from misery and abuse: mental, physical and sexual. Many times throughout my search for the truth, I became so repulsed by what I had learned about Raymond, his family, and companions that I wanted to look no further, fearful of what or whom I might turn up next. But to a large degree I had become possessed. I needed the answers. I wanted desperately to know my true father. And once I got started, I was unwilling to turn back until I found those answers.

Murderer is perhaps an overly-potent word. It is a word the Honolulu Police Department and Detective Ho have chosen not to use. They prefer aggravated manslaughter. Murder appears nowhere in their paperwork or files on Raymond Slack. But murder and murderer are the words that will forever gnaw at my inner being: Raymond Slack was the man who murdered my father, Lee Corbet. There has been a certain closure in having unearthed these events, the events that led up to Lee's killing. But now that all the pieces of the puzzle are at last in place, now that I know Lee Corbet and have come to admire him, I can't help feeling anything more than cheated. And I would guess that my mother must have felt cheated every day of her life, right up to the very end.

Raymond Slack had a brother, Mitchell. Currently Mitchell Slack owns a spice shop, which is simply called Mitchell's. It's a short walk from Waikiki Beach. When one enters Mitchell's shop, there is no question as to what's on the market. The olfactory nerves are bombarded with a plethora of aromas. It takes one's breath away. I'd guess Mitchell is over seventy years old, but he looks to be more in his early fifties. He's reserved, or laid back, depending on the moment or one's perception of him. He can seem spacey at times. He drifts.

Mitchell's is a one-man operation, and when I introduced myself he was arranging various sealed packages of spices in small wooden barrels. He let out a quiet, sad laugh and said, "Well, it's been a long time, a very long time, but somehow, I've always been expecting to meet you."

"Really?"

"I know more about you than you'd expect. I've actually seen some of your work in a magazine, I think. And I'm at that point in life where I read the obituaries. Your father was famous, which in turn made your mother notable. Notable enough to have her death mentioned in the *Star-Advertiser* a few weeks ago. I met her only once. She was a lovely person. Strikingly beautiful. She loved hot red cherry peppers. Quite a bit, in fact. Did you know that? I'll bet not. I've never been able to lose the image I have of her eating them. She was ravenous that day. And given the events of that evening, I'm not likely to forget her. Ever."

He took the cash drawer out of the register and placed it into a small safe under the counter. "And of course, the newspapers had a field day with all of it. I didn't save any of the clippings, but I'm sure you can find them at the *Star-Advertiser*." And then, after a slight pause: "Come with me. I want to show you something. It won't take long."

Mitchell closed his shop, took me to his car, and we drove in silence to Diamond Head Memorial Park. We then walked about a hundred and fifty yards and stopped. He pointed to a brown-gray lava-stone grave marker. It read: Raymond G. Slack, 1945 – 1979.

"He's dead."

"It was Lieutenant Ho who told me where to find you."

"Well, then yes, of course you know he's dead." He stared at the marker for a full minute before he looked at me and spoke again. "Every now and then I wake up in a cold sweat and think that maybe it was all just a gruesome nightmare. On those mornings, I come out here as a way of confirming that it wasn't a nightmare at all, that it really happened. I thought you might want that same confirmation." He glanced back at the gravestone. "At the time, I borrowed $175 from my boss to purchase that marker. I was broke and essentially homeless at the moment." Again he paused for a minute. "He was older than me, and I'd called him Ray since the day I was born. It seemed so odd to put Raymond on the stone, but I guess that's the way things are done. At least, that's what the funeral director said, anyway. So that's what I did. Even now, it doesn't look right." He was quiet for another minute or two and then added, "Have you talked to Trace?"

"I don't know who he is."

"I'm sorry. Tracy. I call her Trace. Have for years, but I'm probably the only one who does. She's not a he; she's a she, a woman. She took me in for a bit after Ray died, kept me off the streets. I'll put you in touch with her. You need to talk to Tracy."

After a year, two more trips to Honolulu, and a number of lunches with Mitchell and Tracy, this is what I learned:

On August 13, 1979, at slightly after two in the morning, Ray Slack walked out to his Chevy pickup truck. He purposely dug the heels of his blackened boots strenuously into the oil-soaked asphalt that made up the rear parking lot of Cookie's Joint. This swagger put undue strain in his faltering knees, but the sound of the hard rubber striking the macadam with a uniform precision had become familiar to him, so that's how he walked. I suppose it reminded him of days gone by, at least that has become my conclusion. There was a crispness to his walk that clearly comforted him. It may have given him an illusion of a discipline that had somehow managed to elude his life in recent years. I will never know.

Cookie's Joint, a strip club labeled CJ's by its regulars, sits a quarter of a mile outside the U.S. Naval Reservation on Puuloa Road, just to the west of Pearl Harbor. An hour of watching young women in various stages of undress had left Ray in a semi-aroused state despite the five Blue Ribbon long-necks he'd absorbed. However his mind wasn't simply on naked women, not on this night. Not like it had been a few nights past when he tried to rape Tracy Tillis, his younger brother's girlfriend, on the seat of his pickup in this very same parking lot. No, this night his mind was chewing over the information that Tracy had just fed him regarding his brother Mitch and how Tracy had tossed Mitch out of her apartment on Tuesday, effectively ending their relationship and then changing the locks to keep Mitch from getting back into her life—ever. Their relationship was officially over and done.

"Splitsville," Tracy had said with a small frown that seemed to suggest she was unhappy that it had come down to this. "Yep. Me and Mitch are done with. There's no goin' back. He crossed the line."

"What line's that?"

She only gave Ray a shrug.

"What'd ya throw him out for, Tracy?" Ray asked, drilling his steely eyes into her as she gyrated her pelvis less than a foot from his nose.

No answer.

"Well, where the hell is he? Where's he been sleepin'?"

Still no answer. She had nothing more to say to him.

"It ain't because I tried to screw ya, is it? Is that what this is all about? About me and you? Or is it about you and Mitchie? Which is it? Or you just gettin' sensitive? You don't want to make this a family affair?" Ray winked at her and wagged his tongue. "You think you'd be the first babe Mitch and me ain't both nailed? At the same time? Hell, we done 'em together lots of times in the old days. Ain't nothin' new to Mitch and me. 'Fraid you might learn a trick or two?"

Tracy didn't answer those questions, either. She just removed her halter top, waved her breasts in his face, gave him a slow wink of her own, and then danced down the bar and postured herself in front of a lanky Black sailor just in off of the USS Quepaw.

Tracy, whom I'd met a few days after Mitch, had told me she believed Ray would have cracked her in the mouth right then and there if CJ's hadn't been jammed with an assortment of GIs, half of whom she believed probably would've never seen things Ray's way.

Giving up on her, Ray tossed a dollar on the bar and walked out to his truck. He spent the next fifteen minutes perched stonily behind the wheel his pickup, engine idling, listening to a Crystal Gayle tape and trying to figure out where his brother might have gone, and where Mitch had been sleeping since the past Tuesday night. At one point, he reached into the glove compartment, pushed aside a loaded .45 caliber pistol, and removed a leather strap that contained a collection of talisman-like trinkets, items surviving from isolated episodes in his life. He hung the strap from the rearview mirror and every now and then proceeded to tap the objects with the backs of his rough knuckles, as if the items contained some mystical powers that would miraculously point his Chevy in the direction of his wayward younger brother.

Ray ran his fingers through his thick black hair and then smoothed his equally dark mustache down onto his upper lip, matting the few erratic hairs into the bushy Fu-Manchu. The stale odor of beers swallowed drifted into his nostrils. He lit a cigarette and tossed the match out onto the asphalt. Mitch was only a year younger than Ray but there was an emotional, as well as a physical, lifetime separating them—so much so that one might wonder if they had the same father. Ray was square-jawed, sinewy, and muscular: a chiseled man who appeared to have covered a good deal of ground in his thirty-four years. Men would avoid Ray, sensing there was a brutal or violent side that was better off left alone. But this rawness, this animal-like demeanor, had a way of attracting certain women, women who thirsted for a measure of dominance in the men they dated. Ray had sized up Tracy Tillis as one of those women. I would later learn that his instincts about Tracy weren't far off the mark.

Ray's brother, Mitch, appeared the eternal teenager: slight, impressionable, soft-spoken, fair-skinned with sandy blond hair; bartenders still asked him for I.D. when he ordered a beer. And even in 1979, with both of them in their thirties, Ray felt that with no real parents to speak of, it had become his obligation to take on the burden of safeguarding his flighty younger brother, though apparently this safeguarding didn't apply when it came to bedding down his brother's girlfriend.

"Kaluamoi Drive," Ray said under his breath as he flipped his cigarette out of the truck. "Why not? The stupid bastard has no imagination." He then dropped the Chevy into gear and pulled out of CJ's parking lot, certain of his brother's whereabouts.

Kaluamoi Drive is just off of Highway 99 on the northern edge of Pearl Harbor. The USS Arizona Memorial rests less than a mile across the black water. Mitch had spent a week roaming this same strip of land five years earlier when he'd first arrived on Oahu, his tail tucked between his legs, ultimately unwilling, or perhaps too intimidated, to call his older brother for assistance one more time. By his own admission, Southern California had got the best of him. He'd run out of hiding places and Hawaii seemed a salvation, just as it had for Ray four years before that. It had been the police who'd picked up Mitch back then—they'd called Ray only after Mitch had reluctantly confessed to having a brother living on the island. Kaluamoi Drive: that's where Ray Slack would find Mitch Slack, once again passed out on a bench.

**

Ray scrutinized his brother's scrawny sleeping physique. He didn't look any better on this night than he had when Ray'd picked him up at the Honolulu police station in 1974.

He shook his head, disgusted at the pathetic image before him. He then forcefully kicked the bench where Mitch had curled up. He snarled a tenacious, "Get up."

The bench was concrete and didn't so much as vibrate under Ray's assault. Mitch didn't stir either, so Ray grabbed the back of his brother's shirt and dragged him off the bench where he fell onto the pebbled walkway. He pushed the tip of his boot into Mitch's ribs three or four times—not serious kicks, but enough to inflict a stinging pain.

"Aw, fuck, man," Mitch groaned.

"Get up. Get in the truck. You can sleep on my couch for now. Move it. It's late. I gotta work tomorrow."

"Shit, Ray, leave me alone, will ya? I'll figure this out."

Ray reached down and grasped Mitch's shirt once more. He yanked him to his feet as if he were working marionette strings and pushed him towards the pickup. Mitch stumbled forward. Ray placed his boot on the small of Mitch's back and kicked him, harder this time. Mitch tripped and sprawled out once more on the gravel, scratching the side of his face on the small stones.

"Get up, ya little bastard. Ya think I ain't got better things to do than to look out after you, ya shit? Get in the fuckin' truck. Now."

Like an abused dog, Mitch did as he was told: silently, with no follow-up complaints. He sat quietly in the passenger's seat while Ray stood outside the truck and smoked a cigarette. Ray lit a second cigarette from the first and smoked that down as well. Eventually he crushed the butt into the dirt and slid in behind the wheel.

Mitch mumbled something, prompting Ray to spit out the window and say, "What the hell'd you say?"

Mitch's voice was tenuous and lacking in any sincerity. "Thanks..." He looked straight through the windshield, avoiding Ray's still steely stare. "I guess." Then as Ray slipped his key into the ignition, Mitch motioned to the leather strap that hung from the rearview mirror. His hand shook slightly. "I've never seen this thing before, Ray, what the hell is that? A finger?"

Ray started the truck. "Goddamn right it is. What's it look like?"

Mitch pushed his face even closer to the dark leather thong that hung like a warlock's necklace, back-lit by the white, blue, and yellow lights that illuminated the sunken war memorial in the distance. The light beams jounced and reflected off the choppy water of the harbor, seeming to hit the objects from all directions at once. The Pearl Harbor breezes that blew in through the truck's open windows had no effect on Mitch's long, greasy, and plastered-down blond hair, but scraps of moonlight shone onto his face, accentuating his angular features and scraggy beard—a beard that said nothing more than he hadn't shaved in close to a week. He was a better-looking man than his present condition would indicate, but there was no hint of a family resemblance to Ray. There was nothing fierce about Mitch.

Attached to the leather thong, along with the withered and dried human finger, was a collection of seashells and beads, a silver ring with an orange stone, a chipped piece of tortoise shell, a small hawk's feather, a set of military dog tags, and a 7.62mm bullet.

"This from Nam? The finger?" Mitch asked shakily, bringing his own finger up to touch it, but then pulling back out of fear. Not fear of the mysterious finger per se, or the voodoo-like image the collection on the leather strap seemed to represent, but out of fear of what violent reaction Ray might have if he actually did touch the finger.

"Well, what do you think, dipshit? 'Course it's from Nam. Some skinny little Gook pointed it at me, screamin' and yellin' like there's no tomorrow, just 'cause I greased his damn kid and dog, the little fucker. So's I just hacked that sucker off his hand with my K-bar and shoved it straight up his skinny yellow ass."

"No kidding? You never told me about that. Did ya hafta pull his pants down? I mean to do it? How'd ya get it out of there? Wasn't it all covered with crap?" Mitch was very serious in his asking.

Ray just stared straight ahead as he eased his truck onto Route 99. In reality, Ray's Vietnam tales were mostly fabricated, like this particular version of the finger story and how he'd acquired it, but this was the first time anyone had suggested to him that a person would need to remove another person's trousers in order to shove something up their rectum. No one but Mitch could pursue the logic of a statement that far. The comment caught Ray off guard, something Mitch's naiveté was prone to do. And Ray wasn't happy about it. He'd been trapped in yet another one of his falsehoods. His response in situations like this was almost always overly aggressive. He loved playing the "whacko" Vietnam Vet to the hilt, especially with his younger brother. He enjoyed seeing the fear his behavior created in the eyes of others, and he relished in taking advantage of the emotions he was able to stir up in the people who were terminally attracted to his brutality.

But Ray was now reminded of how burdensome life with Mitch could be, and already beginning to second guess his decision to search for his brother and offer up his couch.

"A week. That's all ya got, ya little shit. You don't find a place in a week, I'm gonna throw you right back onto that fuckin' bench. Ya dig?" They were silent for over five minutes until Ray lit another cigarette and said, "'Pull his pants down.' What a dumb shit," as the smoke left his lungs by way of his mouth and nose.

In reality, Raymond G. Slack had technically served in Vietnam, but records show that his combat experience was completely nonexistent. He'd been a military policeman in Da Nang with the First Marine Division, and had lasted "in country" a little over nine months, six months of which were spent doing time in his own brig for dealing opium-treated marijuana sticks to the Sea Bees who were working on the airstrip. Upon release from the brig, he'd been shipped straight to Camp Pendleton in Southern California and had been summarily drummed out of the Marine Corps with a Bad Conduct Discharge, ducking serious jail time only because the Marine Corps had its hands full with more important issues in 1968. I later found that the United States Marine Corps was happy to be done with the likes of Raymond G. Slack.

"Them Gooks sure got some small-ass fingers, don't they?" Mitch said, ignoring Ray's 'dumb shit' comment.

"It's a pinky, doofus."

"Oh... Yeah. I'll tell ya, Ray, you know I woulda been right there alongside of you in Nam, you know that, if it weren't for my allergies. Remember me tryin' to get in? And no one would have me? Air Force, Navy, Coast Guard—nobody. You laughed at me, called me a pussy and a faggot? Remember? But there wasn't nothin' I could do about it. Man, I'd sure as shit would love to be able to say I was a Marine over there... Like you." As with the finger story, Mitch knew nothing of Ray's less-than-stellar service, brig time, or Bad Conduct Discharge until many years later.

"Well, you sure as shit can't say it, junior, so don't even think about it. You got to walk the walk before you can talk the talk."

Forty years later Mitch was still unable to come to grips with the fact that the only "walk" his older brother had ever made was the walk from a Da Nang whorehouse to a brig cell.

When they arrived at Ray's ground-floor one-bedroom apartment it was nearly three in the morning. Mitch lit a Kool and dropped onto the couch—a couch that would become his bedding for the foreseeable future. The cushions had been stained with an assortment of fluids, from coconut oil suntan lotion, to Blue Ribbon beer and Dr. Pepper, to take-out hot-and-sour soup, to the damp mementos deposited by the occasional prostitute or loose woman Ray would entertain, women who would never rate a visit to the sanctuary he called his bedroom, a bedroom that would be off limits to Mitch as well. The couch had previously belonged to a wannabe frat house at Kapi'olani Community College where it had no doubt seen the same sort of action, and before that was anybody's guess. The couch's wooden framework squeaked under Mitch as he shifted his slight weight and hoisted his flip-flopped feet onto a spice crate from Ceylon that served as Ray's coffee table. The ash from his Kool fell onto the couch and he brushed it onto the floor.

"Ah, shit. Sorry, Ray." He then inhaled deeply, shook his head, and eventually sighed emphatically. "Fuckin' Tracy..."

"Yeah, fuckin' Tracy. No shit, fuckin' Tracy. So what gives? What's with that bitch, anyway? She gettin' sensitive all of a sudden? What I'm wonderin'."

"She's got some balls throwin' me out like that, that's all I can say. Gluin' up the locks so's I can't get in, then changin' them while I'm off washin' pots and makin' me miss a whole week's work at the damn Pickering Club tryin' to get my head together. Tryin' to figure out what the hell's goin' on; which end's up... Man, I never beat up on her like you did Bobbie. I never hit her in the face, Ray, never. That's where I draw the line. I smacked her on the ass, that's it. Thought she'd like it, really. Thought she'd like to try something different. Broaden her horizons." He choked on his cigarette slightly. "The world's changin'. Know what I mean? Gotta try somethin' different to keep it fresh. She's got some 'nads, that's all I can say." He took a long drink from the can of Blue Ribbon Ray had handed him and then shook his head dramatically from side to side in an effort to emphasize his not-so-believable bewilderment.

"Hey," Ray said, pointing a finger at his brother, "I didn't let Bobbie get away with no crap. You gotta nip that kinda shit in the bud quick. These babes will walk all over you if ya don't. I busted the windows out of her damn Camaro, remember? She learned her lesson."

Mitch laughed. "Yeah, she sure did... So scared of you she moved back to the friggin' mainland. I wish you'd just passed her on to me. Bobbie had some great tits. Remember her tits? I woulda loved to take a roll with her before she flew the coop."

Ray's jaw tightened noticeably. "Look dickhead, alls I'm sayin' is, we can do the same thing to Tracy if you want. I don't give a shit, 'cause... Well, I don't care no more. Especially about Tracy, if you know what I mean. You ain't the only one she's done wrong, I'll bet... You know what she's like. Yours ain't the only set of balls she's messed with. She's the type just waitin' to screw up a man's head." He picked up Mitch's cigarettes from the crate and lit one for himself. "I got no use for these babes think they're so damn smart. Think they got some right to push their men around. We go bust the windows outta that apartment, and she goes running back to daddy in... where the hell's she from, anyway?"

"Minneapolis."

"Yeah, that's right. Minnie-fuckin-apolis. She goes runnin' home and you take over the pad. Then ya bring a babe in on your terms. Then you're the one throws them out when you want. You shoulda never got yourself set up like this in the first place." He pointed again. "You get your own place this week. That way you don't need to get down on your knees for no one. Ain't no reason to let people push you around like you been. Ya gotta draw the line. 'Specially with someone like Tracy, damn ball-buster. Ya gotta grow up, Mitch. Stand tall. Be a man."

Ray downed what remained of his beer, walked over to the kitchen area, and tossed the can into the sink. He then crossed into the bedroom and returned a minute later with two baseball bats. "Finish your beer. We're gonna go take care of that fuckin' Pinto of hers."

Mitch held up his hands. "Nah, hold on, hold on, Ray. It don't mean that much to me. I don't need no more run-ins with the boys in blue neither. I'm walkin' the straight and narrow from now on. I'm a changed man. A couple nights on a bench'll do that for ya. Helps ya clear your head. See things ya didn't see before. Realize your life's gotta change. Besides that road out there sucks the big one, and I ain't slept real good for a week."

Ray threw the smaller of the two baseball bats at his brother. "Who said you were driving, dipshit? Grab a coupla beers for the ride. I'll be out in my truck. I got some weed in the glove compartment."

McCracken

G race drew the stiff hairbrush slowly through her long auburn mane and studied her murky reflection in the still-steamy bathroom mirror. A plush white towel with the Pickering Club crest embroidered in pale pink and gold clung to her chest and dangled loosely over her tanned thighs. Behind her, on the other side of the bathroom door and above the large bed, the ceiling fan rotated lazily, doing nothing more than shuffling the hot humid morning air from one corner of the bungalow to the next. She looked down at the sink, and the countertop that had been fashioned out of jade-pigmented ceramic tiles. There was a teak tissue box and a compatible teak tray where she'd emptied out the contents of her makeup satchel, and next to those items sat the .38 caliber revolver Nick had given her for her *protection*. Its wooden handle matched the tissue box and tray so well that it seemed to be part of the ensemble. Her wedding and engagement and rings sat next to a jar of face cream like unwanted prizes from a gumball machine.

I should have just taken the damn rings off in the L.A. airport. It's over. Nick's shacked up with someone else… Again. Why did I even wear them over here? Even Sally told me to leave them behind. Why didn't I take them off three weeks ago? Four weeks ago? Two years ago? What do I owe Nick? Do I need to take these things to my grave, for God's sake? I mean, really, what do I owe Nick?

Her mind then settled on the previous evening and how Lee had walked her to her room and then lingered, not keen to walk off. How she'd stood in the doorway, un-anxious to end the day, despite being on L.A. time. It seemed ironic that she'd started it all by asking him about his missing finger, and then it had ended with him focusing on her finger, her ring finger, her damn wedding ring. He'd remarked on the ring itself, though he didn't seem to give a damn who she was married to; he never asked, he didn't care. *But he had taken the time to look at my left hand.* At least he found her attractive enough to do that, which was all she really needed at that point in time. She needed to know she wasn't a discard, Nick's castoff. She needed someone to be interested in *her* for once, and not Nick. Even if it was for just a day... or maybe two.

"It's over," she'd said to Lee at last. "My marriage is over," It was the first time she'd voiced that sentiment aloud, although the seeds had been planted twenty-some months earlier when Nick had been working on his film set in Morocco. The tales of his infidelity had reached California with lightning speed. Los Angeles could be a very small town when it came to slinging the dirt from one shindig to the next. After all, what good are friends if they can't keep you up-to-date on who your husband's sleeping with? Of course Nick had denied every sordid piece of the gossip upon his return. She wanted so much to believe him then. She needed to believe him.

"I should have taken the ring off a long time ago."

"Do you still love him?" Lee asked.

The question surprised her into a dazed silence. She didn't know if she loved him, if she had ever really been *in* love with him, and she didn't know how to respond. She couldn't recall ever having said those words to Nick, nor could she remember Nick saying them to her. It was a strange sensation for her: again, this inability to speak, this inability to pull a fistful of fittingly glib words out of thin air at a moment's notice. She'd struggled for an adequate answer. "Who knows what love is?" seemed so trite a reply. Once again, she was feeling an overwhelming desire for a cigarette. And for some unexplained reason it had become paramount not to lie at this juncture in her life. She wanted no more lies lingering on her soul. If this was to be a finale, she wanted it to be a clean one.

"Because your marriage isn't over," Lee continued, "until that moment you discover that you're not in love any longer. You'll know when you're there... So will he."

"I—"

"And don't dare mistake hatred and loathing for not loving someone." He leaned against the porch's support post and she remained in the doorway of her bungalow. A good four feet separated them, but they might as well have been lying in bed together, she felt that close to him already. "Because love and hate are all the same ball of wax. You know that of course. Everyone does. It's no newsflash. But it'll come back to slap you in the face if you're not careful, if you're not prepared for it. If he's a callous person he'll play on that and suck you dry. Walk you around on a leash."

"You're speaking from experience, I take it?"

He only shrugged, and Grace remembered smiling and looking down at her shoes. "No, I could never hate him. Despite all of his problems, all of what he's done to me... He did save me. He took me out of O'Rourke's, out of Long Beach, got me away from my..." She stopped for a second and again thought, *I don't even know this man.* She then sighed. "He brought me to L.A. He's worth millions. He wants the divorce. It's all his making. I'm surprised it hasn't come earlier. Maybe he's finally decided this affair is the real thing? Maybe he's been struck with a sense of... Who knows what? He just said, 'Take what you want.' Except any of the paintings of course." She forced a smallish chuckle that lacked any sign of emotion. "He has no taste in art... How can I hate him? He's a child. He buys toys. Things. If someone else wants it, he wants it more. Especially when it comes to some crappy piece of art."

Lee didn't respond to that.

"The funny thing is, out of all the women he could have had in L.A, which is anyone—believe me—he's just shacked up with another waitress."

"How old is he?"

She looked him in the eyes and tilted her head. "Does that matter?"

He laughed. "No. I guess not. I'm sorry, I shouldn't be sticking my nose where it doesn't belong."

"Twelve years older than me. He's in his forties." Grace smiled at him. "You really don't care who he is, do you?"

"No." Lee looked off to his left. "Should I? Is he here? In Honolulu?"

"Thank God, no."

"Then I could care less."

"Well, it is his year. He's been hard to miss. His picture's been in the newspapers and all supermarket checkout stands," she said, thinking, *How could anyone not have been sucked in by Nick's PR Machine.* "Back in March, anyway. You couldn't help seeing him."

He slipped his hands into his pockets and shrugged once again. "I can be pretty dense at times... But then, on the other hand, you haven't told me your last name, and you haven't told me your husband's name. You live in L.A., I live in New York—two different worlds. So, I have an excuse really. What'd he do? Murder someone?" He let out a small laugh and looked up at the porch rafters. "No, I would guess not. He wouldn't be shacked up with any waitresses if he had. He'd be shacked up with someone named Rocko in cell block thirty-seven."

Grace then walked over to him and kissed him lightly on the cheek and said, "Good night. Thanks for the cigarette. Thanks for talking to me. Thanks for being kind. Thanks for acting like a friend."

"No act. I would ask you who your husband is, what his name is, out of politeness... But I think I know what your answer's going to be."

"What's that?"

"We're both here for a week?"

Grace laughed at that. "You know me a lot better than you think you do... But like I said, don't get your heart set on a full week. You're a nice person. I don't think I would want to hurt you."

He glanced at his left hand and said, "I've been hurt. You've been hurt. What do you say nobody gets hurt anymore?"

"A world without pain?"

"Sure, why not? That's what the Pickering Club is all about."

"I like that idea." She smiled at him, then added a second, "Good night," and closed the bungalow door behind her, leaving him alone on the porch in the moonlight with the rustling palm leaves and the small night lizards and moths that had been attracted to the yellow overhead lighting.

**

"God," she barked at herself in the fogged bathroom mirror. She then slapped her hands on the countertop. The move made her wedding ring jump from the tiles and forced the Pickering Club towel to fall away from her breasts and drop to the floor. "God, when will I ever learn to keep my mouth shut?"

Grace left the towel where it had fallen and walked naked out to the small private patio behind her bungalow. The hot morning sun caressed her form like scalding bath water. She edged her way over to the long wooden deck chair, and then stretched out flat on her stomach, allowing the rays to burn into her flesh from head to toe.

Every man Grace had ever met, bar none, had wanted to sleep with her simply because she was Nick Rolston's wife. Peripheral Star Fuckers she liked to call them. The moment Nick's back was turned they were all over her. Some of them too old and too far gone to do anything even if she would've said yes. She despised it, she despised them, and she hated the incestuous lifestyle they represented. The clan—Nick's clan. The Hollywood Gang. She despised their lack of morality.

"Goddamn it." She pounded her fists into the padded cushion of the deck chair. "The one man... The one man who doesn't know who the hell Nick is, doesn't care... knows nothing about me, and I've got to wear my stupid wedding ring, and then go on and on about the shit. I need to have my head examined."

This isn't the setup. I'm not following the script here, she thought. *I should be closing the door and locking it, escaping and not opening a new door. I can't get involved with this guy. I can't.*

Grace rolled over onto her back, placing her left forearm over her dark eyes, blocking out the brilliant rays of the Pacific sun. After a time, small beads of dewy sweat formed on her chest, stomach, and thighs. She ran her hands over her body, massaging the salty moisture into her flesh, gliding her palms and fingers over every bump and curve. The slickness, the warmth, the total exposure to the elements, exposure to the hot sun, to the world—it all charged her sexually. She allowed the sensations to consume her, to transport her to another universe—a place where absolute solitude prevailed. Every pore of her skin became an open receptacle. No fear, no anxiety. No one could touch her; everyone could touch her. She was a molecule in space. Sweat poured from her hypersensitive skin. She cupped her breasts with her slick palms, pinched at the stiffened tips with her fingers, and then moved her hands between her thighs and her dripping patch of full red hair. She was lost. She was at last alone: a person with no family, a person with no pain. She remained there as long as she possibly could.

**

Grace laughed out loud, but no one turned in her direction. The Pickering Club dining room looked identical to the way it had twelve hours earlier. Instead of being ten at night, it was now ten in the morning and only four tables of diners remained. Everyone else had clearly trotted off to the golf links or ambled down to the tennis courts or swimming pool or health spa. She wouldn't swear to me that it was the exact same group of late eaters she'd witnessed the night before, but their hair was just as sandy-white or salt-and-pepper gray, and their skin was just as lined and overly tanned. They all still wore near identical garish shades of pink and green, and they all smoked cigarettes. And Lee—he sat at the far corner of the dining room next to a set of French doors, the same table he'd been seated at twelve hours earlier. The differences: he was no longer wearing a dinner jacket and only a cup of coffee sat in front of him. He was reading a copy of the *Honolulu Advertiser.* The dinner jacket package had been replaced by a flowered shirt, a pair of navy blue shorts, and tattered black and brown docksiders worn with no socks. He set the newspaper down and smiled at her almost before she'd spotted him. She smiled back and said, "I think I'll sit with Mr. Corbet this morning," to the hostess. She pronounced his name, *Cor-Bay.*

But it was not to be. As she crossed the room, weaving in and out of the tables, Grace was blind-sided by a man in his mid-fifties. He grabbed at her elbow more firmly than seemed necessary. She stopped and turned, and he placed his other hand on her shoulder. He was the same man who'd given her the creeps the night before, the one who'd prompted her decision to escape out to the veranda. The man who'd driven her to Lee, which she later thought to be a bizarre piece of irony. He wore a Kelly-green blazer with brick-red trousers and a yellow polo shirt. His knit belt displayed a yacht club's burgee, and his hair was parted no more than a half an inch above his left ear. It was heavily greased and combed over to the other side of his head in an attempt to dupe the world into thinking he wasn't completely bald. He said, "Mrs. Rolston, isn't it?" and his coffee-and-cigarette breath was something she was not prepared for. It made her body shiver, and she jerked her head back and away to avoid the fetor.

"Yes. Do I know you?" What she wanted to say was: *Why in God's name do you have your hands all over me?*

"Well, no, of course you don't know me, but my wife and I couldn't help but notice that you dined alone last night and thought that perhaps you might need some introductions. I know everyone who's worth knowing at the club. As my father-in-law used to say, 'Stay away from the New Yorkers.' Fortunately we don't have many of that type here." He chuckled and moved his arm around and over her shoulder and began walking her towards the table where he and his wife had sat the previous night, not far from the kitchen door, all the while squeezing and fondling her upper arm. "Naturally we recognized you from the Academy Awards ceremony. We were pulling for your hubby all the way. That was a hell of a movie he served up."

"I wasn't at the Academy Awards ceremony," Grace said pointedly. "I never go. My husband doesn't invite me. He prefers to go with his current female lead, or lead female, whichever that may be, and even if he did invite me, I still wouldn't go because I don't like those people. They're far too touchy-feely for me." The not-so-subtle grievance was lost on him.

"Well, well, it must have been some other function." He scanned the dining room, not seeming to settle on anything, doing a poor job of miming a search for the missing Nick Rolston. "I gather your husband's not joining you this morning either? I was surprised not to see him last night. Although my wife thought that maybe, just maybe, you came to Hawaii on your own, that he might be off... lensing? So it seemed only polite, if that was the case, to ask you to join us. It's no fun eating alone, I can tell you that much. Groups are far more entertaining, don't you think?" He laughed but it wasn't a happy sound. "Pickering Club humor. Don't mind me; you'll get used to it. We're all friends here, assuming—of course—you're no fan of that dim-wit in the White House. We never talk politics at the club."

"You just did."

"What?"

"Talk politics."

They had reached the table before Grace had a chance to lay any of her political opinions out for him. She guessed they might not be on the same page.

"This is my wife, Bunny. And I'm Tug. Tug McCracken. Bunny and Tug McCracken. We're from Michigan. Grand Rapids. Please do have a seat. I insist. We're film buffs, don't you know."

Grace turned and looked across the dining room at Lee. He hadn't lost his smile, and after they made eye contact he mouthed the words, *We have a week?* and shrugged.

She shook her head. She felt numbed. She'd been found out. These old-timers would never let her sit by herself, none of them would once the word got out that she was married to *Nick Rolston*. And if she chose to sit with Lee, they'd never forgive her. It would be as if she'd personally drawn a scalpel and castrated the Great Director before their very eyes. She sunk into the dining room chair, looked at Bunny McCracken, and said, as politely as she could, "It's nice to meet you."

"Oh, indeed, my dear. Of course it was *Tug* who first noticed you last night." She gave Grace a thin smile. "You actually look quite a bit like Tug's first wife, dear little Margot. That must have been the real attraction for him."

Tug shot Bunny a sharp look that she laughed off, giving him a dismissive and well-practiced wave of her hand. "Oh, yes, my little *faux pas*. We don't like to talk about dear *Margot,* now do we? Margot and her ways. Margot has become a bit of a sore spot, so to speak... Always has been, really, but she's been acting up lately so we've had to deal with her and that daughter of hers. A bit of a tramp, if you must know. But who couldn't have surmised that? Anyway, Tug wanted to run right over to you last evening, but I wasn't positive you were *The* Mrs. Rolston, and I certainly didn't want him to make an ass out of himself." Bunny loaded her pronunciation of the words *Tug* and *ass* with more venom than Grace thought humanly possible. She forced herself to smile, thinking, *I'd probably like the trampy Margot much better than these two.*

"I have a friend named Margot—quite a nice person, really."

"Really? Hopefully not the same Margot, for your sake." Bunny seemed truly surprised. "Well, let us not dwell on that."

"No, no, I think Margot moved out to L.A. from Michigan. Maybe it is the same person?" A total lie, but Grace couldn't resist it.

"As I said, let's not dwell on Margot."

"Okay. I'll give her a call later, you never know."

"Not necessary."

"You know, I'm still not all together clear on how you seemed to recognize me?" Grace said. "I don't think my picture's been in any newspapers or magazines since our wedding day, which was quite a while ago."

"Well, of course not. I mean, it's not like the wife of a world-class director is front-page news. Hardly. Who cares what the wives are up to? But if truth be known, I had the tiniest inkling," Tug held his thumb and forefinger up, squeezed them together, winked, and then placed his clammy hand on Grace's wrist.

"Inkling?" Grace could feel a major falsehood coming on.

"The tiniest inkling that you just might not be Mrs. Nick Rolston, as Bunny suggested, so I checked with Guest Registry this morning—just to be certain. And it said Rolston. Rolston is all it said, no Mr. or Mrs., but the handwriting was clearly a girl's, so naturally I wasn't sure if Nick was even along."

Instead of saying, "*Nick* is it, now?" Grace said, "Oh? I was told that all of that information would be kept confidential here at the Pickering Club. Apologies for my *girly* handwriting."

"Yes, of course. However I'm on the Admissions Committee, and so I have certain... privileges, shall we say? Access to registration cards, and so on." He leaned into Grace and lowered his voice. "Not that we're not all thrilled to have you with us, dear, but I couldn't help but notice that Mr. Rolston is not a member of this club, and the 'guest of' portion of your room card was left blank."

"I guess you can blame me for that," Grace replied. "I hadn't expected that the card would be inspected so closely, and to be perfectly honest with you, I was a little... let's say, jet-lagged. Out of it, maybe. And I was told the information had been sent on ahead of me—which it had, by the way, if you care to check. All I did was sign *Rolston* on the card. The Mrs. part must have slipped my mind for some unknown reason. These things happen." She paused, but clearly McCracken expected more information. "Okay... A very good friend of mine, Sally Fulton, is a member of this club. She has been for many years, and her mother before her, and before that her grandfather. She arranged the bungalow for me. Sally felt a week in Hawaii would..." Grace paused, and then added, "but if that's a problem, I'm sure I can find accommodations elsewhere on the island." She considered following it up with, *Better yet: why don't I just go shack up with Lee Corbet over there? That way I'll only have to move my clothes over to another suite. Won't even need to call a cab.* She didn't say it, but later she said she so wished she had.

"Oh, we wouldn't hear of it. Sally is such a dear friend of ours as well," Bunny gushed, giving her reading of Sally far more regard than she had for her own husband's name. "We've dined with her a number of times here at the club. And how is dear Sally?"

"Dear Sally is... Sally. She's fine. She's actually more than fine, she's wonderful." Grace's eyes began to water slightly and she trembled as a wave of hot blood surged through her body. "Sally's been very kind to me. She's a very thoughtful person." And for the first time in her life she thought, *what would I ever do without Sally Fulton?*

"Oh," Bunny said, patting Grace's other hand, "then you're very close, I take it?"

"Yes. Very. She lives across the street from me in California."

"It's so important to have good lady friends. They can be such a relief and comfort when the boys become oppressive. I never knew Sally had such young and attractive acquaintances."

"Well, I'll tell you," Tug interrupted, as he still massaged Grace's wrist, "I just loved the way your Nick handled that Porsche in *The King's Gold*. He was masterful, that's all I can say."

I'll bet that's not all you can say. And would you two please stop touching me? Grace held that thought as well and stuck with, "Actually a stuntman drove that car. The Hollywood talk that the director did all the driving scenes is apocryphal, I can assure you. But anything that revs up the old PR machine would never be denied."

He squeezed her wrist then ran his hand further up her arm to the elbow. "Ha. You'll never convince me of that. Nobody out-studs Nick Rolston in my book."

"Ah, here comes our waiter," Bunny said. She reached into her purse as if the waiter's arrival had triggered some Pavlovian mechanism. She removed a package of Kent filter cigarettes and lit one.

The vision of this hard-edged, lined, and baked in the sun woman from Michigan drawing her cheeks into her skull until she looked absolutely skeletal, inhaling thick blue-white smoke into her mouth, nose, and lungs so disgusted Grace that she realized she'd never light another cigarette, no matter how long she lived. *Praise Jesus, something to be thankful for.* Bunny looked more like the Grim Reaper than any person Grace had ever encountered; she looked worse than her grandmother when she was stretched out stone-cold dead at Wilke's Funeral Parlor in Anaheim.

"What would you like for breakfast, dear?" Bunny said.

The words blew across the table toward Grace like a deep echo saturated in tobacco smoke. She glanced up at the waiter and the pot of coffee in his hand and said, "Just some of that for me, please."

He filled her cup and topped off Bunny and Tug.

"So, now, where is Nick?" Tug's hand was now stroking Grace's forearm. "Will he be joining you later in the week? I'd love to talk to him about a little something I've been noodling around with, a great idea for a flick about some low-life line workers in Detroit. Good car stuff. I'm with Chrysler. I've seen these dopes in action."

"No... No, he won't be coming to Hawaii."

"Well, maybe I can write it up and you can give it to him later on... What was that back in March? His second or third Academy Award?"

"First."

"Really? First? Are you sure about that?"

"Fairly certain, yes. We've been married for over ten years. If he'd won three Oscars I'm sure he would have told me about it by now. I might have even seen the statues lying around the house somewhere. They're very shiny."

"Didn't he win one for *My Son, My Father?*"

"Only nominated."

"Are you sure about that? That was a film and a half. That was stud stuff for damn sure. What's-his-name, that actor, didn't take any guff from that kid, either. Nick gave that relationship some serious meat. Kids now-a-days are getting out of hand. He really deserved an award for that film. Golden Globe anyway. You tell him that for me, okay?"

"Next time I see him."

"Who played the son, again?"

"Alden Campbell."

"Right. What the hell ever happened to him, anyway? Never heard a peep out of that kid after that movie."

Alden Campbell. Alden Campbell's mother had taken the majority of the money Alden had earned from *My Son, My Father* and spent it on heroin. Not content to ruin her own life, she'd introduced her son to the drug. He'd been in and out of rehab clinics for the last six years. Alden had been a bright kid with a terrific and quirky sense of humor. Grace fell in love with him the moment she met him, she really did. She would have traded almost everything she owned, which wasn't much, to have a kid just like Alden Campbell. But Nick wanted no part of that sort of thing. No, no, not Nick. No kids for Nick Rolston. Might as well tie an anchor to your leg. It's not easy convincing starlets a body is free and easy when there's a kid in the picture.

"Right, Alden Campbell. I heard he was a junkie," Bunny said.

"*Morocco Sands.* That was a hell of a film. Nick should have been nominated for that one."

"He was," Grace said, beginning to lose her patience with these two. "That's why he was at the Oscars." Grace dropped five sugar cubes into her coffee cup until the hot liquid spilled out into the saucer. "I'm somewhat confused by your 'film-buff' remark, Mr. McCracken? You appear to have some comprehension gaps in the brilliant career of the brilliant Nick Rolston?"

"Well…"

Bunny sighed. "Good Lord, Tug. Nick and Carla Thompson were both nominated, don't you remember? And they both won awards. That's the girl he was with at the ceremony last March, not this girl here. He won Best Director; she won Best Actress. Remember the sapphire gown she wore? She was the star, remember? She was lovely in that picture, absolutely smashing. Don't you think, Grace dear?"

"Well, if you ignore the fact that she was balling my husband for the ten weeks they were in Marrakech… Yeah, I guess her performance was pretty good. Personally, I had a little trouble watching it."

Bunny and Tug laughed knowingly, but it was Tug who spoke. "Well, there's nothing wrong with a little extracurricular activity to keep a marriage fresh. A man just needs to be subtle about it and then no one's the wiser. All in the family, so to speak. Men do need to stretch their wings. Especially creative ones. The girls? Not so much. As long as he keeps it under his hat, that's what I always say. Don't get the neighbors talking. Besides, I understand her costar on *Morocco Sands* is a fruit. That couldn't have been much fun for her. Probably spent his days running around chasing after all those little A-rab boys."

"Fuck. Fuck. Fuck."

"Pardon me?"

Grace eased her arm from McCracken's grip and dropped her face into her hands. "I'm sorry. Did I just say, fuck?"

"Well… Well, yes you did, dear," Bunny stammered. "Three times. Rather loudly."

"I'm sorry, I really am." Grace stood. More coffee spilled into the saucer as her thigh bumped the table. "I just remembered something. I just remembered why I came to Hawaii." She looked down at the McCrackens. They seemed dazed. "I have to deliver a message. It's a matter of life and death."

"But... But our breakfast, dear," Bunny said.

"Do either one of you know Sally Fulton's nephew? I believe his name is Lee Corbet?" Grace turned and scanned the dining room until her eyes fell on Lee. He was still focused on his newspaper but laughing at the same time. Ronnie later told me that Grace's f-bomb was even heard in the kitchen, much to the delight of the staff.

"Never mind. I see him. Would you please excuse me? This is very important. Sally would never forgive me if I didn't contact him immediately and deliver her message."

She didn't wait for an answer. She tossed her napkin onto the table and crossed the room. Lee raised his eyes from his newspaper when she was about ten feet off.

"Do you know those two?" she said as she collapsed into the chair next to him.

"No. But I remember seeing them there last night. Same table. What's up? Whatever they said, your reaction didn't seem to be quite up to club standards."

"I thought you came here all the time?"

"I only said I'd been here before. I'm not a member."

"Well, I hope you filled out your room card properly. You didn't skip the 'guest of' line, did you?"

"Nobody ever reads those cards."

"Why doesn't that surprise me?" Grace sighed and fiddled with the empty coffee cup in front of her, then set it upside down in the saucer. "I think I might have already outstayed my welcome."

"That's not hard to do here at the Pickering Club. And yelling 'fuck' three times in the dining room, loud enough to be heard out at the reception desk, seems a good start."

Sally

Grace tapped the heavy restaurant-grade silver-plate teaspoon on the pink table cloth four times and then casually nudged Lee's fork with it. "It doesn't look like you've eaten anything. Or are you fasting for some reason?"

"No." He tossed the *Honolulu Advertiser* onto the empty chair to his right. "I was waiting for you."

She studied his eyes and mouth and considered her options—thinking whether to say, "That was nice of you," or what she believed was more likely the truth, "That's a complete crock of shit." She settled on, "Do you feel like sitting outside? This room is closing in on me again. I hope it's not becoming a pattern."

"It's hot out there."

"Is that a complaint or a warning?"

"I've got nothing to complain about."

"Lucky you."

They stood. Lee signaled to the waiter for more coffee and they stepped through the French doors and out onto the tiled back terrace, out of the air-conditioning and into the thick and humid atmosphere. The temperature was already approaching ninety, and although large umbrellas fashioned out of dried palm fronds shaded the exterior tables, they did little to cool things. The light breeze forced the fronds to rustle, creating a sound not unlike winter leaves blowing down an empty country lane, but even this sound had no imagined cooling effect.

"Were you really waiting for me?"

"No."

She laughed.

He added, "I figured you'd already finished breakfast and had left for the day."

"So you lied to me? I'm shocked."

"Not a lie, really. The assumption was that you would've recognized the outrageous dose of sarcasm in my voice. I'll have to work on my delivery, I guess."

"My mind was on something else. Your delivery may have been just fine."

The waiter arrived with a pink porcelain thermos and filled their matching pink coffee cups. Lee asked him to leave the pot, which he did, along with two pink and green breakfast menus. Grace took a small sip from her cup, leaned back, kicked off her sandals, and placed her feet on the empty chair next to her, before adjusting her skirt and halter top to keep both items from pinching at her flesh. She cocked her head toward Lee without really looking at him.

"I was wondering if you could do me a slight favor?" she said.

"Don't lie to you anymore?"

"Hey, you're a man. It comes with the territory." Grace winced slightly. *Why do these things come out of my mouth?* "I'm sorry, I didn't mean that. I really didn't. It makes me sound like such a... bitch. And I'm not. I'm just at a low point. I'm feeling beaten-up. I'm not choosing my words very carefully." She let out a small laugh but kept her gaze on a mammoth fire-red and green hibiscus bush swaying gently on the other side of the terrace railing. "The fact is: I was going to ask you to back up one of *my* lies, one I just passed off to my new-found friends, the McCrackens from Grand Rapids, Michigan."

"That should be no problem, given my gender."

Grace twisted her torso so that the upper half of her body now faced him. The move accentuated her tight and firm stomach muscles, though that wasn't entirely her intention. "What do you do for a living? And don't tell me stand-up comedy because you would have starved to death a dozen years ago. George Carlin you are not."

"I own a restaurant in Manhattan."

"You're kidding? You're a little young for that sort of thing, aren't you?"

"Thirty-five? It's not that young."

"Hah. It's been my experience, and believe me I have plenty when it comes to this, that all restaurant owners are well into their sixties. They are all overweight, either bald or have horribly dyed brown, black or orange hair, and spend nearly all of their time pawing, fondling, manhandling, groping, or better yet, *if* they can pull it off, banging their waitresses. That's how it was at O'Rourke's and every other place in Long Beach. I can't believe New York City is any different."

The waiter arrived, and Grace ordered scrambled eggs, a local sagey sausage, toast, and half a grapefruit. Lee ordered the same.

"Mr. Originality."

"Give me a break, will you? It sounded good."

"Huh. So, what's the name of your restaurant?"

"Saintes Maries de la Mer. It's on East Fifty-Second Street, just off Second Avenue. Seafood, *à la française* for the most part."

"You're kidding? That's kind of well-known, if you don't mind my saying so. Doesn't someone give it *stars* somewhere? And a lot of them?"

He shrugged. "Depends on whose guide book you read."

"I've been to New York a couple of times, but I'm sorry to say, I've never eaten there."

"I know."

"You know? What do you mean, you know? You remember everyone who walks in the door?"

"Pretty much. That's my job. I don't forget things and people easily. A restaurant isn't just about food. It's an intimate place. People expect to be recognized in Manhattan. You're not going to get heavy-hitters walking in or stars in a book if you don't. And I'd definitely remember *you*."

"Yeah? What if I was to stop in today? You're in Hawaii. You would've missed me altogether."

"It's closed. I'm on vacation, so I close the restaurant. The staff is on vacation, too. They're all back in France right now telling their mothers and fathers about the fancy restaurant *they* own in New York City on East Fifty-Second Street called Saintes Maries de la Mer. We're closed for August."

"You just shut the place down?"

"Yes."

"For a whole month?"

"Yep."

"And you're planning to spend that month in this dump? Are you out of your mind?"

Lee laughed. "No. I'm only here for a week. Then I'll be going to the South of France for the other two weeks. My parents have a house there. I rent some digs nearby. It's a nice spot."

A small yellow bird flew in and landed on their table and began scouring the surface for leftover crumbs.

"Come back later," Grace said to the bird. "We haven't eaten yet. You'll do well by me. I'm a sucker for the disadvantaged." The bird ignored her, so she refocused on Lee. "I'm a little confused. If you're off to France, why the hell did you come out here? It's not like it's on the way."

"It's a long story."

"Ah, right, you and your long stories. I'd forgotten about those." She took another sip of coffee. "My husband's eaten at Saintes Maries de la Mer quite a bit."

"Then I probably know him."

Grace's stomach knotted. *Did I really bring up the subject of Nick again? Did I do that all on my own? With absolutely no prompting? I'm nuts. I'm out of my fucking mind.*

Every time Nick Rolston visited Manhattan for work or to "hook up" with his New York agent he ate at least one dinner at Saintes Maries de la Mer. Grace told me it was one of his favorite restaurants in the seventies. He raved about it constantly. No kidding Lee Corbet knew Nick Rolston. Even if he *didn't* pay attention to who walked through his front door, nobody missed Nick Rolston, ever. Nick Rolston made certain of that.

Grace decided to keep her mouth shut for a while and feigned enjoyment of the warm morning. It was not an easy task. Beads of sweat began forming on her chest and then rolled lazily down between her breasts and through her halter top before settling in her navel. The waiter saved the day by arriving with their eggs.

"I gather the McCrackens are the old folks who corralled you by the kitchen door a moment ago?"

"Right, the McCrackens. The lie. I forgot I was in the middle of perpetrating a falsehood. I don't like doing it. I'm making a serious effort to change my ways, but sometimes it's the only way out." Grace tossed a corner of her toast to the yellow bird that had been sitting on the railing and waiting patiently for their breakfast to arrive. "Not that I really care what the hell the McCrackens think, it's just that I'd hate to make life difficult for... Wait, let me back up a bit. There's a woman who comes here all the time. Her name is Sally Fulton. I don't suppose you've ever run into her?"

"She's my aunt."

Grace nearly choked. "Sally Fulton is your aunt? Get the hell out of here. *The* Sally Fulton? From Pacific Palisades? In California? How does that work? She's only forty-five years old."

"She's my mother's brother's wife. Ex-wife to be more precise. She never took his last name, but that's Sally."

"You mean that schmuck, Louis Simone, is your mother's brother?"

He laughed and added a facetious, "People usually speak very highly of Uncle Louis."

"I've met Uncle Louis. He's a jerk. He's more than a jerk. He tried to screw me one night at a party in their own house while Sally was out by the swimming pool with the other guests. He said it would be safe because we could keep an eye on Sally from the bedroom's bay window. As long as we kept the lights out, she'd never see us. He seemed proud of the fact that it would only take six or seven minutes."

"Yep, that's good old Uncle Louis."

"So you're saying that phony-baloney French accent of his is real? That the turd was actually born in France?"

"Fraid so. Lyon."

"Jesus."

"Technically, I'm Aunt Sally's guest here."

"Did you write that in the 'guest of' line on the room card? You might be looking at some serious jail time if you didn't."

"I told you, nobody ever looks at those, so what's the point?"

"But I'm a guest of Sally Fulton, too." Grace shook her head. "She arranged this for me. That's how I know Louis Simone. Sally lives right across the street from us."

Will you stop with this 'us' business? Grace remembered thinking. *Nick's moved out. He's taken his underwear and his shaving crap and moved into his tacky furnished office/ apartment in Westwood.* There is no us. Us is *over. He still wants his house in the Palisades of course. He just doesn't want the wife that comes with it.* "Hey, keep what you want, except the paintings. You just need to find a new house, that's all. Preferably not in the Palisades, baby. That's going to be a little tight. Try Malibu. You like the beach, don't you? You're always threatening to go there. Hell, I'll pay for it. I don't see what's the problem? I'll pay for the damn thing. How much can a house in Malibu cost, for Christ's sake? A half a mil? I'll buy you a house—furniture and all." *Isn't that what he said?* "He has the money, he calls the shots. He found someone new, Gracie. He's serious this time. It's really for your own good. He doesn't want to hurt you anymore than he has. He means it. But he calls the shots. He has the money, he calls the shots." *That's what Nick's lawyer had said on Friday. The shit didn't have the balls to tell me himself, had to run it through legal before he offered to buy me a house. As if I don't know who she is? Jesus, I was with him when she first waited on us at the Ocean Front Grill in Santa Monica.* "Oh, the great Nick Rolston; I can't believe I'm waiting on Nick Rolston. I'm an actress. Really, I am." *She'd actually jumped up and down in her little tennis shoes. Really jumped. Probably peed in her hot pants, too. Who was looking? It was enough to make me sick.*

"Well, she's waiting on him now," Grace said, her mouth full of sausage.

"Pardon me?"

Grace rolled her eyes. "Did I just say something out loud again?"

"Yep. I gather you weren't talking about Aunt Sally. Aunt Sally doesn't *wait* on anybody. Not even Louis. Before he moved back to Lyon, that is."

"Is she really your aunt? You're not making this up, are you? It would be an awfully cruel joke if you are."

"Nope. I've been in love with Aunt Sally since I was five years old. She came to New York, gave me a toy squirrel. I still have it. If you ever come to New York I'll show it to you. It's a little threadbare, but I have hard evidence."

"Okay, I believe you. And I don't doubt you love her. She's a very special person; everyone loves her... So, the other times you've been here, Sally set it up for you, too?"

"Uh-huh."

"I don't know why she's never mentioned you. I guess it's because you're on the schmuck's side of the family. Poor you. You know she's engaged again, don't you?"

"She told me. Jesse. I haven't met him. Have you?"

"Yes. Nice guy. He's a surgeon. He adores her, too. Sorry to tell you she's not going to miss your uncle for a second."

"No one does."

Grace pushed a forkful of eggs into her mouth. The chef had mixed onions, fennel, and dill into them. *Nice touch,* she thought. She tossed another piece of toast to the yellow bird.

"How many times have you been here?"

"In total?"

"Yeah. I think you could interpret *how many* as *in total.* Yes."

"Once in 1968, and then again in 1975."

Grace finished her eggs and then pushed her plate towards the bird who hopped onto it and began clearing off the remaining crumbs.

"See, that would have been enough of the Pickering Club for me," she said. "I would have had my fill. Probably just the one shot in '68 would have done it. I wouldn't have needed to come back in 1975 to be certain. And definitely not now in '79. Too much Pickering Club for me. I really don't see what Sally sees in this place."

"Her mother was a member. She's been coming here since she was in diapers. The place does a good job of holding memories, it seems. Good and bad."

She refilled both of their coffee cups from the thermos. "Did you come here alone the other two times or did you drag along some unsuspecting individual to entertain you? If you did, I notice that *they* weren't dense enough to be duped into a return visit, memories or not."

"I was alone in 1975. With my wife in 1968."

"Ah, now we're getting somewhere. The wife. I knew there had to one lurking around in the shadows. You're not still married, are you? Slipped the old wedding ring into the pocket? Looking for a little something on the side? She's not waiting for you in France by any chance?"

"No. I'm no longer married. Free as that yellow bird."

"Good." She held up her hands laughing and shook her head. "Sorry, I didn't mean *good*, like you're available. I meant *good*, like it's nice to meet someone else whose marriage is completely screwed up... Or was screwed up, I guess. We can compare notes. You didn't come here to kill yourself, did you? That would be too much."

There was that odd smile again, just like the one he'd given her when she'd asked him about his missing finger. He didn't say anything at first. He just sat there playing with the sweat on his water glass. Then finally: "Hey, I'm sorry. I get quiet at times. It's one of my shitty qualities."

Did it again, didn't I? That finger's not the only thing he's lost. What is it with my mouth?

Grace reached over and placed both of her hands on top of his broad wrist. His watch had been sitting directly in the sun and felt remarkably hot to the touch. So much so that she almost withdrew her hands for fear of being burned. But she didn't pull back. She held on. *So what if I get burned? It wouldn't be the first time.*

"Your wife's dead, isn't she?"

"Yes."

Tracy

G race and Lee were not the only Haoles whose senses had been charged by an overly sultry Hawaiian morning. Tracy Tillis, considering her overall numbness, was also keenly aware of the August heat. Forty years after the fact, Tracy now owns and operates a breakfast spot on Kalakaua Avenue called The Morning Glory. Breakfast and lunch only: no dinners, no booze.

Free coffee goes out to anyone who walks in wearing a military uniform.

"Hell, if they're cute enough, I don't even charge them for the bacon and eggs."

Remarkably, Tracy seems to know the first name of nearly everyone who walks through her door. But despite the sunny disposition she serves up to her customers each morning, the three days in August, Sami's Chevron Station, and the malevolent events of 1979, would forever remain crystalline in her mind.

"Yeah, I grew up real quick that summer. Hell, all of us did. It changed my outlook on life in an instant... And Mitch? I'm glad he's come around. I didn't think he would. He wept like a baby. He was in a state of shock... Anyway, I only met your dad once, but I knew Ray Slack much too well. It still makes me sick when I think about it. I guess it always will. What he did to your dad, and mom, was unforgivable."

I visited Tracy in the early afternoon. Business was winding down for the day and she took me by the hand and led me to a corner booth. She has a big heart, Tracy: she loves life, she loves people. We talked for over two hours, and despite the fact that I was not wearing any type of uniform, she refused to let me pay for my lunch. I've never considered myself to be exceptionally "cute."

"It's funny you should stop by today. I was just thinking about all this crap. I drove by Sami's this morning on the way in—the place hasn't changed a bit. It must have been the way the sun was hittin' the gas pumps because it was like a shitty dream. Just made me cry all over again."

"Look, if you don't want to talk about it that's fine. Or I could come back tomorrow if you like."

"No, I'm good."

It was August fourteenth, 1979, and by Tracy's account, she'd been sitting on a wood-slatted concrete bench across the street from Sami's Chevron Station for well over an hour that morning. She said she believed she looked calm enough, all things considered: dark glasses glistening in the bright sunlight, fresh makeup, tanned legs crossed, a large purse clutched to her bare midriff, with her enhanced breasts snug in their halter top and resting peacefully on her folded forearms. The breeze carried her feathery blonde hair in all directions, but she never attempted to control it or push it from her face. It resembled the ratted yellow mane of a stuffed toy lion by the time the wind was done with it. Every fifteen minutes or so she would light a cigarette, smoke it down to the filter, then flip the butt out into the traffic and watch as the tires of the passing cars crushed it like a frightened firefly. These were her only real movements. It was hot, but she had all day, there was no rush. She wasn't due to begin her shift at Cookie's Joint until eight that evening.

Might never go back at all, she thought. After the previous night she wondered what the point was. Having men like Ray Slack sticking their fingers into her panties, throwing money on the bar like they were multi-millionaires. They were mostly one-dollar bills, not even fives. It was no wonder her friend, Bobbie, went back to the mainland. She'd grown sick of the raunchy tattoos on their grubby arms and having them push their unshaven faces between her tits. Most of them wouldn't know what to do with a woman if one walked up and sat on them.

"Hell, Ray proved that last week. After all that pushin' and shovin', couldn't get nothin' up. I should tell Mitch all about what really happened in that damn pickup truck of Ray's—serve him right, that limp dick bastard... Jesus, the fucker's now got me talking to myself."

She knew Ray would return to the gas station by noon. Sami and Ray were as predictable as garbage pickup as far as Tracy was concerned. They'd order a Shakey's Pizza, split it fifty-fifty, and throw the crusts out onto the searing asphalt for the seagulls. Sami kept a pellet gun below the cash register, and on those slow days, days when there were no customers needing gas pumped or pedestrians out front hoofing it down to the bus stop and traffic was minimal, Sami and Ray would take turns shooting at the gulls as they unsuspectingly pecked at the pizza crusts. Real sportsmen, those two. If they nailed one, which was exceptionally rare, they'd flip a coin to see who was going to go out, pick up the carcass, and cart it over to the dumpster. Sami was convinced the blood stains on the macadam contributed greatly to the fact that his gas station had never been knocked off.

And sure enough, just before noon, the green and yellow

tow truck with *Sami's Chevron* scrawled in red, white, and blue, pulled into the station. It idled for a minute in front of the office windows, then pulled around and backed its payload: a small two-tone brown and white Datsun station-wagon, halfway into the second work bay. Ray got out of the truck, lowered the Datsun, unhooked a series of chains, and parked the tow truck in the side lot under a bank of short palm trees next to his pickup truck. He stepped from the truck's cab, lit a cigarette, and strolled into the office. It was time for lunch.

Tracy rubbed at the soft leather of her purse, feeling the handle of the combat-style knife she'd purchased earlier in the day at Sears. Apparently, the housewares department didn't have a blade she deemed sturdy enough or sufficiently sharp to take care of the job she had in mind, so she'd been forced to check out the sporting goods section. "It's for my boyfriend," she'd told the salesclerk, giving him a bright smile. "He's an ex-Marine." She'd been shown a knife that looked more like it had been designed for commando opera-tions: hard black rubber handle with a seven inch, dark gray, razor sharp steel blade protected by a canvas sheath done in camouflage shades of greens, blacks, and browns. "I'll take it." The knife set her back thirty-eight dollars. *Water under the bridge.*

After seeing the tow truck, Tracy stood, walked down to the crosswalk, and waited for the light to change. In her mind it seemed to take an eternity. Her heart was racing and her antiperspirant had long since outlived its usefulness. The cars passing in front of her became blurs of bright colors. Someone honked. The noise came from the bulbous white clouds for all Tracy knew. She ignored these slight interrup-tions to her senses and focused her gaze on the streetlight, watched as the cross-traffic's signal turned yellow, then red, and finally hers went to green. She traversed the street. A car making a left hand turn nearly hit her. She didn't see it. The driver only shook her head and drove off toward Downtown Honolulu. Tracy walked past Sami's gas pumps. There were no customers. The air seemed hotter and damper here. A biting smell of gasoline and motor oil mixed with radiator coolant drifted up through her nostrils and created a stinging sensation.

"Hey, Tracy, how's it going?" It was Phil, Sami's mechanic. Like clockwork, he was off to get some lunch. A nice guy, Phil: not into popping seagulls, not into watching the other two pop the gulls either. That's why Phil went to Harpo's for lunch or sat in the park. Tracy didn't answer him. She just walked past and into the office.

Sami was sitting behind a gray Navy-surplus metal desk. He was a large Hawaiian: six feet one and well over two hundred and fifty pounds. He had a bright smile with perfect white teeth that did a wonderful job of screening a tenacious and somewhat sadistic personality. A cash register was perched to his left along with a sliding credit-card imprinter. The rest of the desk was scattered with a few *Penthouse* magazines and newspapers already yellowed by the searing sun. Behind him, the wall was covered with posters of bikinied women shilling various automotive parts and Italian sports cars. The gray linoleum flooring was coffee stained, chipped, and torn up in spots exposing the concrete underneath. Ray was sitting in a folding brown metal chair opposite Sami. He was dialing the telephone, no doubt ordering up their pizza. He dropped the receiver into the cradle when he caught sight of Tracy.

"Well, if it ain't Miss Slutski of 1979. What's the matter, babe? Too early to be pullin' tricks?"

Tracy was surprised at how calm she'd now become. She

knew either one of these guys would just as soon slap her in the mouth as look at her, but that seemed unimportant. Instead she found herself wondering if Ray's blood would be red or if it would come out yellow or black even, or if he had any at all: if his skin would open and there would be nothing but dryness and a skeleton made of pressed concrete.

"Why'd you do it, Ray?" seemed a good way to start, and it was really the only question she needed answered before she went to town on him.

As expected, Ray played dumb. Something that Tracy maintained came to him naturally. He could have been an actor; he was a lot smarter than he ever let on.

"Do what, toots?" he said.

"Mitch woulda never thought to trash my car like that. You had to put him up to it. Why? I never had no fight with you. What's done is done. I ain't pointin' any fingers. I didn't go public with what I know. That's not me. I don't make nobody feel small, no matter who he is."

Sami laughed. "Something wrong with your car, Tracy? Bring it in. I'll have Phil take a look at it for you. No charge." He then rubbed at the crotch of his flower print shorts. "Well, maybe a blow job. I hear you and Mitch is broke up. That's what Ray here says, anyway. You must be missin' it already. So what do ya say? I could really go for a decent blow job right about now."

Ray laughed. He stood and reached for her right breast, thinking Sami didn't have a half bad idea. She smacked his hand off to the side.

"Ooh, she's got a nasty streak, don't she, Sami?"

He reached for her chest again, and again she pushed him away, keeping her eyes fixed on his.

"Let me tell you how this works, Slutski: you service our schlongs with that fat mouth of yours, and we'll get Phillie-Boy to service that piece of crap you drive."

Sami stood. "Two on one, you could get into that kinda action, couldn't you, Tracy? I got a real nice cot in the back, what do ya say?"

She remained focused on Ray. "I just want to know why you pushed Mitch into it. I need that car, you shit. I can't be takin' the bus home at three in the morning. It ain't safe."

"Well, maybe you shoulda thought about safe before you threw your man out."

"I'm me; I do what I want. It's my place. I pay the rent. I got my reasons," she shot back at him. "Besides, Mitch is... Forget it, what do you know? And I don't let nobody threaten to hit me, if that's where you're goin'. You don't scare me, neither one of you. I've outgrown that, shit. I don't—"

With the speed of a rattlesnake, Ray slapped her across the face with his opened right hand. "How's that for *outgrown*, bitch?"

The blow snapped her neck back. Her sunglasses flew from the bridge of her nose onto the linoleum floor and blood instantly oozed from the corner of her upper lip and rolled down to the end of her chin. She grasped her purse tighter and licked at the blood with her tongue. She made no attempt wipe any of it away as she bent to retrieve her glasses.

"You dickless fuck," she said calmly, straightening her spine.

Sami grabbed at Ray's arm before he could hit her a second time. "You want to beat her up, take her somewhere else. I got a business to run here. Someone comes in here and sees you slappin' a broad around, I'm screwed."

"She's a crazy bitch, Sami. Got a hell of an imagination, too. Thinks I pull the strings on her boyfriend."

"I know you found Mitch. I know he's stayin' at your apartment," she snapped. "He was with you last night. You don't think people talk?"

"Yeah? So what? That don't mean I smashed the windows outta your Pinto, now does it?"

"I didn't say nothin' about no windows. I guess you're psychic all of a sudden, is that it, limp dick?"

Instinctively, he moved to crack her again, but Sami held onto his right arm with a steel grip. Ray reached up with his left hand and grabbed her jaw. He squeezed her face, distorting it and smearing her lipstick and the fresh blood across her cheeks. He shoved the back of her head up against the station's plate glass window. It rattled as if a surprise gust of wind had just kicked up.

"You got a witness, bitch?" he shouted, his eyes now bloodshot and bulging in an almost animalistic rage. "Because unless you got a witness, you ain't got shit. Don't come 'round here accusin' people of stuff you don't know nothin' about. I'll skin you alive, I swear to Christ, I will."

Ray released her and Sami pushed him into the chair. "Call Shakey's, damn it. Order us up some lunch. Get some anchovies on the side. And chill out, ya lunatic. This ain't the place for this shit. And don't get no sausage on it neither. I can't digest that crap, keeps comin' up on me." He then turned to Tracy. "Get the hell out of here. I don't care what you two got goin' on, or what's goin' on with you and Mitch, but it's ugly. Keep it away from me. I don't need no family squabbles on my turf. This is a business I'm runnin' here."

Tracy stared at Ray, now sitting in the metal chair, looking like a rabid coyote in an undersized cage with Sami—his keeper—standing over him, the one who decided when, and if, he was to be fed. She'd come to cut him, cut him bad, but her heart was no longer in it; he suddenly looked small and pathetic sitting next to Sami. She slowly backed out of the doorway and walked down the north side of the building past the mechanic's bays, turning around three times to see if either Ray or Sami might be following. When she reached Ray's pickup truck she stopped and leaned against the right front fender. She pulled her purse tightly into her midriff once more.

She stood like that, fighting off tears for fifteen minutes, until the Shakey's delivery kid came and left. She then set her purse on the hood of the truck and removed her Sears commando knife. She pulled it from the sheath and tapped the tip against the back of her hand. It was needle sharp. She stepped to her left and studied her reflection in the passenger's side window. She had yet to wipe the blood from her mouth and chin and it was beginning to dry to a crusty red-brown. Tracy raised the knife until she could see its dull image in the window alongside her slender neck. She wanted to smile. She had devised a course of action, but no smile came.

She believed she should be enjoying this retribution. And wondered why she wasn't getting her jollies off on this.

Once again she found herself mumbling aloud. "I'm not stuck on this bastard, I'm not. That's crazy. Christ, he just punched me out. How could I be stuck on him? He can't even get his pecker hard."

Tracy ground her teeth together and drove the butt of the knife into the pickup's side rearview mirror, shattering the glass. Seven years bad luck, she thought. Time would tell. She then carved, "Limp Dick" into the paint of the door panel with the tip of the knife and rounded the truck and repeated the action on the driver's side. She stepped back to look at what she'd done. The handwriting was rocky and uneven but clearly readable. She stepped up to the front wheel, pushing the knife tip into the rubber at the high point. The balding tire offered little resistance to the cold-tempered steel.

She expected the tire to blow like a child's balloon; creating a loud pop, an explosion of sorts; a noise that would certainly alert Ray and Sami. She was now ready for the possibility of another confrontation, but believing that standing out in the open, exposed to the lunchtime traffic, offered her a certain amount of protection; she could run to a passing car or down to the McDonald's if need be. However no real noise came. The tire simply hissed. She twisted the blade, the air escaped with a long whoosh and the left front corner of the truck dropped down onto the metal wheel rim. She walked to the pickup's bed and flattened the rear tire, then crossed over and finished off the other two.

Tracy slipped the commando knife into its canvas sheath and returned it to her purse. She walked around Sami's tow truck, out onto the sidewalk, and down to the bus stop. A bus headed for Downtown Honolulu arrived five minutes later. She worked her way to the rear row of seats, sat, and began crying so fitfully that the driver stopped the bus after only five blocks. He set the brake and turned on the emergency flashers. He then walked back, sat on the seat next to her, placed his arm over her shoulder, and asked her if she needed to see a doctor.

Chico

The major I spoke with at the Marine Corps Records Center in St. Louis, Missouri was surprisingly accessible. Apparently he gets requests like mine all the time, mostly from relatives trying to learn how a loved one lost their life in some far off godforsaken war and has never been fully accounted for. Or they'd like to know more about *Dad's* war experience because *Dad* never talked about it before he died.

The file on Raymond Slack is as short and pathetic as I expected. The file on Lee Corbet, not so much. Their time in Vietnam overlapped, but I couldn't see where they might have had any connection with one another. The major couldn't see it either, but he supplied me with a list of six names: Marines whose paths had crossed Lee's in Vietnam and were known to be still alive. Since Chico Lowery was now working at the PX at Camp Pendleton, California he was by far the easiest of the men for me to locate. When I offered Chico the few historical items I'd learned about Lee and mentioned that he was my father, he agreed to meet me at Butler's, a bar frequented by military types, just outside the base in Oceanside. It was more than obvious to me that Lee was a man Chico would never forget.

This was a hot and unusually steamy Saturday afternoon in Southern California—much like, I would imagine, that day in 1968. The sun was scorching, but Butler's clings to a dark and depressing atmosphere. I wouldn't recommend it. It's a drinker's bar. There's no music. Chico is now in his early seventies, nearly completely bald and has taken to buzzing off what little hair is left on the sides of his head to bristle-like snow-white stubble. He's in remarkably good shape for a man his age, but his eyes are those of a man in his nineties. He wore a tight-fitting red polo shirt with the Marine Corps emblem embroidered in gold on the left breast. His biceps are as well defined as any twenty-five-year-old. And despite presenting himself as the poster boy, "Once a Marine, always a Marine," there was a clear reason he wanted to meet me at Butler's: he was a serious drinker and by his own admission needed a little "lubrication" to loosen any Vietnam memories to the point where he was willing to talk about them in any real detail. And even at this afternoon hour the slight trembling in his hands was much in evidence before his first Wild Turkey came to rest in his stomach. He honestly believed he would have lost his life many years ago in a soggy clearing in South Vietnam if it had not been for the actions of Lee Corbet.

"I owe my life to Lieutenant Corbet, I truly do. It hurts me to learn that he's gone. And that he died so young. We all have to go sometime, but he seemed somehow immortal to me. I believed no one could take him out. I never for the life of me thought I'd outlive him. He may have been the most honorable man I met. And to be honest, I've never really talked much about that day to anyone, not even my wife and kids. That said, you deserve to know what kind of a man your dad was... If I start to stray or go silent bear with me, I'll get on track. It's just that nobody likes to see an old Marine cry."

According to Chico, this is how things "went down" that day in 1968:

He freely admitted that he was scared shitless. He had arrived in Da Nang three weeks earlier and this was his first patrol. Lee's previous radio operator had his shoulder shattered by a sniper and had been shipped home. Chico was his replacement. He said stupid stuff goes through your head when you're eighteen. And right about then he was thinking, "How the hell did I get myself into this shit? It all sounded so fucking romantic back in Tulsa. The slick recruiter with his dress blues saying I'd likely get embassy duty, maybe even the White House. His absolute 100% guarantee that I would be stationed with an *aviation unit* on the *off chance* I was actually sent to Vietnam. Some fucking *aviation unit* this is." He said he was ready to strangle the son of a bitch. He had never experienced that kind of heat and humidity. His mind was in a fog. The radio got heavier and heavier with every step. The forest was layered with low-lying vines entangling his boots and tripping him up every chance they got. There were chest-high bushes, then taller trees, and then still-taller trees. The foliage was so thick the sunlight couldn't get through. Two marines, Cokley and Wall, were walking point and slashing away at the underbrush with machetes. All of them were soaked in sweat. Chico was about as far away from the dust and flatland of Oklahoma as he could get.

Lee forced a large dying branch away from his face with his left arm. The moment he dropped his hand, the branch returned with a vengeance. A thorn nicked his earlobe out of spite it seemed, forcing a small drop of blood to form. It instantly mixed with sweat and dripped onto his shoulder leaving a pinkish stain on the weathered green cloth while another bead of blood emerged from his earlobe to take its place. This branch's minor assault created no more than a small ticking sound. Lee touched the new blood with his finger. The liquid was far thicker and stickier than the river of sweat that poured through his eyebrows and rolled down his cheeks. He licked the blood from his fingertip, savoring the saltiness—so much cleaner tasting than the gritty perspiration that had found its way into his mouth throughout this oppressively feverish morning.

"Sir?"

"Not now, Chico."

"Sir, I need to—"

"Can it."

Chico fell silent. When Lieutenant Corbet said, "Can it," most people canned it, no questions asked, at least that was Chico's position. At this point in his tour of duty Chico didn't ask questions; he just did as he was told. It was the first thing he'd learned at Parris Island, but it was also Chico. He was *New Guy* and he didn't ask questions, so he peed in his pants and kept his mouth shut. The warm liquid rolled down his leg and into his already drenched sock. Chico said at the time it seemed his only available option. "If nothing else, I was salty enough to realize that when your CO says, 'Can it,' it was not a good time for me to pull out my pecker."

Lee ducked under the thorny branch and took three steps forward and stopped again. Chico followed closely, silently shaking out the leg of his trousers as he did. The only discernible noise came from the birds. Four different varieties, Chico guessed, though he couldn't see any of them through the thick canopy of broad leaves that blocked out most of the searing sunlight. The birds seemed so incredibly loud—in flight now, their wings striking the vines and foliage that grew at an even higher level.

Chico found himself wondering if they spoke the same

language. Were they communicating? Are they at war, too? Hawks eat doves, right? Do they foretell the future?

"These birds are driving me nuts, lieutenant."

"Can it."

Lance Corporal Hanratty stepped up behind Chico and whispered into his ear, "These birds have seen all this shit happen before, New Guy. A gazillion times. They're up there in the trees with their birds-eye view. Waitin' for the shit to happen. Waitin' for you to shit your pants. They can see it all develop through the cracks in the canopy, and they're laughin', that's what they were doing. They ain't sayin nothin,' they're laughin.' They think this shit is one big fuckin' joke. Funny as hell. A hoot: the birds are laughin' their asses off at you and me."

"Can it, Hanratty. Let him be."

He ignored Lee. "And you know what, New Guy? My heart's also racing like there's no fuckin' tomorrow because I can feel it coming, too. It's just like being in love, ain't it? Your heart's pumping blood faster than you thought was humanly possible. And I know what you're thinkin', New Guy, 'cause I'm thinkin' the same thing. You're thinkin', 'God, please don't let me die in this fuckin' place. I'll do anything, I swear I will, just don't let me die here.' But you know what? You are gonna die here, boy, so don't waste your time prayin'. God done forgot about you and me a long time ago."

If the birds did know what was about to happen, they would have been prudent to get out while the getting was good. And although all of the men felt it in their blood, in their veins and arteries, in their hearts, under their fingernails, there was no real warning. The earth erupted like a geyser of red-orange flame and molten shrapnel, and a horrific black-gray smoke. The noise was deafening. Chico dropped to the ground instantly, wrapping his arms over his head and helmet. Lee remained standing, but crouched low. The explosive flash of light and chunks of searing hot metal came and went in an instant, as did the noise, but their ears rang and the smoke billowed and floated upward as pieces of turf rained down from above. The concussion knocked a hole in the tree line fifteen feet wide. Sergeant Wall, totally out of breath and with blood streaming out of his right ear, raced toward them. He tripped and fell twice, scrambled to his feet, and finally crouched alongside Lee.

"Shit, lieutenant, Cokely stepped on a fucking mine. It had to be a set mortar shell. Maybe something bigger. Maybe an arty round. No way it was just some piss-ant Chicom. The tree line's wide open up there."

Carl Cokely was a Black kid from Atlanta, sixth of eight children, parents both worked for Coca-Cola, nineteen years old, eternally homesick, knew the lyrics to "Georgia On My Mind" backwards and forwards, twenty-three days left in country. They called him "Momma's Boy," and Cokely just rolled his eyes and laughed, he knew better. And he loved to walk point. He said it kept his mind sharp and not thinking about when he'd get to go home.

"Not Cokely," Lee mumbled when the dust finally settled. "He's a good kid. Please, God, don't let me lose Cokely. Not this late in the game... Jesus, I hate this fucking war."

Lee turned, signaling his platoon to take cover, a move that was totally unnecessary—this was a salty group of young Marines. They knew an ambush when they saw one coming. He reached behind him and slapped at his radio operator's helmet.

"Chico, get *The Six* up. Tell him we've run into some shit up here. We need a medevac, ASAP. And a gun-ship if he can find one." He looked at Sergeant Wall. "How bad is he?"

Wall shook his head only slightly, but the move clearly indicated that Cokely was never going to see Georgia again. "Is he still alive?"

Wall didn't answer that question either. Lee pushed past him, and the sergeant grabbed at his arm.

"Lieutenant, this is a fucking ambush, you know that. That tree line is crawling with Gooks. Cokely's not going to make it, sir. There's nothing left of his leg. I saw him fly through the goddamn air. They're just waiting for us to go up there after him."

"We're not leaving him there."

"No, sir, we're not. But he's dead meat, sir. We need to get around these cocksuckers. We need to come up behind them and take 'em out. But if we go straight in after Cokely we're fucked. Nobody goes home. You know how this works."

Lee yanked his arm free from Wall's grip. "I'm going up. If he's not breathing, we play it your way. If Cokely's alive, we're getting him out. Get Cooper, Hanratty, and Ramirez and follow me up."

"Sir, we cannot take our corpsman in there. It's hot like a motherfucker. You hafta know that. You can't put Ramirez up front like that." Too late. Lee had already taken off toward the smoke. Sergeant Wall looked down at Chico. "I should have popped this son of a bitch six months ago when I had the chance. He's gonna get us all killed. Goddamn officers."

Nonetheless, Sergeant Wall did what he was told. He rustled up Cooper and Hanratty, and the Navy corpsman, Ramirez. He then told Corporal Tasker to take the rest of the men and circle around the tree line. "Let's try to get these cocksuckers in a crossfire. They're in there—I saw them. There's a shitload of them, too, so watch you asses. And try not to shoot *us* for Christ's sake." He turned to the radio operator. "Chico, you come with me. If we can save this bastard, you're gonna need you to talk-in the medevac."

When Lee came across Carl Cokely, his stomach turned over and his eyes filled with water. He clenched his teeth together, tightening his jaw until it ached. Chico agreed: it was a nauseating sight.

Cokely was lying in a patch of weeds and a puddle of blood and mud only a few feet from the deep crater the blast had created. He was groping at his hip on the right side where his leg had once been. His trousers had been ripped away from his left leg as well, and there were countless areas where the flesh had been torn from his body, stretching from his remaining booted foot all the way up to his groin. His black skin couldn't camouflage the fact that everything that was left of him, from the waist down, had received second- and third-degree burns and shrapnel hits. His hipbone was partially exposed and looked like something that belonged in a butcher's waste can. His decimated testicles and penis hung from his body by a single thread of tissue. His bowels had been ripped open, and blood shot from his leg artery like a runaway fire hose. Lee dropped his rifle to the ground, threw off his flak jacket, ripped his shirt open at the chest and balled it up. He jammed the material into Cokely's gaping wound in an effort to stop the bleeding, and then it came—the pop-pop-pop, zip-zip, chink-a-chink-a-chink, the metallic crack of the AK-47s. Slowly at first, then all hell opened up. Lee dragged Cokely into the crater, leaving his M-16 and flak jacket where he'd dropped them.

"I'm fucked up, lieutenant. Jesus, I'm hurtin.' I'm on fire." Tears flooded from Cokely's eyes and streamed down his face.

"We're gonna get you out of here."

"Where's my leg, lieutenant? Get my leg for me, will ya? They can put it back on, I know they can."

"We're getting you out of here. Ramirez'll be here in a

second. We'll get you some morphine. Just hang in there. You'll be higher than a kite before you know it. A medevac's on the way. Hang in there, Cokely. Just hang in there, okay? You're going home." Lee tightened the pressure on Cokely's groin. It had no effect, but it was all he could think to do.

The crater was deep enough to protect them both from the small-arms fire, but Lee knew it was only a matter of seconds before enemy troops would emerge from the tree line and be down in the hole with them. The heat on his bare chest suddenly became more than oppressive. It became a furnace.

He would later tell Grace he felt he was in a dream. *Lying in the hot sun with your shirt off. Four weedy hairs sprouting from your chest. Eyes closed, just listening to the waves roll in and WABC. Jones Beach in August—gotta love it. Workin' on that tan. Now watching the girls go by in those skimpy little two piecers. Titties bouncing this way and that. The Four Tops. The Stones. The Under Assistant West Coast Promotion Man. Smoking butts and putting them out in the wet sand with your bare feet because you were so damn cool then. Didn't know from pain. Just take what you want—the whole world is there for you. More girls. Tossing a pinky ball in the breakers. Emptying your bladder in the ocean because you were too damn lazy to walk all that way to the public john.*

"I don't want to die here, lieutenant."

"Piss on it, nobody's dying, Cokely. Nobody dies in my platoon today. Nobody. Hang in there—we're going to get you out of here ASAP."

"I'd really like to see my mom... I just want to see her just once, okay, lieutenant? Just one more time? Don't let me die in Vietnam. Anywhere but here. Sir, I don't want to die in Vietnam. I don't want to die on this piece of ground. The

Devil lives here. There's no God here. God has turned his back on us all."

"Don't you worry, Momma's Boy. Ramirez is on his way."

As if on cue, Ramirez, Cooper, Hanratty, Chico, and Sergeant Wall tumbled into the crater with them.

"Goddamn, lieutenant," the sergeant said, "this hole ain't big enough for seven grunts. How's he doin'?"

Wall didn't wait for the answer. He propped himself up, raised partially out of the crater, and fired eight or ten rounds into the tree line. "These cocksuckers are going to be on top of us in no time, lieutenant. The rest of the men are coming in from the rear, so be careful who you shoot at. Chico peed his fucking pants."

"I peed my fucking pants before the shit hit the fan, lieutenant. Don't listen to that crazy son of a bitch."

Sergeant Wall was back up, his entire torso out of the hole this time. He finished off the remainder of his ammunition clip, slid down, ejected the magazine from his M-16, and jammed another in its place. He looked at Hanratty and Cooper. "You guys need an engraved invitation? There's a fucking war goin' on."

Lee pulled his .45 caliber pistol from his belt and mimicked Wall's move. He rose on his knees, unloaded the entire clip into the tree line, and dropped into the hole. "I don't see shit out there, sergeant."

"Well, who the hell do you think's shooting at us, lieutenant? The little birdies? The Wizard of Oz? They're all over the fucking place."

Ramirez removed Lee's shirt from Cokely's wound. Blood shot from his artery straight into the corpsman's face.

"Jesus."

He quickly grabbed a medical clamp from his pack and locked it down across the artery, stopping the flow of blood.

Cokely's face was now turning ashen. He began trembling uncontrollably. Ramirez next pulled four morphine doses from his bag and jammed them one at a time into Cokely's flesh. It was a futile effort.

"He's gone into shock, lieutenant." Ramirez's voice became soft. "He's not going to make it, sir."

"Nobody dies here today, Ramirez, nobody. What's the status on that medevac, Chico?"

"They won't come in until we have the area secured, lieutenant. It's too hot for them. They're holding a half a click south of here."

Sergeant Wall, Cooper and Hanratty were rising up and ducking down on an alternate basis; each time firing off ten rounds into the tree line. The North Vietnamese returned every volley with equal intensity. Cokely was now holding on to the pocket of Lee's trousers. Although shaking radically, his grip remained iron tight, keeping Lee from crawling high enough out of the hole to get off more shots of his own.

"Ah shit, here the fuckers come," Wall growled. "Tasker must be forcing them out. Make sure all your shots clean. Our guys are right behind these cocksuckers. Cooper, stay to the right. Stay left, lieutenant. You can't hit shit with that fucking .45, anyway, and I don't think there's any of the bastards over that way."

Lee felt a strong stinging sensation rake across the side of his face. He ran his hand over his cheek. It was covered in gritty blood. He felt his cheek again. There was no real pain, just the sharp sting, as if he'd dragged his razor too close to his skin. He felt the area once more searching for the wound, but found nothing. The blood wasn't his. It belonged to Gary Hanratty. A bullet had passed through his throat, and he was lying at Lee's feet motionless. It had been the shattered pieces of Hanratty's spine that had stung the side of Lee's face. And at that moment, Carl Cokely dropped his grip on Lee's trouser leg. The two had died within seconds of one other.

Vague and garbled, like some voice echoing from another world, Lee heard Sergeant Wall scream, "Goddamn it, lieutenant, get that cocksucker. I can't get this fucking clip out." He kicked his boot into Lee's ribcage to be certain he had his attention.

Lee scrambled to his knees and looked to his left. A North Vietnamese regular was advancing toward the crater, but firing his AK-47 toward the tree line and Corporal Tasker who'd just emerged behind him. The soldier then spun his rifle in the direction of the crater, continuing to fire on semi-automatic. He looked to be no more than twelve years old. The bullets kicked up the earth at the edge of the hole and flew between the Marines, whistling and cracking like hyped-up honeybees as they went by. Lee brought his .45 around just as his radio operator's head rose up, blocking his view. He slapped his left hand aggressively onto Chico's helmet, forcing him down to the ground. He raised himself higher and squeezed off three rounds. The soldier dropped to his knees, leaned backwards, and then lurched forwards as his body was raked with bullets from behind by Corporal Tasker. Again Lee felt a strong stinging sensation, this time in his left hand. He looked at it. It was now also covered in blood, and he wondered which one of his men he had lost this time.

In less than a minute the world would become silent—no more rife shots, no more grenades, no more explosions. Just voices that blurred into a horror house soundtrack, and the distant whomp-whomp-whomp sound of an approaching helicopter.

Chico began yelling, "I can't hear shit. I can't hear shit,

lieutenant. What's going on? I called for the medevac, told them it was clear, but I can't hear this fucking radio. The radio's dead. We gotta find a spot for the slick, gotta throw some green smoke for him." He began pounding the side of his PRC-25 radio with the hard black rubber handset. "Can anybody hear this fucking thing. I don't hear shit. Somebody say something for Christ's sake."

Sergeant Wall slid down the edge of the crater. There was a dazed look in his eyes. Thick red blood covered the front of his flak jacket as a small stream of crimson rolled from the corner of his mouth.

Cooper slid down beside him and said, "Are you hit, sarge?"

"Jesus mother-fucking Christ."

"Are you all right?" Lee asked, scanning Wall for any sign of an open wound. From his waist up he was saturated in human blood, but other than his mouth and ear, none appeared to be coming from within. It was as if he'd been spray-painted in the stuff.

The sergeant slowly closed his eyes. "Bit my fucking tongue." He leaned to his left and spit a huge wad of blood into the earth. "Man, I don't ever want to go through this shit ever again, I swear to Christ. I'm too old for this shit. I'm too short for this shit. This is not short-timer duty. I shouldn't be here. And I want my God damned mother-fucking Purple Heart. I don't give a shit, Lieutenant, I'm bleedin'..." He stuck out his bloody tongue, "...and I want my third Heart. I want out of this fucking hellhole. Jesus, if I see my twenty-first birthday it'll be a fucking miracle. Might even start goin' to church if I can get home. Jesus God, give me that third Purple Heart and send me back to Philly. Please, God."

Wall then opened his eyes and looked down at Lee's bloody hand. He smiled at first. It developed into a chuckle. Finally he laughed out loud. "What happened to your fucking finger, lieutenant?"

Chico told me he firmly believed that the round from the AK-47 would have passed through his brain if his lieutenant hadn't reached up with left hand to shove his head out of his way. As it was, the bullet just clipped the top of Chico's helmet, severed the pinky finger of Lee's left hand at the lower knuckle, and left Chico's gray matter feeling as though it had been put into a blender.

It took twenty minutes for the ringing in Chico's ears to begin to subside.

Lee Corbet's finger would never be reattached to his hand and would eventually end up in Honolulu, Hawaii hanging from the rear view mirror of Raymond Slack's Chevy pickup truck.

And two nineteen-year-old boys, Carl Cokely and Gary Hanratty, would be placed in thick, black plastic body bags. Their names, in the end, would be struck on a granite wall in Washington, D.C., however their mothers would never see their faces again.

Sergeant Wall

Lee had never disclosed any specifics about the day he lost his finger. No one ever seemed to get the details. Ever. Like Chico Lowery, Grace said he believed there was no point in going through it time and time again.

"It's depressing as hell and it's never going to bring Cokely or Hanratty back to their families. Not in a million years. So what is the Goddamned point?" he told her.

Lee considered it all set in stone and opted to leave it there. Like a viper pit, he saw no good reason to go poking a stick into it. Even the official Marine Corps records in St. Louis contain no particulars regarding Lee's missing finger, and very little of what else actually happened that day. Chico said the medevac helicopter had swooped in and taken out the bodies of the two dead Marines. Lee gave his official account to the colonel later in the afternoon via radio. There is no paper trail. The bullet's incision had been so clean, he simply had Ramirez stitch up his lacerated left hand, preferring to stay with his platoon rather than be shipped back to the States after only six months in country. He never received a Purple Heart for the wound because it was never reported. When he was released from active duty two years later the Navy's examining physician had said, "Tell me captain, how the hell did you get into the Marine Corps with onlya thumb and three fingers?" I was told Lee shrugged and said, "I guess somebody at Quantico had trouble with the math. They're Marines, after all."

"Yeah, right, I thought fingers were the only way Marines could count to ten."

Having never met Lee, I'm not certain I'll ever be able to fully understand why combat veterans wouldn't want to talk about their experience, if for no other reason than to get it off their chest. I thought Chico had handled it fairly well, though he did manage to kill off a half a bottle of bourbon in the telling of it. Grace told me that she initially felt the same way—that Lee would be healthier if he got it off his chest. But when she once again asked him, "What happened to your finger?" his answer was boiled down to just a few words: "I lost my finger in Vietnam." Nothing else was offered. End of story. "I don't want to talk about it."

Clearly, he had yet to come close enough to the one person he could trust with the specifics, the hard truth, the emotional damage. In reality no one other than Grace had ever asked Lee for any details. My mother always believed that very few people had any interest whatsoever in those who fought in Vietnam, on either side of the conflict for that matter. It was a dirty war with no visible reward for those who were dragged into it.

Grace and Lee had found their way to the Pickering Club's private beach by early afternoon. It was a chance meeting—both believing the spot would be deserted, both thinking this was a golf, tennis, or swimming pool crowd, not a beach crowd. Both searching for some time alone on a secluded stretch of sand, ultimately the reason they'd both flown off to Hawaii in the first place. Neither one thinking of the other very much. Except for Ronnie, methodically polishing glasses behind the tiny palm-shaded bar, they were alone. At seeing one another, both were filled with the same sense of disappointment mixed with a feeling of amusement, both gleaning the real reason the other had ventured to this deserted spot: that need for solitude.

The sun was high in the sky, eighty-six degrees with a light breeze coming in off the ocean. After exchanging a stiff and clumsy and unusually formal greeting, the couple dragged two green-striped canvas deck chairs to water's edge and allowed the waves to wash up and over their bare feet. Lee wore nothing but black bathing trunks and Grace the two-piece number she'd purchased at a tiny shop on Rodeo Drive. That had been a year earlier. The suit had never been exposed to salt water. Nick hated the beach and only on rare occasions would he step into a swimming pool's shallow end. He never liked the way he looked with wet hair. He also refused to allow Grace to travel to the Malibu beaches on her own, maintaining Southern California was infested with kidnappers, perverts, and rapists. *Now he's pushing me to move out to Malibu. What does that say?* she often wondered.

"Right," she said pointedly to Lee, shaking off an image of Nick, while at the same time seeming unfazed by Lee's declaration of, *I lost my finger in Vietnam,* "but you didn't say *lost* last night, you said *stole*. See? See my point? See what I'm getting at here? How does somebody *steal* your finger?"

"I guess I can't just say, *it's a long story*, and let it go at that, huh?"

"You can say it, but it's not going to do you any good. I'm no longer accepting that as a viable response from you, or anyone else for that matter. I figure the longer someone's story, the less talking I need to do. It severely reduces the odds of me saying something I might later regret."

Lee leaned back in the chair and smiled at her. "You mean you aren't going to feel sorry for me because I spent seventeen months of my life in South Vietnam?"

"No. Why should I? I've spent *ten years* of my life with my husband. You've got to put in another hundred-some months before you're even close to catching up."

He chuckled and said, "At least you weren't being shot at."

"Hey, you were lucky. People were only shooting at you with mortars and bullets. Try getting shot at with verbal slams for ten years. Try living with someone who needs to control your every movement. That's warfare. Chinese Water Torture is nothing compared to—" She stopped and looked at her toes; unable to make eye contact. *I don't want to talk about Nick, I really don't. It's time for another chapter.* "So, who stole your finger?"

"I don't know."

An overly long pause followed. Grace began tapping her fingernails on the beach chair's wooden framework. Finally she said, "Clearly that was the wrong question, Mr. Fountain of Information. Let me step back. Let's try this: *how* does someone steal your finger?"

"You're not going to let this go, are you?"

She didn't answer him. She watched the small waves roll onto the sand for fifteen seconds or so and then stood, without facing him, looking straight out to sea, and said, "You know what? I don't give a shit, I really don't. I came out here to be alone. You take your secrets to the grave and I'll take mine to the grave."

Lee reached for her hand and said, "This isn't easy for me. Can you give me some time?"

"No. No, I can't. I have no time to give."

Grace then walked twenty yards to the far end of the beach and sat on the trunk of a low-slung palm tree that stretched out over the sapphire blue water. She never glanced back at him. They stayed separated like that for a half an hour, until Lee followed in her footprints and sat next to her.

"The strange thing about being alone is... it gets sort of lonely after a while. Maybe we've both been alone for too long. Opening up is something we're not comfortable with, or worse, we're just getting used to *not* opening up. I recognize that. It's not safe. I look at you and I think, *I don't want to play it safe anymore.* I mean, what the hell can happen? We shed a few tears? Something I would guess that isn't new to either one of us."

They sat quietly for another five minutes, until Lee added, "It's actually kind of a funny story, when you look back on it."

"Oh, I'll bet. Tales of people losing body parts have always been a phenomenal source of humor and entertainment for me." Her eyes met his, only by chance. She didn't intend to look directly at him; she wasn't ready, but they shared an energy. She backtracked involuntarily: instantly frightened that her life was changing course, that her reasons for living and for dying lacked any substance whatsoever, any rationale. "No, don't. Don't talk. Don't put yourself through this just because you've met some nosy broad on a beach somewhere and she's asked you a question about something you don't want to talk about. You owe me nothing. And believe me—I have volumes that I'm unwilling to talk about."

He ignored her, breaking the eye contact and looking at the back of his left hand, challenging the gnarled scar to stimulate his memory. It did. It always did. How could it not? But this would be the first time since the day it happened that any words of substance would exit his mouth.

"I guess we all like to play it safe. The mistake we make is in thinking that not sharing is somehow safety... After the corpsman stitched up my hand," he pointed to where his finger once was, "my platoon sergeant, a kid named Wall, found what was left of my finger perched in the mud. It was interesting; the really painful part, the trauma of the wound had been absorbed mainly by the base of my finger, which obviously was no longer attached to my body. The bone was shattered at the end, but I didn't really get to feel any of that happen. It was just pulled off at the knuckle. Sure, it stung, and the tendons withdrew, and that was an odd feeling. And it did hurt, I won't lie about that. It hurt like hell, but no bone chips or fragments were left in my hand. I missed any of the intense pain that should have come along with a broken bone."

My mother said she placed her hand on his, covering the scar, thinking if he couldn't see it, he couldn't go on. As if he'd been looking through a window, and now would no longer be able to detail the images he saw on the other side of the glass. But she conceded the effect was the opposite: her touch only opened the window wider. I somehow felt that she was talking about an event in her own life, which she was. She was there, hearing Lee's words, but somehow it all seemed to be resonating on a much more personal level as she transmitted it all to me, as if she had walked through the minefield with him and was now taking me with them both.

After a silence where he looked across the water to the horizon, he pressed on. "So, anyway, Sergeant Wall picked up my pot and tucked the finger under my helmet band." He glanced up at Grace. Her face conveyed nothing other than a new willingness to listen. "These were straps, more like large black rubber bands cut from inner tubes. We stretched them over our helmets. Guys tucked bug repellent, smokes, photos of girls, whatever was handy under the bands. Whatever was cool, whatever was lucky... Hey, they were just kids. Kinda like putting the Queen of Diamonds into your bicycle spokes to make it sound like a motorcycle, something I'll bet a few of them had done only a few years before they found themselves sweating it out in Southeast Asia. They were kids... And in '68 most of them weren't old enough to vote or buy a beer, but there they were, doing what Uncle Sam had asked them to do."

He paused and looked out over the Pacific Ocean once more, as if the day was now being played out on the sky above the waves. "Anyway, Wall put the finger under my helmet band and said, 'There you go, lieutenant, your personal *Red Badge of Courage.*' It stayed there for almost two months."

"And then someone stole it from you." It wasn't a question.

"Right. I was down in Da Nang at China Beach on in-country R and R and someone lifted it while I was swimming. I gather they must have thought it'd come from an NVA soldier or Vietcong, a war souvenir of some kind. I was stupid to leave it there, but who thought...? This guy's probably showing it to his kids right now, running down some War-is-Hell tale of unparalleled heroics. I'd love to run into the jackass someday... Hell, at least it has a happy home, right?"

"That sounds kind of bitter, if you ask me."

"Bitter?" He tilted his head slightly. "Hey, my radio operator seemed more whacked out about the incident than I ever was. The whole day was his first taste of real war—he got a very early wake-up call. But I have to tell you, it's a piece of your body; you do miss it. Obviously it's not as horrific as losing an arm or a leg, but you'd still like to have it back. You kind of hope that if there is an afterlife you'll meet up with it again. You want to believe that you'll be made whole at some point in time. But we all know that will never happen, don't we?"

"Did your radio operator make it home?"

"Chico? Yep, he's a lifer. Still in the Corps as far as I know. Probably went back over there a few more times. We haven't been in touch."

"What about Sergeant Wall?"

His eyes remained fixed on the horizon. It appeared as if he'd stopped breathing, he was that still. He was quiet for a very long time. My mother told me she could see it all beginning to shut down, but finally he said, "Sergeant Wall," in a voice that was nearly impossible to hear.

"Yes, did he get home, back to the States?"

"Do you really want to know what happened to Sergeant Wall? Really?"

"Yes, I think I do."

After another lengthy pause Lee said, "I wrote up Sergeant Wall for a Silver Star and recommended he be given his third Purple Heart and sent home. He'd only bit his tongue during the firefight, but he was bleeding. He wanted to go back to Philadelphia. He was exhausted, and I wrote him a ticket home. He'd earned it. Troopers get sent back to the States for a lot of different reasons. Mostly they've spent their thirteen months in combat and are sent home. And, of course, fifty-eight thousand went home in a box. But the reason doesn't really matter because they all just disappear from your life forever. You never see them again. Three Purple Hearts was Sergeant Wall's ticket home."

"But he survived. He got out. God bless him."

Almost as if he hadn't heard her, Lee added: "Wall stopped into my restaurant two years ago. I didn't recognize him. He was out of the Marine Corps. He'd let his hair grow out and he had long sideburns and a mustache, but as soon as he spoke I knew it was him. He said he'd stopped by to apologize for any disrespect he might have shown me in Vietnam.

He told me I was a good officer, the best he'd served under. I suspect he was just being gracious, but it was nice to hear. He also said that he always believed his third Purple Heart was a bullshit medal. He said didn't deserve it, it wasn't a real wound, he shouldn't have taken it, and he should have never been sent home early. He shouldn't have left the rest of us behind, and it constantly ate away at him. He wanted to know who had been killed after he left. He didn't like what I told him... There's no reason why he would, but I wasn't going to lie to him. I probably should have. Wall was the most decorated Marine in the entire company. Hell, in the battalion for all I know. He'd been awarded two Purple Hearts and a Navy Cross before I even arrived, but he'd never been able to accept the fact that his last Purple Heart, by his opinion, was less than honorable. He believed he should have stayed and looked after his guys. I couldn't persuade him otherwise."

"And?"

"That night he hanged himself in a hotel room on West Forty-Fifth Street. In his note he apologized for being a coward and listed me as his next of kin. I was called in to identify him at the morgue. He's buried at Arlington."

"Jesus... Were there any winners at all? Any?"

"I don't know, I really don't. These guys were treated like crap when they came home. The 'baby killers.' People spit on them. Just another reason not to talk about it... Don't let them know who you are, where you've been. Get out and try to hide it all behind long hair and a beard." After a small pause, Lee added: "I had a dream last night. I dreamt that you and I came down to this beach, but it was dark, pitch black, nearly three in the morning. We took off our clothes and went into the water. You began swimming out to sea. I tried to follow, but you were a much stronger swimmer than me, and I eventually lost you in the darkness. I tread water for what seemed like hours, not wanting to return to shore alone. Fearful that I'd lost you. Eventually the sun began to rise in the east, and I could see you swimming towards me. You swam straight past and continued to the beach. That's where I finally caught up to you. We stood frozen in place for five minutes, naked, only inches apart, like statues, not touching. I asked you where you'd gone, but you refused to tell me. We then made love and you cried—wept, actually. I couldn't get you to stop."

"Was it a happy crying?"

"No. You were a basket case. You hated yourself for cheating on your—" He stopped, unwilling to finish the sentence, but then added: "You wanted to kill yourself. You asked me if I had a gun."

"And...?"

"And what?"

"Did I kill myself?"

"I don't think so."

"What do you mean, *you don't think so*? What happened after that?"

"Nothing. That was it. I woke up." He squeezed her hand with his three remaining fingers. "I hate to tell you this, but guys' dreams don't go on too far beyond the fucking part."

Grace laughed. "Do you feel like taking a swim? Now?" she asked.

"Sure. As long as you don't decide to swim all the way to China."

"I'm beginning to think I'd come back even if I did."

Teflon

For Mitch Slack that August would play over and over in his mind for the rest of his life like a gruesome video loop. "I can't change what happened. I wish I could, I'd give anything if I could. It was tragic really... and so violent. I'm sorry he killed your father, I am, but my brother was out of control. There was no stopping him. He had been exposed on so many levels, all in the same week, and I guess that's what was eating him up. It's hard for me to grasp, but looking back, I think he simply wasn't mature enough to handle it all. He became intensely paranoid, which translated into rage. My head wants me to forgive him, but my soul won't let me do it."

On the evening of August fourteenth Mitch said he was frying hotdogs in a scratched and dented Teflon pan when his brother returned to the apartment at close to nine o'clock. He'd stopped at Cookie's Joint along the way, where he'd consumed five shots of Jim Beam with follow-up Blue Ribbon longnecks while waiting for Tracy Tillis to show up for work. She never did. She wasn't stupid. She knew Ray wouldn't be pleased about his truck and had opted to hide out. When she'd phoned in sick, Lainie, one of the other dancers, informed her that Ray was hanging out at the bar getting blasted. No real surprise there either. Then Lainie, being a friendly sort, informed Ray that Tracy would be a no-show. Basically, just to get him the hell out of there while he could still walk. Ray had then driven to Tracy's apartment. She wasn't there either. Tracy wasn't stupid.

"How come you're drivin' Sami's tow truck?" Mitch asked, looking over his shoulder, past Ray, through the apartment's still open front door, and into the parking lot. Mitch had cleaned himself up: shaved, showered, washed his hair, and picked up some new clothes at Woolworth's rather than reclaim his own things from Tracy's apartment just yet. He was actually looking forward to getting back to work at the club in the morning. The Pickering Club was beginning to look like his last safe haven. Ray's apartment was getting a little too tight for Mitch. Unpleasant images of their childhood together were already beginning to surface in his mind, and he knew he needed to get out before they surfaced in Ray's mind as well.

Ray walked straight to the television set, turned it on, and then crossed to the refrigerator where he pulled out a can of Blue Ribbon and opened it.

"You don't know where that ex-bitch of yours has got herself to, do you?" he said without really focusing on Mitch's face.

"Nah. Haven't talked to Tracy all week. Good riddance, that's what I say. Screw her. You're right about that, Ray—I gotta just move on. Get a new lease on life. I used some of your deodorant. Hope that's okay? I'll grab some of my own tomorrow. Washed the towels, though." He rolled his three hotdogs over in the Teflon pan with a brown plastic spatula so that the darkened side was now facing up. "What's with Sami's truck?"

"Someone keyed my pickup. I'm getting the scratches buffed out at Tommy's, the detail shop on the boulevard."

Mitch shrugged. "It looked fine last night."

"Yeah, well, it didn't look fine this morning," Ray snapped. "Alright?"

"Sure. Whatever you say."

"Yeah, whatever I say. You're such a pussy, Mitch." He looked down into the Teflon pan. "Looks like you're fryin' up a bunch of dicks for yourself." He laughed and removed a cold and uncooked hotdog from the packaging that sat on the green-flecked Formica counter and ran his tongue along the length of it. "Is that what you're havin' for dinner, there, Mitchie? A bunch of hot cocks?" He moved the frank in and out of his mouth as though he were performing fellatio, bit it in half and then finished the show by ingesting the entire thing. "Yeah, I like mine raw. That's how we had to do it in the Nam, my friend. Ya didn't light no fires over there, buddy boy. Had to be careful just torchin' up a smoke, even during the day. Damn Gooks would be on your ass in no time. Bastards could smell match smoke two miles away." He removed another uncooked frank from the package and ate it. "So you don't know where Tracy is, huh?"

"Nah, she probably ran on back to Minneapolis, like you said she would. What do you want with her, anyway?"

Ray picked up a third frank and tapped it against Mitch's cheek. Mitch jerked his head to the side. Ray laughed, inhaled what was left in his beer can, and gnawed on the raw hotdog.

"You know something, Mitch? I fucked that bitch of yours, Tracy. Yeah, that's right. I wasn't gonna tell ya, but that's how bad she is. That's how low she is: screwed your own damn brother. You should know that. You're lucky to be rid of her. She's been sleeping around like a big dog. Turnin' tricks outta the back of the bar. Ya didn't know that neither, did ya?"

Mitch turned the electric burner off and slid his hotdogs onto a flowered plate, almost as though he hadn't heard what his brother had said. He then pulled a fork out of the kitchen drawer, tore a paper towel off the roll, and walked over to the couch and sat with the plate on his lap in front of the TV. A *Dallas* rerun flickered on the small screen. The bent rabbit ears did little to improve the poor reception, and Barbara Bel Geddes' and Larry Hagman's skin tones were rendered an off shade of orange by the aging color set.

"Course I didn't pay her shit. She's the one came on to me." Ray lit a cigarette and leaned against the counter top. "Last week. Yeah, I was trying to get the hell outta there 'cause I gotta get to work early the next morning, Tuesday or Wednesday night I think, and Tracy slipped out the back of CJ's and hopped into my truck. Said she's horny as hell. Musta been after you got yourself outa her apartment."

Mitch kept his mouth shut and tried to focus his eyes on the TV. He'd heard this story a little differently from Tracy. She said she'd left work and some drunk was waiting for her in the parking lot, tried to rape her in his truck but couldn't get his pecker hard. *She never told me it was Ray, though. Who the hell do you believe around here?*

"Yeah, I gave her a ride like she's never had." He pointed a finger at Mitch. "She spent the whole time tellin' me about how my dick was bigger than yours. You were a smart man to get out when you did, my friend."

"She's the one tossed me out, remember?"

Ray pulled another beer from the box. "Ya want one?"

"No thanks."

"Suit yourself."

He joined Mitch on the couch and took one of the cooked franks from the plate with his fingers and spoke between bites, drags from his cigarette, and pulls from his beer can.

"I'm gonna tell you something about these women, Mitch. They all lie. Just like that damn TV. Ya can't believe anything they tell ya. You can let all that *she threw you out* business be her side of the story if you want 'cause no one's gonna believe her for a second no ways. Not Tracy. See, what *you* tell people is that *you* packed *your* bags and left because the bitch was a whore. And if they don't believe you," he slapped his chest ape-fashion, dropping beer and cigarette ashes onto his jeans, "you send them to me. Because you got yourself a witness, my friend."

Mitch nodded, trying to let it all roll off. He jabbed at one of the franks three times before he could get his fork into it and prevent it from sliding across the plate and onto the floor. He then ate it slowly, not saying anything.

"You know, I been thinkin'," Ray continued, his lips now unable the keep from slurring the words together, "we didn't really give Tracy what she deserved last night, not by a long shot. Busted windows? Hell, that was nothin'. I mean, she needs to be taught a lesson. I mean a serious lesson, for treatin' you like that. I mean where'd she think you're gonna sleep? And then her ballin' me while you're out on your own shacked up on a bench? You couldn't even go into work lookin' the way you did after spendin' all them nights on the street. Am I right?"

"I had to clear my head. My boss understood. That's why he gave me the week off. I'm back in tomorrow."

"Okay, fine, but I'm talking about payback here. You spent what? Five, six days on that friggin' bench before you came to me. You're lucky the damn cops never found you like the last time. They keep a record on who they find and when. Toss your ass off the damn island if you're not careful. Specially someone who wasn't born here. United States or no United States. If you weren't born on the islands, you get shittier treatment. Next thing you know you're back with all them fruitcakes in California, and there ain't a damn thing you can do about it."

"You found me, Ray. I didn't come to you." Mitch was beginning to wonder if anything he said was getting through to his brother. "But I do appreciate you helpin' me out like you've done. I do. I'll make it up to you. I'll even chip in some rent money, once I get back to work and figure out my cash flow."

"Yeah, but we still didn't do Tracy up right."

"We busted the windshield out of her car," Mitch said, raising his voice uneasily. "That's enough. I'm ready to move on, Ray, I really am. I don't want to do nothin' that's illegal no more. It's bound to catch up with me."

Ray took the last hotdog from Mitch's plate, bit off a quarter of it, and waved the remainder in his brother's face. "You know what your problem is? You let people push you around. Man, if I acted like you I woulda never made it through Nam, I swear to Christ. You had to dig in or get blown away. Couldn't do nothing half-assed or you'd be comin' home in a tin can. And ain't nobody looked out for your butt, neither. You had to cover that for yourself."

Mitch set the empty plate on the wooden spice box. Of the package of six franks he'd purchased on his way home from the Laundromat, Ray'd consumed five and he'd only eaten one.

"Look, Ray, alls I'm saying is, I'd like to let the entire Tracy thing drop. I don't know that we shoulda busted up her car like we did. I wish we hadn't done it. She don't have any money to fix it. But on the other side, I think I might have learned something through all this. I don't know. Maybe she was right in doin' what she did... It makes for a clean break—she goes her way, I go mine. Maybe we weren't cut out for each other. I'm gonna look for a place after work tomorrow… I shouldn't have bothered you with my problems. I'll get outta your hair as soon as I can, I mean it. I'm gonna straighten myself out on my own. That's the only way to grow up, like you said."

"You ain't in my hair. Not yet, anyway. Hell, I'm happy to have the company. Like the old days. Almost like when we was kids, right?"

Mitch's body stiffened slightly. Ray slapped Mitch on the thigh and belched loudly. His eyes then widened dramatically. He placed a hand over his mouth, stood, trotted into the kitchen area, and proceeded to vomit into the sink. The beer, the five hotdogs, and the Jim Beam he'd ingested all served to burn his throat and nostrils as they regurgitated from his stomach and passed from his mouth and nose. The gagging went on for nearly three minutes while Mitch stared straight ahead at the television, not really seeing or hearing any part of *Dallas*. When Ray'd finished with the vomiting and the dry heaves, he reached for a paper towel and wiped the remaining slime from his mustache.

"Man I don't know how you can eat that shit, I really don't. Who knows what the fuck's in a hot dog?"

He flipped the garbage disposal switch and the machine rumbled and groaned as it pulverized all that he'd disgorged and sent it into the Honolulu sewer system. He pointed at the TV with his can of Blue Ribbon. Beer slopped out of the opening and onto the linoleum floor.

"Linda Gray. Yeah. I'd like to give her a ride." He dropped a paper towel onto the wet spot on the floor. It became instantly saturated with beer so he dropped down two more towels and pushed them around the floor with the tip of his boot. "Come to think of it, she looks an awful lot like Tracy. I mean her tits are smaller, but in the face. What do you think?"

"I suppose."

"And you know them tits of Tracy's ain't real; you know that don't you? She's had them babies worked over."

"I suppose."

"And you don't know where she's at, huh? 'Cause she ain't at home and she never showed up for work at CJ's. Called in sick. Sick, my ass."

"I just want to let her be, Ray. I don't have any grudge against her no more." Mitch stood and walked over to the kitchen sink where he proceeded to wash the flowered plate and set it in a plastic drying rack. He then scrubbed out the Teflon frying pan and cleaned the sink with scouring powder and a sponge.

Ray positioned himself behind Mitch, grabbed his hips and forcefully pushed his groin into his brother's backside, wedging him up against the counter top. "You're just the perfect little homemaker, ain't you, Mitchie? Doin' the laundry? The dishes? You're gonna make someone a good wifey one of these days. Ever take it from behind?"

Mitch spun away from him. "Cut it out, will ya?"

Ray laughed and tossed his empty beer can in the trash. "Relax. I'm just foolin' around. Come on, let's go find Tracy. I want to give her a good old-fashioned down-home workin' over, what do you say? Just you and me? Do a little twosome on her."

"No."

"You're such a pussy. You're such a damn pussy. Just like when we were kids. You haven't changed a inch." He lit another cigarette from his last. "Okay, the hell with you; I'll go find her myself. 'Cause you know what? I'm gettin' a little horny around here."

Ray grabbed two more beers from the refrigerator, walked out to Sami's tow truck, and started the engine.

Parachutes

The temperature in the Palisades hadn't dropped with the sunset as it was known to do. The bougainvillea outside Grace's bedroom rattled against the wooden trellis in the warm night air and the mild aroma of her roses drifted through the open windows. In her retelling of that evening Grace seemed lost in a dream. I honestly believe she had forgotten that I was in the room with her; otherwise, she would have never gone into such graphic detail. She had transported herself to what was perhaps the most joyful evening of her life. I'm sure she had returned to that point quite often over the years, and I'm guessing there must have been something in the air that had taken her back once again. I had only come in to say goodnight, but she had taken herself to Hawaii. As she spoke, I'd hoped to persuade her to get some rest, but interrupting her at that moment would have only been cruel. I let her go on.

Lee bent at the waist, rolled his trousers up to over the calf, and joined her in the ankle-deep tide pool. They'd left their shoes on a green deck chair alongside the Pickering Club's deserted and darkened beachside bar. There was nothing chance, nothing accidental about their being together on the small strip of sand under the darkened sky. They'd shared a dinner, drinks, and wine and exited the dining room with no real desire to be alone or separated from one another. Their walk to the beach had been slow and quiet, side-by-side, no words spoken. Other than the night's flickering starlight and moon, the low-lying yellow path lights were the only illumination. She wrapped her arm in his when she felt him near. It was the first they'd touched since the afternoon and energy passed between them. Neither one was quite yet able to discern if it was a sexual force or simply a form of brotherly-sisterly attraction, a new- found feeling of friendship and intimacy, and a certain safety. There were no clouds, and the sky was so littered with stars it seemed gray rather than black. The three-quarter moon was still low. They hadn't spoken by choice, each wallowing in a great freedom to be silent. On occasion, a larger wave would possess enough force to send its sampling of frothy sea across and over the small rise in the sand, refreshing the water in the shallow tide pool. There were no sounds other than these waves and the intermittent nocturnal insect or frog or bird. They both felt a sensation that their futures had been mapped out by someone other than themselves, that their fate had been decided, and therefore they had nothing to do but roll with the tide.

"I don't know what I would have done here if I hadn't run into you," Grace eventually voiced. "I had such a clear picture of what was going to happen when I boarded the plane at LAX. I had an illusion that I was a much stronger person than it turns out I am. I've disappointed myself, but I'm not finding the disappointment all that disappointing." She smiled. "Sorry, that doesn't make any sense."

He didn't say anything but she could feel his hold on her arm become more firm. She rocked her feet from side to side, digging them deeper into the grainy bottom of the gully, feeling the coolness of the wet sand between her toes.

"I wondered..." she said after another long quiet period. He said nothing. She decided to wait him out. *Did he even hear me?* she began to think.

"Wondered what?" he said at last.

"I wondered if we were going to end up sleeping together before I depart?"

A small laugh escaped from his lips. "Aren't you forgetting that you're married?"

"No, but I'm trying like hell."

He laughed a little louder and then pulled his arm from hers and placed it around her waist bringing her hips up against his own. There was nothing brotherly-sisterly about the energy that now passed between them. "I'm glad we ran into each other, too."

"I never said I was glad. I didn't say glad. Glad is your word. You've confused me. It's as if I was bringing a steak out of O'Rourke's kitchen and when I got to the customer's table I found that there was a chicken on the plate and I don't know how it got there. I feel that I've lost control of my own destiny. And I can't tell if that's good or bad."

"I guess you could always go back for the steak before it, or the chicken, gets too cold."

"You don't want me to go back into the kitchen."

"No, I don't. I want you to stay right where you are. I don't want to release my hold on you. Chicken's just fine with me. Always has been. Hot or cold."

They again stood quietly for well over five minutes, each a little uneasy, more than ever convinced where the evening would end up, but unsure as to the route it would take. Lee broke the latest silence by asking, "Do you still have family in Long Beach?"

Grace looked away and said, "My dad."

"No mother? Brothers? Sisters?"

"They're divorced. My mother lives in San Mateo. Has for almost fifteen years. I think she might be a lesbian. She lives with another woman." Grace shrugged. "One sister, no brothers. My sister lives in Dallas, I think. She dropped out of high school when she was sixteen. Her boyfriend played football for U.S.C. and was drafted by the Oilers, so she ran off with him. He dumped her a few years after they moved Houston. Apparently he was kind of abusive. Last I heard she was married to a Dallas lawyer."

"You don't talk to her?"

"No."

"What about your mom?"

"No."

"Your dad?"

"My father wasn't a very nice person, okay?"

Despite the warmth of the evening a shiver passed through Grace, and Lee pulled her closer. She leaned the side of her face on his shoulder. "Do you ever feel like you've just jumped from a plane and halfway down you realize you left your parachute behind?"

"You mean like right now?"

She let out a small laugh. "If I say I feel safe with you, will I be proven right or wrong?"

"You're safe with me. I have an extra parachute."

"And you're not just saying that to get into my pants?" He laughed, and Grace added, "Well?"

"You *are* married."

"What are you, a Catholic, for God's sake?"

"Actually, I *was* raised a Catholic, now that you mention it. I've even been to Mass once or twice in the last year— Easter, anyway. St. Patrick's puts on an impressive show."

"Oh, brother..."

"But a French Catholic."

"What does that mean?"

"It means we don't pay a whole lot of attention to what Rome dictates."

"In other words: it's okay to sleep with married women?"

"I believe in France it is, yes."

"What about Hawaii?"

"I don't think your average Frenchman gets too bogged down in border issues any longer. They let the Americans, Chinese, and Russians worry about that."

He burrowed his feet into the sand so that he could feel his toes touching hers. He studied her for a long moment while her eyes seemed to dance, even to make love with his. He then bent and kissed her. Their mouths opened and their tongues found one another, and their heart rates increased significantly. His body became as stiff and hard as hers became soft and compliant. When they broke, she leaned her head on his chest once more and said, "Thank you."

"I've never slept with a married woman."

"That's okay," she said gently.

"It's not a Catholic thing. It's just... It's more of a personal issue. I don't know, I guess somehow it just seems that it's something that shouldn't be done. Because when you've..." He stopped in mid-sentence.

"Are you saying we can't do this, that you can't do this? Because a certain portion of your anatomy is in stark disagreement with you... Lee, I'm getting a divorce. My marriage is over. I'm separated. In fact, I'm separated by two thousand miles of ocean."

I can't believe this. Every man in the world wants to sleep with me for the simple reason that I'm Nick Rolston's wife, and here I am stuck on an island with the only man in the world who won't sleep with me because I am married. Because he has morals? This is not fair. This is craziness.

Grace moved her arms up and around his neck, and their lips met once more. His arms caressed the small of her back and pulled her close while they again explored one another's mouths with their wet tongues. Their bodies rocked intimately, almost as if they were of one being. His hardness pressed against her flat abdomen so forcefully it caused them both some pain. Grace took his sports jacket by the collar and peeled it down over his shoulders, letting it drop into the tide pool.

"That was a $150 jacket," he said after their kiss had ended.

"Was."

She untucked her blouse, vigorously yanking the silk from the waistline of her skirt. She unbuttoned it and slipped it off. The moonlight reflected off the ocean and the light flickered blue and green and silver across her bare chest, her firm dark nipples forming long shadows on her pale untanned breasts. Grace held the blouse out in her right hand and let it drop into the salty water.

"We're even—that was a $150 blouse."

"Was."

He smiled at her and kept his eyes fixed on hers while he removed his own shirt and let it fall. He said, "Twenty-five dollars," and brought his mouth to hers once more.

"Take me skydiving some time, will you?"

"Now seems as good a time as any."

The tips of her breasts scraped and dug into his chest, pushing the hair aside until they met his own hot flesh. When they had, Grace moaned softly as an electric charge seemed to travel from her breasts through the length of her body and finally settled between her legs. Her fingers worked persistently to unfasten his belt and trousers. They fell into the pool, and he stepped away from his pants, his erection was fully exposed through the opening in his white shorts. Grace grabbed at it with both hands, sending similar shock waves up and down his body.

Their lips never parted, but when at last they did, Lee stepped back, removed his shorts, and dropped to his knees in the water before her. He slowly and carefully unhooked the catch at the side of her skirt and lowered the zipper. As he worked the skirt down her thighs, he hooked his fingers into the elastic waistband of her panties and slid them down also, while at the same time gathering up the hem of her skirt. Grace stepped out of the garments, and he handed them to her, attempting to keep them dry. But she let them fall into the pool, preferring to entangle her fingers in his thick hair. Lee pushed his face between her legs and ran his tongue along the inside of her thighs—first the left and then the right, then back to the left. Grace's fingernails played with his scalp as he worked his way up until he met her center. His tongue played at the dampness that had formed on her soft mound of auburn hair. Grace let out another soft moan as she spread her legs and opened herself to him.

Grace allowed Lee to make love to her in that fashion for nearly five minutes, until she could stand it no longer. She then knelt in front of him and held him close. After a moment she brought her face to his and they engaged in another lengthy kiss. They fell sideways along the bank of the tide pool. She rolled onto her back, pulling him on top of her, and he entered her as if all of creation said it was meant to be. Their fingers and hands had played no part in the undertaking. They stayed in that position for a lifetime: smiling, kissing lightly, laughing, kissing deeply, and then again making love with their eyes. Eventually, the idea of raw sex overtook their bodies, and they began to grind their pubic areas together rhythmically. Their movements were not frenzied or animalistic; they were slow and peaceful. The tide pool was just deep enough to cover the spot where their bodies had joined, and their easy rocking motion sent small waves rolling down to the far end of the gully. Ultimately Grace's muscles tightened as her orgasm came upon her. Her fingernails pressed into Lee's buttocks and he stiffened as well. After the intensely passionate shock waves had passed through them, they found themselves totally expended, short of breath, and drained.

"I see that 'not sleeping with a married woman' didn't turn out to be a very strong conviction on your part," she said after she'd kissed a bead of sweat from his cheek.

"You're a temptress. I lost control of myself."

"Hah. That's a new one." She kissed him again, lightly, and he returned it with more energy. "Did you notice," she added, "that I haven't had a cigarette in over twenty-four hours?"

"I did."

"And I don't even want one now."

"Does this mean we'll have to call off the firing squad?"

"Yes."

Tomas

Tomas Pressten is now retired but still living on Oahu, still driving his yellow Jaguar. But by mid-August 1979 he had been the Pickering Club's general manager for almost two years. Nonetheless, many longstanding members still referred to him as the "new" manager, while at the same time retaining fond memories of the "old" manager, Hans Brugger, a cigar-chomping German who had been with the club for thirty-eight years. And where Hans Brugger would never have been addressed by anything other than *Mr.* Brugger, or *Herr* Brugger behind his back, Tomas Pressten seldom got beyond being Tom or Tomas. He was tall, nearly six-four, with manicured blond hair that had been turned into near platinum-white by the Hawaiian sun. Rejecting his Swedish heritage, he had a total disdain for any suggestion of cold weather or ice or snow. After detesting his four winters at Cornell University in Ithaca, New York, he'd escaped to Florida the day after graduation to take a position in Hobe Sound, about as far away from skis and ice skates as he could get. But Florida had worn thin after sixteen years, so Tomas had taken this assignment with the Pickering Club and moved on, leaving his two children behind with a Sunshine State wife who failed to understand, or coexist with, his attraction to other men. Their divorce had been finalized on May tenth of that year.

One of the few people who did call Tomas *Mr.* Pressten was Mitchell Slack, the Pickering Club's pot washer of the past six months. Tomas found Mitch to be an interesting person; often out in Never-Never Land, but a fellow who seemed to have a lot more on the ball than someone willing to settle for living the life of a pot washer in a private club on Oahu. And it was for this reason that he had been disposed to give Mitch a week off so that he could straighten out some *personal difficulties.* Tomas knew all too well what it felt like to be thrown out of the house by a woman. It was a situation he could easily empathize with.

August fifteenth was the day Mitch had promised to return to work. In the back of his mind Tomas told me he thought it would probably never come to pass. Pot washer was low-of-the-low when it came to restaurant jobs. Most had a little gypsy in them, if not a pint of rye whisky, and there were only two directions to go for a pot washer: up, or out the door. And ninety-nine percent of the time, if your pot washer walked out of the door, that was the last you ever saw of him. Under normal circumstances, Tomas wouldn't have held the job open for more than an hour before calling Fletcher's Employment Agency on Date Street in search of a replacement. But he held out hope that Mitch would return, jockeying employee scheduling on a daily basis to make sure the position was covered. And sure enough, just before eight a.m., there was a knock on his office door.

"Come in," he said, a hopeful expression graced his lean face, something Mitch would not immediately detect.

Mitch opened the door and stuck in his head. "I just wanted to let you know I was back, Mr. Pressten. And thank you again for letting me have the time off. I think I have everything straightened out... Sorta."

Tomas stood and walked over to the door and swung it wide. "Come on in, Mitch. Have a seat for a minute. I was just going over the week's kitchen schedule."

Mitch entered and sat on the rattan couch that faced the large teak desk. He wore new jeans and a green-and-white striped short-sleeve Dacron shirt. He glanced beyond Tomas at the office wall. It was covered with black-and-white photographs of Tomas with notable Floridian and Hawaiian politicians and celebrities—none of whom Mitch recognized except for Burt Reynolds, which impressed him significantly. Tomas' diploma from Cornell hung dead center, directly behind the desk and above his dark brown leather office chair. On the teak desk, alongside a gold pen and pencil set in a black marble base, sat two photographs in silver frames. One of a boy and another of a young girl. The boy reminded Mitch very much of his brother, Ray, when he was the same age. His look was very intense, almost hostile.

Tomas instantly became aware that Mitch was studying the photos, so he said, "My son and daughter. They live in Florida with their mother."

"Huh. That's a long way to be separated from your kids. I guess you must miss them a lot."

"Yes... Yes, I do," Tomas said, somewhat surprised by the question and the sensitive way it had been presented. "They were visiting in April for two weeks. I gather your paths never crossed while they were here?"

"No. But you know the kitchen. We don't get out front too often. Only the cooks on buffet night."

"Ah, yes, and my former wife believes that nothing but evil lurks behind the swinging doors of a restaurant's kitchen. My children have been brainwashed to stay out for fear that they'll end up like some wayward waifs in one of those sadistic German fairy tales—roasted on a spit over an open fire by a pack of laughing timberwolves."

Tomas took his seat behind the desk and shuffled some papers around. "Were you able to find a spot to settle into?" he asked, giving it as much of a distracted ring as he could.

"Ah... I ran into a guy I sorta know," Mitch lied, thinking that bunking in with his older brother had a somewhat juvenile sound to it. "I met him a while back at a bar. He's putting me up. I'm on his couch. But it's only temporary. I'm gonna look for a place of my own after work today."

"I see." Tomas cleared his throat. "Are you okay money-wise? You're going to need something for a deposit, aren't you?"

"Yeah, I'm okay, I'd been savin' up for a guitar. It's in a bank account. I got enough." Mitch looked up at the ceiling. "I think. It'll be tight, but I'm okay for now. I just need to budget myself for the next month or two. Put the guitar on the back burner for a while." He chuckled uneasily.

"Let me know if you need some help. We may be able to work something out. The club has a discretionary fund if you need a small loan of some sort."

Tomas again moved some papers off to the side of his desk. His hands shook just slightly as he opened his employee schedule book.

"Well, Mitch, I've been looking things over in your absence, and I'd like to make some changes in the kitchen. Chef wants to expand the dinner menu, and I think it's a fabulous idea. Times are changing and members want something more than the usual club fare of lamb, prime rib, and lobster tails. People want to dabble in something different every now and then. Try something new. If you know what I mean?" He glanced up at Mitch to see if they were on the same page, but Mitch's expression was fairly blank, not giving much up one way or the other.

"Well, I won't bore you with what's all involved with this,

Mitch, but basically Kami will be needed to help out Chef with the fresh-dinner menu, which means I'm going to have to put a new man on as short-order cook to handle the evening bar fare, and finger food for the lounge as well."

Mitch sat quietly. He told me he was totally confused as to why he'd been brought in on this type of high-level executive decision-making.

"What I'd like to know," Tomas continued, "is whether you would be interested in learning how to handle the short-order duties? Sandwich and fry cook, really. That way I could just put on another pot washer to take your place. I've had my eye on you for some time now and I like what I see." He took a small pause. "You seem to know your way around the kitchen fairly well—you're a good worker. Other than this past week, you haven't missed a day or shown up late once, and I believe you're due for a promotion of sorts." Before Mitch could answer, Tomas held up his hands and added the disclaimers. "Now, the raise in pay wouldn't be much, perhaps another dollar or two an hour, and of course you would be working different hours, the noon-to-ten shift. And you'd need to grind down the grill at the end of the night, and clean the steam table and food service areas before going home as well, so you most likely wouldn't get out the door much before eleven or twelve each evening. But you will be paid time-and-a-half for any overtime you might put in."

Mitch was speechless.

"You don't have to make a decision about this right now, but I'll need an answer by the end of the day. I'd like to get Kami off of the evening shift and working with Chef tomorrow morning." Tomas paused, trying to read Mitch's thoughts, but his face was again expressionless. "Now if you do say yes, you'll have to work until midnight tonight and be here again all day tomorrow so that Kami can teach you the ropes. Hopefully, I'll have a new pot washer in tomorrow as well, but if not, you'll be doing a little double duty. In any case you're looking at two sixteen-hour days back to back. After that you'll be on a more regular schedule."

"No. No. I'm hep to this, Mr. Pressten." Mitch was no longer able to restrain his delight with the situation. He smiled broadly. "This is great, Mr. Pressten, I won't disappoint you, I swear I won't."

"Well, that's wonderful, Mitch. I'm very pleased." Both men stood, and Tomas walked around his desk and draped his arm over Mitch's shoulder. "Obviously, this means you won't be able to look for a new place to live until the day after tomorrow. But you will get your overtime, don't worry about that. You're going to be a busy little beaver for the next two days. I'm sorry about that, but I don't see any other way to handle it." He opened his office door, and Mitch stepped into the hallway. "But I'm sure things will work out."

"Yeah. Thanks again, Mr. Pressten. Things are gonna work out. I know it."

"And do let me know if you have any difficulty finding a place to bed down. The club can help. I can help."

Ellen

The moment she told Lee about Nick, Grace said it was like traveling at a hundred miles an hour, the wind blowing through her hair, not a care in the world, and then slamming into a concrete wall. They fell into a dark silence. He said nothing, but she could see the wheels turning at warp speed behind his veiled eyes. She was married to someone he had met on numerous occasions, a man he probably knew fairly well. Grace must have understood the facts. I've often wondered; what *does* one say when learning something as disquieting as that? What should Lee have said to her? What could he have said to her? I can only imagine what might have flown through his mind that moment.

What am I supposed to say to her? I run a restaurant. There's a certain confidentiality that goes with the pursuit. I don't talk about my customers behind their backs no matter who they are, end of story. I don't talk about who comes in with whom and when. Who's groping whom under the tables. I don't talk about who drinks too much. I don't talk about anything. It's the business. Hell, she should know that. She's been in the business. That's the very reason people return. So, what do I do? What do I say? Do I tell her what I know? A guy comes in maybe four or five times a year, and he's with the same woman every time. She's good-looking in a Wall Street kind of way. Very well-dressed, sexy glasses. They're lovey-dovey; must be his wife, right? He returns with her, time and time again. Always the same woman. He's loud. He makes everyone take notice of him. But the other customers seem to enjoy the show—they like to think they're rubbing elbows with a "somebody." So, here I am, swimming in the Pacific Ocean, I'm miles and miles away from Manhattan— in Hawaii, for Christ's sake—and the woman with whom I just spent the entire night, tells me she's married to this guy, meaning the woman he's been bringing into my restaurant all these years. The Wall Street cutie with the sexy glasses is not his wife and never has been. As far as I know he's been cheating on Grace for over eight years with the same woman. I can't tell her that. He's not leaving her for a Santa Monica waitress in hot pants. He's leaving her for Miss Prim and Proper Wall Street Investment Banker, or whatever the hell she is. So, what in God's name do I say to her?

"You're not saying anything," Grace finally said. "I expected more of a reaction, since Nick's eaten in your restaurant so many times." She continued to tread water. "I shouldn't have told you who he was. I knew it was a shitty idea. When will I learn to keep my mouth shut? But I had to, Lee, I really had to." She swam a complete circle around him. "Say something, will you?" she nearly shouted.

"He's a good tipper?"

"Fuck you."

Grace began swimming straight out to sea. But unlike in his dream, Lee caught her after a short distance. He grabbed her around the waist and they went under for a few seconds. When they surfaced they both breathed deeply, in and out, spitting the salty water from their mouths as they did. After she caught her breath, he pressed his lips to hers.

"I didn't need to know that," he said after a lengthy and loving kiss. "I don't care who the hell he is, I really don't. Okay, I would have figured it out sooner or later. You've got the same last name. I thought it might be the case, could be a coincidence, but not likely. I'm not sure what I can say that you don't know already. You're getting a divorce, right? So? So? Of course I know who he is. He's a movie director, big deal. Who gives a shit? I don't get to the movies much. The governor, the mayor: they're in my place all the time. I'm not easily impressed by movie people." They were kicking their legs vigorously in an effort to keep their heads above the small waves while their arms held onto one another, their bodies pressing together from chest to groin.

Grace began rocking her head from side to side as if her neck bones had turned to putty and an invisible hand was pushing her face first left and then right and then back again. "I'm sorry, Lee... I didn't want to tell you... I had to tell you..." She began to cry. "You were going to find out... I wanted you to hear it from me... I wanted you to know before now... I wanted you to know... I didn't want you to ever find out... God, I wish he'd disappear." She was now sobbing.

He held her more tightly. "Don't. Stop... It's okay."

"No," she nearly screamed. "No, it's not okay. It's not. When I got back to my bungalow this morning there was a note from the front desk. Nick is coming to Hawaii."

"What?"

"He's booked a flight for Thursday."

"Why?"

"I called him at the apartment in Westwood... That was the number he left." Tears continued to flow from her eyes. She tried to push Lee away, but he held onto her. "Jesus, Lee, don't you understand? He wants me back. That's the reason.

He's trying to make up. He wants forgiveness. I knew this was going to happen. I knew it. It's not even a week since his lawyer called me. He pulled this same stunt four years ago. Why did I think this time would be any different?"

"Did he say that? That's what he said? In those exact words: he wants you back?"

"No. No. Jesus, he wasn't there. I left a message. But what else could it be? I can hear him now, 'It was all a big mistake, baby. It'll never happen again, I swear.'"

Lee's grip on her slackened. They were quiet for a long moment and he eventually said, "I would guess his... waitress... must have dumped him," stumbling noticeably over the word "waitress."

"Or he's found out about you, which is more like it. That's my guess. Nick's ego couldn't handle that. The idea of me coming here to be alone is something his head can cope with. But me with another man? What if that ever hit *Variety*?"

He pulled his arms from her altogether and they treaded water a foot apart, not touching but with their eyes locked. Tears still drifted slowly across Grace's cheeks. They rolled down and mixed with the seawater like dew from a leaf in early morning. "Tell me about your wife," she said softly.

"What?"

"Please, Lee. Please tell me about her. I need to know who she was."

"It's not important."

"It's important to me. I need to know more. I need to not think about Nick. I need him out of my life. Please, Lee. I feel like I'm drowning."

"Not a good choice of words."

She smiled. "Okay, sinking. Like I've got lead weights on my feet that I can't kick off. Either way, Nick is cutting off my oxygen."

"Not much better." He looked off to his left for a while. He again breathed in deeply and at last said, "Ellen drowned," as the air escaped his lungs, making no eye contact with her.

"Who?"

"Ellen... My wife. That's what she did. She drowned."

"Jesus," she said. "Oh, God, Lee... I'm so sorry." She pulled him in and they were touching once more. "I'm sorry." She dug her eyes into him—more for herself, trying to ignore the water surrounding them, trying not to acknowledge how far out they were, how much in over their heads they were. "Where was this? Were you with her when it happened?"

"You're a good person," he said. "You deserve better than what you're getting." He kissed her lightly on the lips. "No, I wasn't with her. I was in Vietnam."

"So, it was quite a while ago, then?"

"Eleven years."

Again she didn't speak for some time. When she did, she said, "Do you know that Nick supervises my birth control pills? This is absolutely crazy. He's a control freak. He buys them every month. I don't even know what drugstore he goes to. Maybe he doesn't even use a drugstore. Maybe some film-crew flunky gets them for him? I don't even know where he keeps the prescription. If he's on location, he constantly checks in just to be sure that there's a monthly supply. It's really just to check up on me, make sure I'm still taking them. He knows damn well what the supply is. He's a nut about this. He marks my periods off in his date book in red ink. That's how badly he doesn't want to have children. How much he doesn't trust me is more to the point. Do you know what it's like to have someone tell you they don't trust you? With a task as simple as taking a fucking pill? He's said so in those very words, 'I don't trust you.'"

Lee smiled at her. "The queen of the non sequitur."

She kissed him. "Not really. I was just looking at your eyes when you told me about your wife, and I realized that if there were anyone in this world I ever wanted to have a baby with, it would be you... I never really felt that with Nick, even at the very beginning. Maybe that's why I let him get away with it. I don't know."

"You don't really mean that? About a baby?"

"I wouldn't say it if I didn't mean it. I'm a good person. Hell, you're the good person. I trust you." Once again she kissed him affectionately. "Oh sure, I wanted a baby with Nick, I won't deny that, but all I wanted was a kid of my own. I just wanted a child. Any child. I still do. I think in my mind I believed that a baby would love me and somehow that translates into being taken care of. I know it sounds stupid. The baby doesn't take care of the mother. Anyway, something's changing in me. I would really like to make a child with you. I want to create a life that's half you and half me."

"Well, we sure gave it a shot last night."

She laughed. "That we did, good person, that we did." She kissed him one last time and added, "You trust me, don't you?"

"With my life."

"My legs are cramping. Can we head in to shore?"

**

Lee spoke unhurriedly, as if painting a picture on the emptiness in front of his face. "We got together in Hawaii in August of '68. I'd already been in Vietnam for ten months: already lost my finger, already had it stolen." A small laugh escaped from his chest. "She said it made her ill to look at my hand, actually asked me to keep it in my pocket and not touch her with it. It wasn't the perfect picture; I think that's what bothered her more than anything. I had become an aberration in her mind... Anyway, a lot of the married guys did that. They'd take their R and R in Hawaii, and their wives would fly out to meet them. And since Aunt Sally was a member at the Pickering Club; she set up the whole thing for us. Ellen..." He stopped, as if the word was made of raw cotton and had stuck to the roof of his mouth. "Sorry... Anyway, Ellen came out and we had five days here. It was okay... The sex was good at least. It certainly beat ten months of celibacy, which is what I was comparing it to, I guess. But conversation didn't flow. Not like it used to. I don't know, I guess I'd changed. I spent the entire time worrying about my guys. I felt like crap for leaving them, like I had deserted them in some way. I had nightmares, couldn't sleep. I kept seeing them drop like flies, just out of reach. Horrible deaths; the worst kind— their bodies shattered into pieces. Each night they would get younger, until they were all five-year-olds. I'd try to do something, try to get to them... I'd always arrive too late... And what was left of them would slowly melt into the earth and disappear."

He lifted his beer glass and set it back on the bar without drinking any. "Ellen had changed too. She seemed, I don't know, much older to me... And distant in her own way. She was against the war. Hell, by that point I was, too, but we weren't on the same page any longer. I was so in love with her in college. I was in love with her when I left for Vietnam. I could never blame her though. I was a different person, not her. I didn't realize it then. I was angry, I know that much. I despised the people who were ducking the war, men and women alike. It made no sense at all because at that point I realized I could have done the same thing given the opportunity. I don't think I figured it out until I returned to the club in '75. Things seemed a lot clearer... Anyway, that was in June of '68, and she drowned that September. She was out sailing in Long Island Sound with a buddy of mine. Actually, he was Best Man at our wedding, an old college friend. She fell over as he was bringing the boat about. The boom hit her head and she just went under. It took the Coast Guard four hours to find her body." He placed his hand on her thigh and leaned back. "The Marine Corps gave me a week to come home and deal with the funeral... And her parents... I was never so anxious to get back to Vietnam in my life. All of a sudden it looked like the only safe place in the world. I haven't spoken to her folks since. They reacted as if the entire thing was my fault in some way. If I hadn't deserted her, if I hadn't gone to Vietnam, it would have never happened... Hell, maybe they're right."

Grace slid her Tom Collins across the high-gloss mahogany bar to arm's length and let it sit there. She said there was something about the smell of the gin that was making her stomach turn over. The sweat from the glass had totally saturated the flimsy napkin where it perched. The drink had gone untouched. She set her hand on top of his.

"Was he sleeping with her? Your Best Man?"

"Something wrong with your drink?"

"It's just not doing it for me. I've never been much of an afternoon drinker."

Lee pushed his beer to the side as well. "Me neither. But what do you do at a bar? You have to order something. If we'd asked for iced tea we'd be the laughing stock of Honolulu." He glanced at the tab and placed a ten-dollar bill on it. "I suppose they were sleeping together. It makes sense, but I never asked him about it. What's the point? I haven't seen him since our wedding. He lives in Old Saybrook, in Connecticut. I never go up that way, but his job brings him down to New York on occasion and he's never stopped into my restaurant, not even to say hello. I guess that has to say something. Obviously, we'd been good friends at one point. College, you know, all three of us were buds. I'd assumed he had to feel guilty about the incident, but yeah, he probably feels guilty about a lot of things. He did a good job of skipping any military service, had an iffy medical exemption. His old man was a doctor. Set it up for him. So who knows? Maybe that's what's bothering him. Like I could care who went to Vietnam and who didn't at this point."

"That doesn't necessarily jibe with your feelings about those who did duck it."

He laughed. "Good point. Ah, screw it, times change. Maybe I'll grow up some day. Maybe someday the pinball in my head will stop bouncing from one side of the game to the other."

"Trust me, it won't."

They'd spent the afternoon wandering the stalls of the International Market Place adjacent to Honolulu's wide tourist beach and the high-end hotels. The open-air mall had been created around a huge banyan tree whose tendril-like roots hung down from its mammoth arms like anchor lines. The roots had dug into the earth among broad-leafed philodendron and orchid plants that lined the pathways. Colorful tropical birds flew amidst the branches and swooped down between the shoppers to the delight of the smaller children, while ukulele music drifted from camouflaged speakers, creating a permanent holiday atmosphere. Anything Hawaiian was for sale here: from local crafts to the usual tee shirts, dark glasses, and beach toys. They'd stopped into Riki's Tiki Bar simply to get off their feet for a few minutes.

The bartender picked up Lee's ten dollars and returned with two-fifty change, seemingly unconcerned that they hadn't gone anywhere near their drinks. After he ambled away, Grace said, "Are you ready to move on?"

Lee stood and said, "Sure."

She slid off the barstool and took his hand again. "I meant with your life. Have you been able to get past your wife? And her death? Do you feel comfortable with other women?"

"With you?"

"Anyone."

"Something tells me you're not just anyone."

They began to walk slowly toward the mall's exit and the bright sunlight, hand in hand.

"I came back to the club in '75 to try to piece it all together. I had to wait for the war to end. Seeing a bunch of GIs having a swell time with their wives wouldn't have helped much. Plus, I'd taken over the restaurant from my father and it consumed every waking hour for a few years. Sitting out at the Pickering Club alone for a week I was able to realize that neither one of us was in control—Ellen or me. There was nothing we could have done to alter the outcome. We'd become products of our history. Someone else was running the show, pulling the strings, not us. In my case: Johnson, Nixon, The Marine Corps... I'm not blaming them, I'm beyond that now. After all, I did volunteer, there's no getting away from that. But Ellen and I weren't in control; we were just the game pieces. We were who we were. Who we'd become, we couldn't have avoided any of it. It was a car wreck waiting to happen. And in the long run, you have to move on and just try to make yourself a better person. You have to spend time thinking about other people and not yourself. Give a little back. A restaurant is a great place to learn that lesson. You have to learn and grow... I came this time for a refresher course. Actually it was Aunt Sally's idea that I return. She thinks the Pickering Club holds some sort of miracle cure."

"And that was necessary for some reason? A refresher? A cure? After this much time?"

"If you take into consideration that I met you, I'd have to say, yes, very much so." Lee draped his arm around her waist as they strolled toward the Mustang he'd rented. "I just needed to convince myself I was really ready for someone else."

"I hope you're not trying to tell me you haven't slept with another woman in eleven years because I suspect it would have a slightly disingenuous ring to it. You don't seem like you're out of practice. Not to me, anyway."

Lee laughed. "No, I've had a few relationships; they just haven't gone anywhere."

"Why's that?"

"Kinda nosy, aren't you?" She didn't answer, so he said, "Because I'm a jerk, that's why."

"You could have fooled me."

He unlocked the car door and opened it for her, and then crossed over to the driver's side and slid in. "Look, I'm committed to my restaurant. I want it run in a certain way, and for that I have to be there. It's called the American immigrant work ethic. I got it, along with the restaurant, from my father, the French Catholic, the real immigrant. Regular customers, like your husband, expect me to be there to greet them when they walk in the door. If they have a problem, they want to talk to me about it, not a host or hostess. I work long hours. I'm in at nine-thirty in the morning, and depending on what the movement's like, I'm home anywhere between midnight and one. I'm closed on Mondays, and that's it. Not many women are willing to sign on for that lifestyle."

"Maybe you should be a more accommodating to the women you date and a little less concerned about your customers."

Lee squinted his eyes and smiled at her. "That's why I'm a jerk."

Grace leaned across the car's center console and gave him a long and deep kiss, a kiss that said she wanted very much to make love with him all afternoon.

"If we ignore the fact that Nick will be here in forty-eight hours," she said, "if we make-believe hard enough and with all our souls, if we wish on the stars when they come out tonight, will it make it not so? Will it make Nick disappear?"

Lee thought it over for a second and said, "Yes. I think that's the way it works."

Freddy

Apparently Lee knew wine. It's a gene I don't seem to have inherited, and after learning what I have about him, I question if I've inherited anything at all from Lee. DNA for sure, but that's only science. Grace told me I had his eyes, so there's that too. But I'm not a heroic person. I wouldn't have lasted ten minutes in Vietnam, Chico convinced me of that. I don't have the slightest idea of how to run a restaurant. I paint. I'm successful, but that's all I do, I paint. Any personality traits I may possess come from Grace and Nick. As much as I'd like to say there's a part of me that's Lee, I can't do it. That's not to say I don't drink wine; I drink a lot of it. Too much at times, but I select bottles only because I find some labels more attractive than others. So I'm not sure how I would have handled the new Pickering Club wine list in 1979.

Lee was in his element. That evening he opened the leather-bound club dinner menu and scanned the selection of newly-acquired labels, titles that glistened in crisp red ink and were tucked into the glassine leaf inside the back cover. He smiled and shook his head and then set the menu off to the right side of his water goblet.

"Something wrong?" Grace asked.

"A new menu. Their first changes since 1968."

She laughed. "I wondered why it'd been the same offering two nights in a row. You mean this hasn't changed in over ten years?"

"As far as I know it's been the same since 1924. 1968 just happens to be the first time I saw it."

Once again my mother divulged events of those days and nights with such starling and undiluted detail that I ultimately became convinced that she forgot she was talking to her own child, and perhaps she really wasn't. Perhaps she was only calling to Lee. I believe that she'd been desperately trying to bring it all to the forefront of her soul in an effort to keep it fresh. So fresh that it would remain with her for all eternity, and if there was such a thing as an afterlife these ramblings would serve as a roadmap to whoever it was who might be responsible for setting her course.

The two of them had returned to the club from Downtown Honolulu by four-thirty, the sun still high in the sky and beaming down hot on the tops of their heads and shoulders. Neither Nick's name, nor his threatened arrival, had been mentioned for the entire time, but the bad news lingered in the backs of their brains, making all conversation seem trivial. So much so that neither could recall what the other had said on the return drive to the Pickering Club. They'd showered together in Lee's bungalow, which is where they began their lovemaking. They'd then taken it out to the large bed without bothering to towel off, going at it aggressively, almost as if they were possessed by demons, almost as if they needed to hurt one another. When they were drained, they'd fallen into a deep sleep within seconds of each other. But even sleep was not gentle—both experiencing brutal, short clipped dreams infested with more demons. They awakened after an hour, finding themselves locked into another passionate sexual embrace: Grace curled in an almost fetal position with Lee entering her from behind. They seemed to have no recollection of how it had begun or how long they'd been like that. It was as if their bodies were attempting to become one tormented mass, a mass that kept their minds and eyes from being appraised of the situation. They'd went at it like that for twenty minutes, until they'd become beyond saturated, and then showered a second time, not speaking of the dreams that had haunted them until much later in the evening. Lee dressed and walked Grace, draped in his robe, to her suite. She tossed on a sheer yellow-print dress that clung to her body as if it was statically charged, and they'd sauntered into the dining room shortly after nine-forty-five looking very much like a hedonistic couple that had spent the entire afternoon doing exactly what they had been doing. Grace's breasts still hard and pointed and straining at the yellow silk of her dress, Lee's tie crooked and his hair simply pushed off to the side without the benefit of a brush or comb.

"Don't look now," Lee said, "but your friend, McCracken, is giving us the evil eye. Do you think he knows what's up? I thought we looked rather nonchalant."

"Forget it, it's written all over your face. I was hoping that at least *I* would appear somewhat more composed, but my nipples are as hard as rocks. Still."

"It's chilly."

"It's Hawaii, Buddy boy. It is not chilly."

She glanced at the McCrackens through the corner of her eye. They were staring at her lover with daggers, not saying a word to one another.

"It's because of Nick," Grace said. And on hearing his name it was as if he'd appeared out of nowhere, two days early and had pulled up a chair and sat between them. But Grace could see that Lee had no understanding, no comprehension that he could be so despised by another person for doing so little. "McCracken," she continued, "he hates you, and maybe me, with more venom than you would think humanly possible."

"Get out of here. He's just an old man with a grumpy face. He probably doesn't like the way Ronnie mixed up his Old Fashioned."

"No. No. I've spent a lifetime around people like the good Mr. McCracken. It's amazing. His type comes on to me all the time. Age makes no difference. It's beyond odd. All they want to do is bed down Nick Rolston's *woman*. It's some sort of macho fixation, a brotherhood of stags. Nick's friends try it in our own house, even if he's in the next room. Look at your Uncle Louis, perfect example. I guess it's some kind of male dominance thing. Especially these guys in their fifties—they like to prove they can still get it up. But then they seem to loathe the one that gets away with it, and that would be you. Can't you see that? Maybe they're jealous? Maybe that's it. Look at McCracken's face. I kind of figured this would be the way it would work out, but it makes no sense at all, and it all still gives me the creeps."

"He's old enough to be your father."

Grace's whole upper body tensed involuntarily at the suggestion and she shivered despite the warm air. The reaction did not go unnoticed by Lee, but he made no comment. Instead, he said, "I hope you're not lumping me into the category of 'those wishing to bed down a great director's wife' because I didn't know who your husband was until this morning, well past the time the dirty deed had been executed."

"I wish you wouldn't keep calling him *my husband*."

"I'm open to suggestions. What would you prefer?" Lee said, doing a poor job of camouflaging the fact that he would be very happy to see Nick Rolston drop off the edge of the earth.

Feeling the growing tension, Grace turned her face to him with a forced smile, overcompensating on the light side. "Let's try *Nick* for a while. I'll let you know if it begins to bother me."

"Okay... So, how did this McCracken recognize you? I'm a Page Six junkie, I read all the gossip columns: the *Times, Post, Daily News*, and I've seen a dozen pictures of your hus—*Nick*, but never a shot of you."

"I gather McCracken just saw the name Rolston on the incoming guest list. His story's a little vague. Maybe Sally mentioned who I was married to... But yes, Nick doesn't like us to be photographed together. He calls me his *Mystery Woman*. Always has. About six years ago *Town and Country* did a piece on the house in the Palisades and Nick wouldn't let me get into any of the pictures. The style people had me made up to look like the lady of the castle and everything, but he nixed it. I mean, it is his house, his furniture; he put it all together. It's his money, his art, everything's his—so why not? Fine. He can have all the credit. I didn't care that much. But he was really adamant about being the only person to appear in the magazine. Happens all the time with Nick. He likes to project the image of being an unattached man. Never wears his wedding ring. The *Town and Country* writers mentioned me in the article, but Nick always banks on the fact that people in L.A. can't read and only look at the pretty pictures. And it's not too far from the truth. I worked for a number of years writing coverage on screenplays and books at Universal. The studio execs just want things boiled down to a paragraph. They don't have the attention span for much more than that. And it's better if you lay it out for them verbally so they don't even need to read the damn paragraph." Grace laughed. It was a small, very private laugh.

It prompted Lee to ask, "What?"

"I don't know. Just thinking back." She sighed while her eyes scanned the pink of the dining room, and then said, "Do you know Freddy Keeley?"

"The old actor?" Lee replied, and Grace nodded. "I didn't *know* him, no, but I've seen all of those 'Mom and Pop' movies he appeared in with Kay Randall in the '40s and '50s. They're on TV at two in the morning most nights. And he did stop into my restaurant once, about five or six years ago. Shitty tipper. He died recently, didn't he?"

"Two months ago, yes. Freddy was the one who got Nick his first real break in the movies. He was pretty choked up when Freddy passed away, they were great friends. Both grew up in Camden. In New Jersey. Towards the end, Nick threw Freddy bit parts whenever he could. Of course, Freddy was forty years older than Nick, but they had this weird Jersey connection. Anyway, we had our wedding reception at the house. A very private affair, but everyone on Nick's good side was there, which included as many baseball players as it did actors and directors. It was kind of surreal. There were hardly any women there besides me and his New York agent and my maid of honor, who was an old friend from high school. Nick picked the bridesmaids from the girls at the Playboy Club. He thought it would be 'a howl.' I think they were only there to put out for the ballplayers. Though I have to tell you, some of the Dodgers seemed far more interested in the Yankees than they did in any of the Bunnies. Anyway, Freddy Keeley was falling down drunk and at one point he grabbed me by the wrist, and pulled me onto his lap, wedding dress and all. I don't know where the hell Nick was at that point... You know how well Freddy could pull off that sad-sack face of his? He did it in almost every movie at one point or another. Freddy put on that sad face and said to me, 'Do you know why people buy canaries?' I said, 'No,' and he said, 'They don't. People don't buy canaries. People buy pretty cages. Then they need something pretty to put in their pretty cages, something that sounds nice, looks nice. That's where the canary comes in. But nobody gives a shit about the damn bird—the bird dies, they get a new bird. It's all about the cage.'"

Lee looked across the expansive dining room at the McCrackens. They hadn't moved an inch. He said, "Do you want to eat outside again? I can't sit here watching those two scrutinize us any longer. It'll ruin my dinner."

Grace stood and said, "Sure. This is getting to be quite a pattern. Can we leave *Nick* in the dining room this time?"

"No."

Lee once again grabbed the menus, waved to the waiter, and pointed to a table out on the terrace. They walked through the French doors and into the cooling evening, keeping a few feet between themselves. Once they were beyond the purview of the other guests, Lee wrapped his arm around her and pulled her into his chest. He kissed her softly at first, and then with more passion. Eventually they were interrupted by the waiter ferrying their two glasses of water.

"Sorry, Mr. Corbet," the waiter said. He placed the glasses on the table. "Would you care for a cocktail?"

Grace shook her head, and Lee said, "I think we're fine. Give us five or six minutes and we can order dinner, okay?"

"Yes, sir."

"Thanks."

They sat, and he took her hand. "This is better. I wanted to touch you in the worst way, but it just seemed like we were on display in there."

"We were."

"Is that what you've felt like? Feel like? The canary?"

"I don't know… It wasn't the type of thing you like to hear on your wedding day, I can tell you that much."

"Just after my father danced with Ellen on our wedding day, he pulled me aside and said, in his best French accent, which becomes absolutely unbearable after a bottle of champagne, 'You should have married someone in the restaurant business. At least she'd be able to dance.' So…" He squeezed her hand slightly. "The moral being: when someone is three sheets to the wind, never take anything they say seriously. They'll have a much different story in the morning." Lee glanced at the menu a second time, focusing on nothing. He said, "Do you feel like you're cheating on him now?" not wanting to see how her face would respond.

"Oh, please, he's effectively told me to get lost. Move out, remember?"

"Right, but he's on his way here. And you *are* still married."

Grace laughed out loud. "Ah, the Catholic upbringing rears its ugly head. Let us not forget that at this point *you* are as much of an adulterer as I am. It's a two-way street, my friend, so don't split hairs. Better start working on your Sunday morning's confessional speech."

He laughed as well, "If it makes any difference, this is the first time I've done it."

"I gather you're talking about the adultery thing."

"Uh-huh." Lee looked out at the yellow garden lights illuminating the lush greenery from underneath. He said, "Don't you think he's ever cheated on you?" again without making any eye contact.

"Oh, Jesus, yes. He had an affair with at least one of the actresses he worked with, I know that. It was in Africa. Then, four years ago, he tested the divorce waters for some unknown reason. Called it off after a month, but I gather he was balling someone... Other than that..." She pulled his face to hers and kissed him lightly. "Can we talk about something else? Why can't we make Nick disappear? He's not here yet, Lee. Let's not let him infect us. Let's not get him here any sooner than we need to. Let it be just you and me. Can you do that for me?"

"He's treated you like shit. I just want you to know that."

"Who doesn't know that? I've known it since the day I married him. You're not making me feel any better about it, okay? Now, can we change the fucking subject? Please?"

Lee stood slowly and moved around behind her. He bent at the waist and kissed the side of her neck. "I'm sorry. I'm angry. I want this to be different, and there's nothing I can do about it. I can't control this situation, and I want to. I want things to work out the way I want things to work out. I want him to disappear, too. He's not coming here because he loves you. You have to see that—he's coming here because he lost you, and he hates to lose. He hates the thought that the world might find out he lost, that he's a loser. He wants to smother you. If he could preserve you and hang you on the wall with all his shitty art he'd be a happy man."

"Please, Lee, please. Let's talk about something else."

"I won't let him do it to you, Grace. I won't let you do it to yourself. He's going to run into a lot more than he bargained for when he hits Hawaii."

"My hero." She turned her face toward him and kissed him on the lips. It did little to ease the tension she felt in his arms. "Sit down." She kissed him again. "Why don't you tell me about all these relationships of yours that haven't 'gone anywhere.'"

Lee smiled at her. "That's not what I'd call a real change of subject if you ask me."

"Sure it is. *You're* now the thing, and not me. And unless

you had an affair with Nick, he should be effectively removed from the conversation."

He kissed her again and sat quietly for a moment, and then said, "Okay. Fine. Only for you would I do this because I'm not a kiss-and-tell person... One of them was an actress, a Tony winner in fact."

"You're kidding?"

"No. Why not? A Broadway actress, right? We keep the same hours. It makes sense. She's on stage until eleven o'clock each night, she has Mondays off, just like me. And... She was an alcoholic. I think that was her main attraction; I was a man with an unending flow of free liquor. Speaking of which, do you want some wine with your dinner?" He tapped the menu. "Some of this stuff isn't half bad."

Grace shook her head. "I don't think so. The smell of booze seems to be making me nauseous for some reason. I'll get over it."

"Quitting smoking and drinking in two days? We'll have to start calling you the *Iron Willed Woman*."

Grace smiled and picked up the menu. "So who was she?"

He laughed. "Are you nuts? I'm not telling you that."

"Come on, you know who *I've* been sleeping with for the last ten years... Who would think that we were both Star Fuckers? Gee, we have so much in common." She fluttered her eyelashes facetiously. "So did she win the Tony Award before or after you met her?"

"Before."

"Ahh, so you knew what you were getting into, so to speak?"

"Yep."

"So, who was she?"

"I'm not telling you."

"Come on, Lee."

"I'm not."

"Was she a dancer, too, or only an actress?"

"Actress... Well, and a dancer, yes. She started out as a chorus line dancer. And a swing dancer in a few Fosse shows when she first started out."

"And Bob Fosse lost her to you? There's a notch in your gun."

Grace set her menu on the table and looked up at the star drenched night sky trying to visualize the names of the women who had recently won Tony Awards.

"Was it Patricia Forbes?"

"No."

"Dee Tolland?"

"I'm not telling you, so let it drop."

"It was Dee, wasn't it? Yeah, she's your type. Long legs, that crooked smile of hers. I could see you falling for her. Dee and Lee; that's just too damn cute for words. So she's an alcoholic, huh?"

"It was not Dee Tolland... And that just proves why I can't tell you who it was. I don't need the world to know this woman's a drinker, that she has a problem. Last I heard she was dealing with it. She's been battered around a lot, but she's working things out. It's not fair for me to tell the world about her problems. It's not going to help her career. We're still very good friends. I see a lot of her."

Grace laughed. "Life isn't fair. Who told you that? Come on, I'm not going to tell anyone. Who would I tell? What do you take me for? We're a million miles from New York... Okay, if it wasn't Dee Tolland... Who else?" Grace snapped her fingers. "Elizabeth Egan."

"Will you stop?" He was blushing.

"It *was* her. Look at your face. God, I hope you never play poker. You'd lose every cent you own." Grace reached for her purse. "I'm getting out a mirror. I want you to look at your face right now."

"Forget it, will you?"

"The famous Miss E-E. The Wild Woman. Of course it was her. Elizabeth Egan. I can just see you now. Holy crap, you two must have turned some heads walking down Second Avenue together, especially if you were wearing that dinner jacket you had on the other night. I'm jealous already. Yeah, I was wrong about Dee Tolland. Elizabeth Egan is much more you. Her and that *I'm going to eat you up* look she's so good at?" Grace laughed. "I'll bet you fell for her hook, line, and sinker. Who wouldn't? And you still see 'quite a bit' of her? Sounds fishy to me."

"Enough, okay?"

"Deny it. I want to hear you say, 'I was not shacked up with Elizabeth Egan.' Come on, say it."

"I'm not going to..." Lee groaned.

"Look, if I was a lesbian, Elizabeth Egan is the first person I'd go after. You could do a lot worse than Elizabeth Egan, that's for damn sure." Grace took a long drink from her water glass. "I just want to hear you say it was her, that's all."

"I'm not going to say it. What do you want to eat?"

Grace slid her chair back a foot or two, crossed her arms over her chest, and stared at him.

He turned to her and said, "What? What do you want me to say?"

"Nothing. You don't have to say anything... I was just trying to visualize what Elizabeth Egan would look like squatting over your face."

He laughed and threw his napkin at her. "You're disgusting, you know that?"

"No, I'm not." She pulled her chair close to his. "What I am is in love with you. I'm so in love with you that I can't stand it, and I can't bear to think that you've ever slept with another woman."

Angel Dust

"**W**here the hell have you been?" Ray snapped at Mitch, using the most derisive tone he could muster, which only served to conjure up unpleasant memories of a mother's behavior they were both anxious to keep submerged in their psyches. The endless amount of alcohol and PCP Ray'd driven into his bloodstream had numbed his lips and tongue to such an extent the sentence came out as one long garbled word. He glanced over his shoulder at the clock on the kitchen wall, something he'd probably done a hundred times in the past hour. It was almost one in the morning. He seemed compelled to vocalize the fact.

"It's close to..." He pointed at the clock, almost falling backward over the couch. He grabbed at the armrest for support. "It's after midnight."

"Sorry, Ray," Mitch said wearily, "I guess I shoulda called you. I had to work late. Mr. Pressten's promoting me to cook and switching me to the night shift. I gotta work the same hours tomorrow. Eight a.m. to midnight."

"'Mr. Pressten's promoting me to cook,'" Ray said mockingly and in a child's voice. "You're turning into quite the fruitcake, ain't you, Mitchie. I think you got those hotdogs on your mind too much, that's what I think. You and Mr.

Pressten got something going, do ya?" He laughed, but it was hollow and came off forced and practiced. "Yeah, you shoulda called. Like I said, I can't be wastin' my life lookin' out after you. You coulda been dead for all I knew. How'd I know you weren't back on that goddamn bench? Or worse yet, screwin' Tracy again. Ya think I need to be drivin' all over Oahu to find out if you're breathin' or not?"

Mitch told me he'd dropped onto the couch like a sack of rotten pineapples, his entire mind and body had gone beyond the point of exhaustion. He put his feet up on the wooden crate, lit a cigarette, and inhaled deeply. He was in no way ready for another faceoff with his brother.

"I'm sorry about all this, Ray, I really am. I can't start lookin' for a place of my own now until the day after tomorrow, but I'll be out of your way within a week, I swear."

Ray sat on the couch next to his younger brother, took one of his Kools, and lit it. "Any sign of Tracy?"

"Who?"

"Who...? Who...? Tracy. What do you mean, who? Who the fuck ya think I been talking about all this time?"

"I was at the club for the whole day."

"Yeah, but she didn't try to call you? She didn't stop in? She didn't try to make up or nothin'? You ain't talked to her at all in a week?"

"Nah."

"You still got shit in her apartment, right?"

"Yeah. Everything."

He slapped Mitch on the thigh hard. "What say we go over there now and pick that stuff up? I got my truck back. Looks real good all buffed out. She'd probably like to see it lookin' like it used to. Bet she's just gettin' in about now."

"I'm whipped, Ray, I really am. I gotta get some sleep. I gotta be at work tomorrow at eight. Plus, what's the point of moving my stuff twice? I'll get it when I find my own pad. It's just gonna clutter up your place if we move it in now."

"You ain't worried the bitch is gonna skip town? You had a stereo, didn't ya? What if she cuts out with it? Or hocks it? What about your albums? Mitch, ya gotta grow up, for Christ's sake. Some of them albums you got are worth money. Ya gotta stand up for what's yours. You're just lettin' this babe push you all over the place."

Mitch stood and walked over to the TV. "Are you watchin' this? Okay if I turn it off?"

"Yeah, I'm fuckin' watchin' it. Leave it alone." Ray barked. "I gotta be at work at eight, too. You don't hear me pissin' and moanin' about it."

Mitch rubbed at his eyes and said, "How about if I sleep in your room tonight. That way—"

"You go in that room and I'll cut your liver out, I swear to Christ I will. I'll cut your balls of and shove 'em down your throat. You don't believe me, try me. Brother or no brother."

Ray stood and moved his face to within a few inches of Mitch's. His muscles were tight and well-defined, stretching the fabric of his Orlon shirt. His breath reeked of beer and bourbon.

"That's how we took care of business in Nam, Mitchie. Yes-in-dee-dee. We strapped them Gooks to trees and shoved their balls into their mouths. Left 'em there for the other Slopes to find. Scared the shit outta them. Don't fuck around in my room, Mitch."

"Fine, whatever you want."

Ray swung his hips side to side and again put on his child's voice. "'Fine, whatever you—'" He was interrupted by the ringing of his telephone. He walked into the kitchen and yanked it off the wall. "Yeah?"

"I want to talk to you, Ray," Tracy almost whispered into her end of the line.

"Well, if it isn't Miss Slutsky in person. We been looking for you, Sweet Stuff."

"Is Mitch there?" she asked. "Is he with you now? Or are you alone?"

"Yeah, he's here, but he can't come to the phone right now."

Mitch crossed to Ray and held out his hand for the telephone. Ray put his hand on Mitch's chest and pushed him away maliciously and with enough energy to knock some of the air from Mitch's lungs, to bring on a minor coughing spasm.

"Ya see, Tracy, your boy Mitch has gone sweet on you, that's why he can't come to the phone... What I mean is: he's got his mouth full, he's down on his knees giving me some head right now. Real brotherly love, know what I mean? And, man, he's better than you could ever hope to be. This boy really knows what he's doin'."

Mitch again reached for the phone, more forcefully this time. "Come on, Ray, let me talk to her."

Ray relinquished the phone. "Here. She hung up. I think she believed me, stupid bitch. What's she think we are, a bunch of fags over here?"

Mitch listened to the dial tone and then put the receiver back on the hook. "Was she at home?"

"How the hell should I know?"

"What'd she want?"

"Beats me."

Mitch took the phone off the wall and dialed Tracy's number. She answered it after three rings, saying, "Yes?"

"That wasn't true, Tracy. Ray was just foolin' with you."

"She's home?" Ray said in a coarse whisper. He then picked up Mitch's Kools from the wooden crate and staggered out the door.

Tracy sighed into the receiver. "I called to talk to Ray, Mitch, not you. I don't want to talk to you, that's why I hung up the friggin' phone. I want to make a peace with him. I know you didn't do nothin' with your brother. I just don't want this to go any farther. Put him on. I need to talk with him."

"He left. I think he's on his way over to your place. He's really shit-faced, Trace. You probably shouldn't stick around much longer. He wants to fight, and I don't think he cares who with. You know how he gets. He's off the wall, and he's dangerous like this." Mitch opened the refrigerator, looked at the two remaining cans of Blue Ribbon, and shut the door without taking one. "Why didn't you tell me he's the guy tried to rape you last Tuesday?"

"I never said rape... Just let it drop, Mitch. I didn't say rape. Nobody said rape."

"Actually you did, you did say rape, and he tells it different. He says he rode you like a stallion. Is that right? Just because of that business the other night, just because I tried to teach you something new, you went out and screwed my own brother? What's that prove?"

"Yeah, well maybe I did. Maybe he gave it to me good like he says. Maybe that's what I'm lookin' for, ever think about that? Maybe I like a man who's in charge."

"If you stick around that apartment any longer, you *are* gonna get it good, I can tell you that much. 'Cause Ray's comin' to get you. But, hell, if that's what you want... Knock yourself out. I got plans of my own. If you think I'm gonna sit around and watch the world fall apart, you're crazy. My life's takin' a different direction. I got it all worked out."

Mitch hung up the phone, crossed over to the TV, turned it off, and flopped once more onto the couch. He was asleep in less than fifteen seconds.

8:00 a.m.

Sami Awapuhi has not aged well. He is dangerously over-weight and rarely rises from his chair or walks from behind his desk at the Chevron station. He lets Phil pump gas for the customers, but even Phil moves at a snail's pace these days. I can't say Sami and I hit it off. He doesn't care to talk much, especially to strangers.

"Who wants to know?"

"Ray Slack killed my father."

"How the fuck does that work? All that crap was forty years ago."

"Right. I'm forty years old."

Sami looked me up and down. "Yeah, well you look pretty good for forty. Coulda fooled me. What's the secret?"

"Wine."

"Hah. Funny... Listen, I don't give a shit about Ray Slack. Never did, but whatever the world thinks... *or thought*, of him, the one thing he wasn't: he wasn't lazy. He wasn't afraid of a day's work. He believed that if you wanted to get by in the world, you ought be ready to put in your forty hours, and if you had a job, you'd damn well better do it right and show up on time—hangover or no hangover. This is a service station. The operative word is *service*. You can get gas anywhere, and Ray understood that. And that's the only reason I kept him on. He treated customers with respect. Other than that, he was a class-A fuck-up... And a real bullshitter, especially when it came to all that never-ending phony Vietnam crap. I know too many guys in Honolulu who are the real deal. It wasn't hard for me to recognize that Ray was full of shit when it came to what he did in Vietnam." And then as an afterthought: "I understand the guy he killed, your dad, I guess, was the real deal."

"From what I've learned, I'd have to say yes. That's why I wanted to talk to you. I'm still trying to piece together what exactly happened."

"Yeah, well, I never met your dad. And I sure as hell wasn't a fucking eyewitness to that bullshit."

"I understand that. I want to know the man who killed him. I want to know how they ran into each other that night." I said it with much more intensity and volume than I intended. I've never been particularly good at hiding annoyances.

Sami leaned back in his chair, laughed, lifted his beefy hands, placed them behind his head and gave me a malevolent look. "I don't like to be pushed."

"Sorry, I'm just getting—let's say, frustrated."

He again looked me up and down. I had no idea what was going through his mind. Despite his expansive frame and age, he was an intimidating figure. He seemed capable of becoming abusive in the blink of an eye. I was concerned I might have poked him too hard. I was surprised when it seemed I hadn't.

"Okay, fine. Sit down. I like you for some reason. Maybe I'm getting soft. But I don't know why anyone would want to waste their time on a jackass like Ray Slack. He's just the bad guy."

Ray Slack's predisposition to work may have been the only thing that compelled him to pull into Sami's Chevron Station at eight a.m. since he'd logged in only four hours sleep the previous night. Sami and his mechanic, Phil, had been there since seven. Tracy Tillis had been there since seven-thirty thinking Ray wouldn't dare touch her in front of Sami, not again. In an effort to ensure this, Sami said she'd offered to take him back to his cot for an early morning roll. He maintained that Tracy had always considered him to be a hot property, so why not? He admitted he'd declined to take her up on the offer that day.

"Maybe some other time, Tracy. I don't wanna get in the middle of this. Maybe in a few weeks, after Ray cools off. I don't need that nut-case comin' after me some night in the dark. Let me think about it. I'll let you know... Look," he added, thinking there was no point in blowing her off completely, "what I will do is this: I'll keep Ray from smackin' you while you're here, but I'm not gettin' in any deeper than that. Say what you gotta say to him and hit the road. I don't appreciate you two draggin' this garbage into my station. It's not good for business."

So she sat in Sami's office in silence until Ray walked in at eight. He'd showered, shaved, and wore a laundered blue-and-green-striped shirt and washed but faded button-up-the-front black jeans. He glanced at Tracy quickly and then purposely ignored her, lifting a stainless steel clipboard from Sami's desk and flipping through five or six of the thin yellow carbon copies it held. He looked at his boss deferentially.

"This the same damn Mercedes I dragged in from Waimananalo three weeks ago?"

"Nope. Different one. Same problem, though. The starter motor's shot. I don't know why the GIs and swabbies buy these Benz diesels from the Haoles. They're all on their last legs. That's the only reason the cheap bastards are willing to part with them. These kids should be wiser than that. They'd be better off getting something from the damn junk heap." Sami shrugged. "But hey, more business for me, right? The kid who owns this one don't get off duty 'til noon, so there's no point hookin' it until after lunch. Be sure you get the registration papers from him in case he ships out before Phil can pick up a reworked starter."

"He's a squid, then?"

"Yeah. Says he ain't on a ship, though. He's stationed at the base. But that don't mean the damn Navy won't pack his ass off before I get my money, so get the title." Sami cocked his head toward Tracy. "You got a visitor."

"So I see."

Tracy tried to sound businesslike. "You know, Ray, it cost me close to three hundred dollars to get the windows fixed on my car."

"I don't know nothin' about your windows. I told you that. Besides, it cost me damn near that much to get a set of new retreads and have my doors buffed out, and I'm still waitin' on the side mirror glass. Shit's outta stock." Ray was tempted to lay into her about the message she'd left on his truck's door panels but decided it wasn't a subject he needed to have batted around in front of Sami.

"And that's my point," Tracy continued, "I can say I don't know nothin' about your tires, too, but where does that get us? I don't need this, I really don't. Can't we just say we're all even and move on? I don't think Mitch gives a damn. I know he doesn't."

"He's still got stuff in your apartment, don't he? And where the hell were you last night?"

She raised her voice slightly. "Where I was ain't none of

your damn business... And I'm not goin' anywhere with Mitch's stuff, so just forget about it. It'll be there whenever he wants to get it. I ain't no thief. Let me handle Mitch, okay? You don't hafta big brother him your whole life. He ain't your responsibility. He's a big boy. Let him be. He knows why I locked him out. That's between him and me, and not you. He's ready to move on. So am I."

Ray reached down, grabbed her wrist, and pulled her to her feet. "Let's talk about this out in my truck. Sami's got better things to do."

She yanked her arm from his grip. "I don't want to be hit no more."

"I ain't gonna hit you, ya stupid bitch, I just wanna talk in private, that's all."

Tracy looked at Sami who raised his hands and shook his head. "I'm nobody's babysitter. I want no bullshit in this office. But you walk out? You're a big girl, you're on your own."

Ray took hold of her wrist once more. "Come on. I just want to talk. That's it."

"If I scream, will you come out, Sami? I don't want to be hit no more, and I mean it."

Sami sighed deeply. "I need this shit like I need another goddamn hole in my head." He leveled his stare at Ray and said, "Don't hit her on this property. You wanna do some damage, take a drive. I don't wanna know nothin' about it."

Ray removed the keys to his truck from his rear pocket, unhooked the clip from his belt loop, and tossed them onto Sami's desk.

"There," he said, looking at Tracy. "I can't drive off the lot, and Sami won't let me smack you while I'm here. Happy? Now, come on."

Ray pulled her by the wrist, and she reluctantly stumbled

on her high heels behind him. They crossed the hot asphalt looking like a jailer dragging a doomed prisoner off to the gallows. When they reached the right side of Ray's truck he opened the door, pushed her in, and crossed over to the driver's side. He slid in behind the wheel, slammed the door, leaned into her, and promptly ran his left hand up her thigh and under her short skirt. Tracy grabbed his forearm tightly but made no effort to remove his fingers, which pressed against the fabric of her lace panties.

"Don't, Ray, not here."

He groped her more clumsily, and then pressed his lips into hers, forcing her head to collide against the truck's metal doorframe. She responded by accepting the kiss, letting his tongue enter her mouth, and parting her thighs to his hand. He pulled back.

"That fat lip I gave you makes me hornier than hell, sweet-stuff. Looks good on ya."

"I don't want to be at war with you, Ray, if that's what this is all about."

He reached out and took her hand and placed it on the buttons of his jeans and his new erection, while an arrogant and unsympathetic smile formed on his lips.

"Yeah, well, you know me, baby, *make love, not war*. You don't want no war, that's fine with me. I say we just kiss and make up."

He pushed her hand tighter into his groin, and again she made no move to pull away, even squeezing him softly.

"I was drunk as a skunk last week," he said, "that's why I couldn't get it up. Can't hold that one time against me. Besides, you were too damn ready. Like a little pussycat in heat. I like some more fight in my women. Nobody likes a bitch to just roll over like you do. That's why you end up gettin' slapped around so much. You gotta learn what men want, baby, how to please 'em."

He reached out and pinched the end of her breast, and she pushed his hand away.

"That hurts."

"See, that's what I'm talkin' about. That's what makes my dick hard. A woman with some balls."

Ray once again forced his lips on hers as he slid across the seat and pinned her against the door. Again she made no real effort to stop him. He eventually pulled away, clumsily unbuttoning his jeans and exposing himself. He then placed his hand on the back of her head and attempted to force her face into his crotch. She pulled away, shoving his arm off to the side. He laughed.

"I don't want to do this here," she said. "I'll give you what you want, but not in your truck."

"Hey, this truck was good enough for you last Tuesday."

"It was dark in CJ's lot, Ray. It was nighttime. I'm not going to do this out here in broad daylight. I'm not. Anyone could walk by. It'd make me look like a whore." She dropped her hand into his lap and grasped his penis. "Let's go back to Sami's cot. I want to do you right. Whatever you want, but I don't want to fight, I don't want to be hit no more."

He pulled her hand away from his softening erection. "Forget it. That cot mighta worked for a little two-on-one, a little freaky-deaky. I could get into that, but I don't like someone in the next room listenin' to me while I'm goin' at it. You wanna bring Sami in on it, fine, but it ain't gonna work just you and me."

"Let's go to my place then. Go get your keys. I'll wait for you here."

"This is a work day. I'm workin'. I got a job to do." He started to rebutton his jeans. "You don't just walk out on your job because some babe needs a good fuckin'." He reached over and swung her door open. "Go on. Get outta here. I ain't gonna hit you. You got your peace treaty. I'll leave your car alone."

Tracy sat quietly for a moment, and then said, "I want to do this right." She leaned into him and tried to kiss him, but he pulled back. "I want to take care of you, Ray. I do. What time do you get off work?"

"Five."

"Okay. I don't have to be to work 'til eight." She rubbed her hand across his chest. "You tell me what you want. You wanna push me around a little? You wanna get a little rough? Get me from behind? We'll find some middle ground. I just don't want to get slapped no more. Not hard anyways. It don't look good for work, me havin' bruises."

"What about Mitch? Man, you don't think about nothin', do ya? How's it gonna look me comin' home after ballin' his girlfriend all night."

"First off, it ain't gonna be all night because I've got to be at work at eight. Second, Mitch ain't my boyfriend no more and he don't give a damn. It's over between us, I told you that. He wants to move on, and I want to move on. And if you don't want to tell him we've been together, you don't have to. I don't see where there's any problem."

"How come you threw Mitch out?"

"That's between me and Mitch. Just stop playin' big brother, will ya?"

"Yeah? Well, I got no desire to set myself up for the same treatment. You think you're some hot-shit chick that can just lock a man outta your apartment whenever you want? I don't play that game. Don't be dumpin' Mitch and me in the same basket."

"And that's all I'm sayin'. Mitch's different than you, and that ain't gonna happen to you and me."

"Yeah? What're you talkin' about? He's a skinny runt

and he ain't got an edge because he ain't spent any time in Nam... Or the stir for that matter. Other than that, he ain't half bad. He's a good kid and he don't hurt nobody, and he don't deserve to be treated the way you did to him."

Tracy shook her head and sighed. "He's different. That's all."

"Says you. What do you mean, 'different?'"

Tracy was quiet for a moment. Eventually she sighed again and said, "If I tell you, you gonna keep it to yourself? You're not gonna tell Mitch I told you? You ain't gonna go give him some big brother lecture or beat him up or nothin'? 'Cause it would kill him if he thought you knew."

"Hell, no. He told me all he did was slap you on the damn ass. I know all about that. You think we don't talk? You don't think we communicate? Mitch and me is close, okay? Who hasn't slapped a broad on the ass? Hell, that's what they're looking for half the time."

"It's more than that." Tracy glanced out the window and tapped her fingernails on her purse.

"What?"

She looked at Ray. "Please don't tell Mitch I told you this..."

"Tell me what?"

"Lainie... She's one of the nightshift dancers at Cookie's—"

"I know Lainie. Who don't know Lainie? What, has Mitchie been bumpin' Lainie on the side? So what? Ya gotta learn to live with that shit, baby. That's what men do. Ya can't be stickin' it to the same piece night and day. Gets too damn borin'."

"No, that ain't it."

"What, then?"

"Lainie... and this guy, Eddie, she met down at Barbers Point wanted to go out on a double date with Mitch and me.

We went to see that new movie with De Niro, and then went back to Eddie's place and smoked some weed." She focused her eyes on Ray and lowered her brow. "You're not gonna tell Mitch I told you this? I'll kill you if he ever finds out I told you."

"I ain't gonna tell nobody nothin'. Jesus. I know this Eddie guy, nothin's gonna surprise me there. He's a real freak."

He reached out and pinched her breast again, and she pushed him away.

"So what happened? Lemme guess," he said with a cold laugh, "you all start fuckin' like rabbits and the next thing you know Eddie is suckin' on Mitchie's dick?"

"Yeah. How'd you know?"

Ray straightened up in his seat and vigorously shook his head from side to side. "What do you mean, 'yeah'? I was just messin' with ya."

"Yeah's what I mean. That's what happened. And Mitch didn't even push him away. The two guys started goin' at it with each other. Sixty-nining. Suckin' each other off. Tellin' us girls to do the same thing."

"You're shittin' me? You are shitting me, right? You ain't makin' this up?"

"No." Tracy reached over and grabbed Ray's forearm. "You can't tell Mitch I told you this. You really can't."

"What'd you do?"

"I left. I left the three of them there and went home. I squirted Crazy Glue into my lock so's Mitch couldn't get in and slammed the door. Had the lock changed the next day. I haven't let him in since. And that's how it happened. I like Mitch, Ray, I really do, but what he did ain't right. And right in front of me like that? Lainie ain't talkin' to Eddie no more neither. He's the one cooked the whole thing up."

"Man, this is something. I gotta get my head together."

"You can't tell him I told you."

"So, Mitchie goes both ways? Who woulda guessed? After all these years..."

"He said it was the first time he did it, but I don't wanna be with someone who's not all man. It ain't right. That's why I like you, Ray. You know how to treat a woman like a woman, how she wants to be treated."

"You ain't never done it with another broad?"

"No."

"Like I believe that."

"I haven't, I swear."

"You better not be lyin' to me about all this."

"I ain't. Just don't tell Mitch I told you, okay?"

Ray lifted his arm as if he was planning to hit her with his open hand.

"You talk too much, baby, ya know that? That's the kinda shit ya gotta keep under your hat. I don't care who you think you can trust. Ruin a man's life if the world knew he dabbled in that queer stuff. That's a secret you don't tell nobody."

Tracy flinched, and he slapped her lightly on the cheek.

"How's that? That man enough for ya? That ain't too hard for ya, is it?"

"No."

He slapped her again with slightly more force.

"How's that? Like to get some of that man's hand on that tight ass of yours, wouldn't ya?"

"I don't like being hit on the face, Ray, I really don't."

He laughed at her. "Yeah, that's what they all say. I'll see you at five-thirty at your place. Now get the hell outta my truck. I got work to do. And you tell anybody my little brother's been suckin' cock I'll cut you from one end to the other, I swear to Christ, I will."

10:20 a.m.

Bunny McCracken died of lung cancer twenty-three years ago. Her husband, Tug, is wheelchair-bound, living in the Cedar Point Retirement Community just outside of Grand Rapids, Michigan. Time has not been kind to him, though I see no reason why it should. He is one of the more unpleasant individuals I have ever met. But I was ready for him. My mother and a few Pickering Club employees had given me fair warning. And in truth, I believe it was simply my stubbornness that made me make that trip to Michigan because I learned very little from him than things I didn't already know. Before he died, I wanted this spiteful old man to understand that the love Grace and Lee shared had produced a child. His reaction to learning this didn't surprise me in the least.

"So you're Corbet's kid and not Nick's? The son of a bitch knocked up your mom. I shouldn't be surprised. I guess he got what was coming to him then, didn't he?"

In 1981, McCracken had sold a screenplay concept to Nick. It eventually became a very successful film, making them both a tremendous amount of money. Nevertheless, when I spoke with McCracken he had not one nice thing to say about Nick, and he clearly thought even less of my mother.

"She was nothing but a tramp. Sorry, kiddo, but that's the truth," were his very words, though he was incapable of looking me in the eye when he spoke. I wasn't about to let my eyes do anything other than drill into him with abject loathing, hoping beyond hope that Grace was right when she said I had Lee's eyes. McCracken's side of the story was quite a bit different than my mother's telling of it. I prefer to believe my mother.

After what must have seemed an eternal wait, nearly twenty-five minutes, Tug McCracken spotted Grace strolling toward him down the overgrown trail. According to Member Services she'd scheduled a massage for ten a.m., and since the pathway was the sole route to the Pickering Club Spa, McCracken was certain this would be the ideal place to entrap her. What he hadn't figured on was her being twenty minutes late, which maddened him even further. Grace wore a flowered sarong, matching halter top, and tan sandals: all of which she'd purchased with Lee's American Express card in Downtown Honolulu the day before. She carried no purse and her bungalow key dangled loosely from her index finger. Her face was still flush from a morning of lovemaking. "She looked like a goddamn street walker," was how McCracken would remember her appearance that morning.

When she approached him, Grace said, "Hello," as politely as she could, making an attempt to maintain her stride and hoping to dodge an extended exchange of pleasantries. She tried to squeeze past to his left on the narrow path, but she nearly fell into a large-leafed philodendron in her effort to avoid touching him in the slightest.

McCracken took her small stumble as the green light to reach out and grab her arm. "Whoa. Better watch your step, little lady. These pathways can be uneven, some of them."

"Thank you," she said coolly as she removed her arm from his clammy grip.

"I was wondering if I might have a word with you? In private?" he asked.

"Private?"

"A place where we won't be disturbed."

"Meaning no witnesses? I think I see where this may be leading. I don't think so, Mr. McCracken. To put it succinctly, you're not my type."

McCracken creased his bushy eyebrows. "You have a rather coarse mind, young lady, and that's precisely what I'd like to talk to you about. However it's only for your reputation, and your husband's, that I choose to keep our conversation from becoming public discourse."

"My reputation?"

Grace looked up and down the wavy path. Underbrush encroached from all sides and short thick palm trees blocked out the bright morning sky giving the feeling that they were isolated in thick, dark, and overly dense jungle. *Jesus, I've been ambushed.* They were completely alone, and she pointed this out to him.

"There's no one around. What do you want to talk about? I have an appointment at the spa."

"You're late." He reached his hand out and she stepped back.

"Don't touch me, okay? Just... don't... touch me. I don't like to be manhandled." She raised her hands, palms open and shaking. "Just keep your hands to yourself. I don't like to be touched, alright?"

He forced a tight laugh. "Watching the way you and Mr. Corbet have been frolicking about the club, I'd say that's a bit of a misstatement, my dear. I wonder: does your husband have any idea what you've been up to? My guess is that he might be very interested in finding out."

"Who are you, mister?" Grace snapped. "I suggest you

mind your own damn business." She attempted to slide past him, and he grabbed her arm once more. Again she pulled herself free. "You touch me one more time and I'll scream, I swear to Christ I will." She then began to walk away from him.

"This is a very serious matter, Mrs. Rolston, and I suggest you hear me out."

Grace turned and faced him. "Alright, fine, say what you have to say, but don't come any closer and don't call me Mrs. Rolston."

"What would you prefer? Grace? That seems a little inappropriate, if you ask me."

"Why don't you just try, Miss?"

"I believe I'll stick with Mrs. Rolston. I, for one, have maintained a respect for the institution of marriage." He took a deep breath and started in a slow, practiced speech. "As you are well aware, I am a senior member of the Admissions Committee for the Pickering Club. Not only does this committee review all applicants who wish to join the club, we also review existing memberships to be certain our members are comporting themselves in a fashion worthy of club membership."

That had to be straight out of the bylaws, Grace thought. "What's your point?"

"My point, young lady, is that your behavior, as a married woman, is unacceptable and beneath club standards. It's clear to every member vacationing here that you and Mr. Corbet are having some sort of *fling*, if you will. In my day, this sort of an affair was handled with far more discretion. Husbands were not publicly castrated by their wives. Virtually everyone at the club has come to me at one moment or another to express the opinion that your conduct, and that of Mr. Corbet, is totally inappropriate and unacceptable."

"Like what? Sharing a few meals together? From that you jump to castration?"

"No. I'm talking about the noises that pour forth from both of your bungalows at ungodly hours, the not-so-sly groping of one another in public places, and that episode on the beach the other night."

She took two steps backward and stammered. "You saw us? Wait a minute, you were somewhere in the bushes watching us? The entire time?"

"Well, of course. I was out for my usual evening walk. It was nearly impossible to not to see the both of you. You were hardly quiet about the incident."

"'Nearly impossible?'" Grace gritted her teeth. "I'll bet it was. I hope you got your cookies off... You know what, Mr. McCracken? I'm not a member of this fucking club. And as far as that goes, Lee Corbet isn't a member of this club either. We are adults, in case you hadn't noticed, and we will behave any way we feel like behaving."

"I'm afraid that's where you're wrong, Mrs. Rolston. And I would appreciate it if you would refrain from using such vulgar language for the time you remain on the Pickering Club grounds."

"What do you mean by, 'that's where I'm wrong'? You're not my father..." Grace paused. She placed her hands over her ears and bent slightly at the waist. Her body shook. Her teeth became more clenched. After a second, she straightened and dug her eyes into McCracken, feeling herself in a position of strength for a moment. "You are not my father, and even if you were, you have no right to tell me how to behave. None whatsoever."

"Indeed, but as you so rightly pointed out, neither you nor Mr. Corbet are members of the Pickering Club; you are simply guests. You are only granted certain privileges out of the generosity of club members—privileges that can be revoked at any time."

"You old fart, do you honestly believe that either Lee or I give a shit about you, or your fucking club? We are not children." *I am not a child. I am not a child any longer. I can say no. THEN SAY IT, GRACE.* She took in a deep breath and let her words out slowly. "Well, not to worry, Mr. McCracken. Rest assured that Lee, Mr. Corbet, and I will pack our bags and be out of the Pickering Club before noon today."

Tug McCracken laughed. It had a calculated and sadistic tone to it. "And what would you like me to tell your husband when he arrives tomorrow afternoon. Or haven't you thought that far in advance?"

"You... You know Nick is on his way?" Grace again stammered. "You've read my messages, too? Have you spoken to him? Are you the one who told him about Lee?"

"This is a private club. Decorum must be maintained."

"No, no. Don't change the subject. You read a confidential note, the one that said Nick was coming in on Thursday. How else would you know? Where do you get off?"

McCracken stepped toward Grace, and she took another step back. He stared at her for nearly thirty seconds, not saying a word, and then pulled a pack of Winstons from his breast pocket, shook a few of the filter tips out of the opening, and offered her one. Grace waved him off. He lit one for himself, tossing the match into the shrubs, and said, "I was up a good deal of the night pondering how I was going to handle this situation, how I was going to make you understand that you cannot flaunt your adulterous behavior in the faces of decent people without incurring serious repercussions. Deeds such as yours cannot go unpunished."

"What the hell are you talking about? This is the seventies, not the fifties, in case you haven't looked at a calendar recently."

McCracken inhaled deeply from his cigarette and blew the smoke directly into Grace's face. "It may surprise you to learn that you're not the first unruly young lady I've dealt with in my day. Does your husband approve of you sleeping with other men? Rhetorical question. Of course he doesn't."

Grace stomped her sandal into the pathway and clenched her fists at her side. She spat her words at him. "I don't give a shit about my husband. I don't give a shit about you. I don't give a shit about your fucking club. If I could figure a way out of here, I would. He's canceled my credit cards, the shit. And do you know why? So I can't change my plane ticket to get off this goddamn island. I'm trapped here."

He smiled at her and said, "Very well put."

"Pardon me?"

"You may not care about your reputation at the Pickering Club, you may not care about your husband's reputation, but I'm sure your host... I'm sorry, *hostess*, Sally Fulton, cares deeply about the standing of her membership—"

"Leave Sally out of this. I told you we'd be leaving, so just let it drop."

"I have no intention of making this easy for you, and I will not let you derail my game plan. I will not let it drop. I have an opportunity at hand and I will not look this gift horse in the mouth."

He moved closer. Grace held her ground, but she could now feel his hot breath on her face, and she could smell the stench of his cigarette and the shot of rye whiskey McCracken had taken for courage. The odors gnawed at her brain, and as much as her psyche tried to fight it off, she was beginning to feel like a child in front of him. His breath seemed to come from the same source as her father's, and it made her tremble.

"Not only *won't* you be leaving the Pickering

Club," McCracken continued, "but you will remain here until your scheduled checkout day. I believe that's Saturday. You will greet your husband in a ladylike fashion when he arrives and you will both sit down for dinner tomorrow evening with my wife and me. This engagement will be of your suggestion. Believe me, I have no intention of letting this opportunity slip away. During the remaining time before your husband does arrive, you will not associate with Mr. Corbet in the slightest. You will not be seen with him. You will not so much as talk to him. I will have the club switchboard monitored; under no circumstances will your rooms be connected by telephone. If you fail to obey these few simple rules, I will suggest to the Membership Committee, with the strongest possible language, that Sally Fulton's membership in the Pickering Club be permanently revoked. As a former club president, I have a great deal of sway with this committee. Quite simply, and to use your own vulgar language, you've just been fucked, my dear. How do you like it? How does it feel?"

"You..." Grace started, but found words were now failing her. Her mind sped in circles and her mouth quivered and her nostrils flared as an emotion for which she had no understanding raced through her body and weakened it to such an extent she felt she was no longer capable of standing. It was an emotion that literally took all of her breath from her. Eventually, she said in a whisper, "You can't do this to us. You just can't. Don't..." *Please, Daddy, don't. Don't hurt me.* She was begging; she could hear it in her voice no matter how hard she tried to make it come out differently. *What's going on? I sound like a twelve-year-old,* she thought. *What's happening? How did I end up in this position? Where the hell am I? This can't be my father. I've run too far.*

"Oh, but yes I can. I'm very much in the driver's seat, Mrs.

Rolston. You may have the morals of an alley cat, but the members of the club don't need to have our faces rubbed in it."

She raised her hand to slap his face, but he latched on to her forearm with surprising agility. He squeezed her wrist until he could see by the tears forming in her eyes that he was causing her real pain.

"In the long run, you're getting off easy, my dear. The other punishment I had in mind was to force you to service me sexually. The idea was certainly intriguing, I must say, and I suspect that you may have been willing to go along for the ride. Something tells me I can handle your type much better than Lee Corbet could ever hope to. But do you know why I opted for this other course of action?"

Grace remained motionless, still unable to decipher the messages her brain was sending her way. Nevertheless she was conscious enough to drill her wet eyes into him with absolute loathing.

He dropped his grasp on her arm and said, "I decided not to take you, Mrs. Rolston, because, as with my daughter, Margot, I really have very little taste for used goods. Think about that, why don't you. Think about who has used you and to what extent. Corbet is a man like any other. I'd guess he's already got what he wants—a quick roll in the hay. My guess is he'll go back to New York and forget you ever existed. You might think a bit about how your behavior affects other people. And then think about what you'll be left with in the end... That's my prediction, Mrs. Rolston: when all the chips are counted, you'll be left with nothing, a washed-up hollow tramp." He then turned and left her standing alone on the path.

10:45 a.m.

Mitch Slack looked an altogether different person in his Pickering Club whites. He said Chef had been reluctant to issue these accouterments on his first day behind the range, not being completely convinced that Tomas Pressten was correct in his assessment of the young man's hidden talents. *Why lose a perfectly good pot washer?* was Chef's thinking. *Fry cooks are a dime a dozen.*

But Mitch had proven himself to be somewhat of a surprise in the kitchen. He was in no way fearful, or even shy, of the intense heat that radiated from the broilers, ovens, deep fryer, and steam table. He seemed to enjoy it. And he was lean, not much of a sweater, which pleased Chef immensely. Few salty beads of moisture formed across his face and none ever rolled down onto the cutting boards. No damp, sticky handles on Chef's collection of Swiss knives. And with only one day's experience, Mitch could chop onions, potatoes, and parsley with the best. He could lay a freshly-cracked egg into a skillet with one hand and never break a yolk, unless he intended to. He could determine whether a steak was rare, medium, or well-done simply by tapping it with a finger. He never burned bacon. He could build the notorious 'Pick-Club-Club-Sand'—three slices of toasted white bread, crusts trimmed of course; white-meat turkey; crisp bacon; lettuce; tomato; sweet pickles; and Russian dressing—with remarkable ease and speed, and arrange it on a platter in the exact manner that the Pickering Club had been presenting the sandwich for the last fifty years.

"Chef tells me you're a natural back here, Mitch," Tomas said in an uncharacteristically loud voice as he entered through the padded doors that led into the kitchen from the main dining room. A warm smile graced his tanned face. His teeth appeared as white as the trousers Mitch wore, and his stride and posture mimicked that of a triumphant Viking Warrior rather than a hotel manager.

The major portion of the breakfast guests had already passed through the dining room. The pandemonium that the waiters were so splendid at creating was over and done, which effectively made Tomas the focal point of everyone's glances. He crossed over to where his new recruit was running raw, peeled potatoes through a handpress that sliced them lengthwise into French Fries. Tomas eyed Mitch head to foot. He found his mouth watering; Mitch looked more like a fifteen-year-old British sailor than a fry cook.

"I must say; these whites serve you very, very well. You look as though you were born in them. It's fortunate for us that we don't have any waitresses at the club; they'd be all over you. Here—"

Tomas reached over and undid the top two buttons of the starched tunic, allowing the flap to fall open. He creased it at the fold and pressed the flap firmly down onto Mitch's chest. "There. That's how it's done in Europe. It gives one that devil-may-care appearance. Anything goes. Next thing you know we'll be sending you off to Escoffier to learn some new tricks." He then moved his hand behind Mitch's neck and gave his ponytail a small flip. "We have to do something about this hair of yours, though."

"I know, Mr. Pressten, I'm sorry. Chef told me to get it cut yesterday, but I haven't had any free time to find a barber. I'll do it first thing tomorrow morning."

Tomas stepped back a few paces and studied him from a distance. "I'll tell you what—I think we can give you a few hours off this afternoon, can't we, Chef?" He said this keeping his eyes fixed on Mitch, and paused only briefly while waiting for Chef's all-too-predictable reply.

"Whatever you say, Boss."

"Wonderful. Why don't I take you out to the fellow who does my hair, then? There's no point in having someone making a hash of it, now is there?"

"Well..." Mitch looked down at his pile of sliced potatoes and uttered a slight sigh. "Is he expensive?"

Tomas laughed. "I think it's an expense that the Pickering Club can pick up this once. The members do like to have their employees well-groomed, especially if we're going to have you out on the line for buffet night. And Bruno loves to get his hands on a full head of hair like yours. He adores having something to work with. I believe he jokingly calls it, 'fresh meat.'" He moved close to Mitch once more and lowered his voice a spot. "How are you coming on your apartment search?"

"That's another thing I can't get crackin' on 'til tomorrow, Mr. Pressten. But I got the *Advertiser* today on my way in and circled a few things. I'll find something."

"And this fellow you're bunking in with? How's that working out?"

"It's kinda tense. The sooner I get out the better, I think. It's kinda close. I mean, it's okay, he just has some problems to work out, that's all. But nothing I can't handle."

Tomas patted Mitch on the shoulder. "You let me know if the club can help out in any way, alright?"

"Yes, sir."

"Well, I'll see you... shall we say... at two, then?"

"Sure."

"Wonderful." Tomas turned and headed toward the padded doors. "Don't work him too hard, Chef. We don't want him exhausted, now do we?"

"Whatever you say, Boss."

11:00 a.m.

Perhaps it was because there was a real fear of having his dentures crammed down his throat, or the possibility of having his comb-over loosened from its anchorage, but Tug McCracken opted not to confront Lee Corbet personally with his threat to expel Aunt Sally from the Pickering Club. Instead, the moment he'd awakened, he'd inked his intentions out on a piece of club stationery. He'd refrained from showing it to his wife or illuminating her as to his plan of attack, knowing full well that Bunny would have no part of tarnishing the reputation of her good friend, Sally Fulton. *Besides*, he thought, *it will never get that far*.

McCracken had quietly slipped out of his bungalow at nine-fifty and headed straight to the path that led to the spa, where he'd accosted Grace. The moment he'd finished outlining his intent to her, he'd trotted down the overgrown path and headed directly for Lee Corbet's bungalow. He waited, and once he heard the shower begin to run, he'd slipped the paper under the door and strolled off to the dining room where he found Bunny idly gazing at her English muffin crumbs, sipping her coffee with her right hand while a half-smoked Kent cigarette dangled indiscriminately from the fingers of her left. He approached her with a "mission-accomplished" smile. She hardly noticed or even bothered to discern what might be going on in his head. The coffee and cigarettes had yet to pick up where the Old Fashioneds and brandy had left her spirit the previous night.

**

I'm guessing Lee stepped from the shower imagining Grace getting her massage and feeling mildly jealous that someone else was at that very moment caressing, pressing and compressing, squeezing, and generally fondling her body. Maybe smiled at his reflection in the mirror and shook his head, thinking, *Life could be a lot worse than this*. In the solitude of the steamy shower, his first moment alone since hearing of Nick Rolston's pending arrival, Lee had found an answer, a solution to all the obstacles. Everything would work out. His face beamed with almost the same self-satisfied grin that Tug McCracken had used to greet his wife only ten minutes earlier, though the emotional justification was altogether from a different world.

Lee toweled off and ambled, still naked, out of the bathroom. He crossed over to the door and retrieved the piece of stationery that had been deposited there. He then sat on the edge of the bed, unfolded the letter, and read it. He read it five times in all, each time finding it more and more grotesque and harder to absorb. And with each reading his hands would tremble more and more while more salty water would collect within his eyes.

Lee had traveled the spectrum of emotions in less than two hours. The height had been lifting his eyelids at eight-thirty to find Grace still dead to the world with her head resting peacefully on his chest. Then the soft and slow lovemaking they fell into after she'd begun to stir and her insistence on finishing him off orally.

"I have a massage at ten. It's not very polite to go in there stinking of sex," she'd said with a smile that seemed to take lewdness to an altogether new level.

And now Lee sat on that same bed, still unclothed, with his sensibilities bouncing like a tennis ball between self-pity and rage. He told Grace he was shocked at how quickly his mind presented him with myriad violent and murderous solutions. He visualized himself pounding McCracken's head into the base of a palm tree until there was nothing left of it but a gray mush, of pushing his face into his cereal bowl until he drowned in sour milk, or staking him out and slicing him to a slow tortured death with a straight razor. Lee wasn't the sort to just roll over, and he did not like this feeling of being someone's whipping boy. He sat on the bed for ten minutes squeezing his hands into the sheets and mattress, pondering possible adjustments to the foolproof solution he'd arrived at only moments earlier. He was not about to give up on Grace so easily, but at the same time he was unwilling to sacrifice his Aunt Sally.

At last, he stood. He carried the letter over to the writing desk. He placed it unedited into a Pickering Club envelope, which he sealed and addressed. He made one phone call and then slipped on a pair of khaki shorts and a polo shirt, neglecting to tuck it into the shorts or put on either underwear or shoes. His mind was elsewhere. He walked out and down to the Pickering Club's reception desk.

"Good morning," he said, doing his best to place a smile on his face. "May I have a first-class stamp, please?"

"Certainly, Mr. Corbet." The receptionist was a petite Hawaiian with a near perfect figure, straight white teeth, flawless skin, and silken black hair down to her waist. She handed Lee a stamp. "I can post that for you here if you like?"

"No, thank you. I think I'll just drive it straight to the

post office myself. I'd like to make sure it gets to where it's supposed to go without any assistance from past presidents of the Pickering Club."

"I understand..." She released a small sigh, looking first to her left and then right before continuing. "I just would like you to know that the entire staff is very upset about all of this, from Mr. Pressten on down. We all know what's going on."

"Yes, and I'm sorry. We didn't realize that our behavior was that extreme. I guess that's one of the pitfalls of being in love. I—" He stopped himself. *It's not her fault.* He turned to leave, but she called him back.

"No. No. I mean none of us want to be involved with this... this... this psychotic behavior of Mr. McCracken's. He was the worst president this club ever had. The switchboard operator has been in tears all morning. But the problem is this club is still run like a warship. Mr. Pressten, as nice as he is, is essentially powerless, and the board of directors doesn't look favorably upon mutiny or signs of disloyalty from the crew. None of us wants to lose our job, so we're all frightened *not* to carry out Mr. McCracken's directives. I just wanted to apologize, that's all. It's out of our hands. I want to apologize for all of us."

"I understand. I do." He smiled at her with a bit more sincerity. "Thank you for telling me that. It makes me feel a lot more comfortable with what I'm about to do. Thank you."

Lee marched across the expansive lobby and into the dining room. He had no difficulty in locating the McCrackens. They were seated at their favorite corner table with the sweeping view of the other guests. As he approached, he could see Tug's entire body stiffen. Bunny gave him a squinty and lined smile and inhaled deeply on her cigarette. Lee did not ask if he could join them, he simply pulled out a chair and sat. He tossed the envelope onto the table, address side up.

"I have nothing to say to you. I believe I've made myself perfectly clear," McCracken said nervously. "I'd rather you not sit at our table."

Lee told Grace he was tempted to throw his arms in the air like the bogeyman just to see how far the old guy would jump back.

"Oh, goodness me," Bunny said with a touch of excitement in her voice and seemingly unaware that Tug had spoken or possessing any cognizance of the tone he'd taken. "I see by your envelope that you're writing to your Aunt Sally Fulton? Well, I do hope you've given her my best. I do so enjoy Sally's sense of humor. She can laugh at almost anything."

"Actually, Mrs. McCracken, I'm simply forwarding her a piece of mail I received this morning. Something that was clandestinely slipped under my door while I was showering. I thought my Aunt Sally would find it interesting. But you're right—I'll bet she finds it somewhat amusing as well. She does love to laugh."

McCracken reached for the envelope, but Lee was much too quick for him.

"I don't think so, *Tug*. You see, I'm banking on the fact that my aunt is a far more decent individual than you are. In fact, I know she is, so that's a moot point. And I think I have a fairly good idea of how she'll respond to this letter, but only time will tell."

"Don't cross me, fella. I'm warning you."

"I think you've made your position very clear here." Lee tapped the letter on the knuckles of his left hand. "Now let me tell you where I stand."

"What's going on, Tug?"

"Shut up, Bunny."

"Don't you tell me to shut up."

"This is none of your business, Bunny, so just butt out. It's between me and Corbet here."

"Ahh," Lee said with a tight smile, "you didn't tell your wife what you were up to, huh? Extortion can get so ugly, can't it? You never know how the jury's going to respond. Well, I guess that's something you two will have to iron out later." Lee twisted his chair to a forty-five degree angle to the table and crossed his legs. "Now, there is one part of your list of suggestions that *Mrs. Rolston* and I are going to agree to. We are going to stay here at the Pickering Club. And you know why? Because I like the private beach. I like the new menu; I haven't tried the veal yet. I like the privacy of dining late, al fresco, with no one else around. The waiters here are a very pleasant bunch. I like not having to hear traffic noises. I've traveled six thousand miles to get here; I really don't feel like listening to car horns. And lastly, I want to rub your hateful, grizzled face into it. Go ahead: call me bitter if you like; you won't be the first person. And if you want to make this a personality contest between you and my Aunt Sally, if you want to see who the members of your fine club line up behind, you go for it, Mr. McCracken. But I would suggest you don't try to find out who your friends are—I'd wager you're going to be very disappointed with the results."

Lee stood, and as he walked away from the table he could hear Bunny say, "What the hell is all this about, Tug? And don't you ever tell me to shut up in front of another person again. Ever. You'd do well to remember whose trust fund it is that pays for our membership at this club."

Lee walked out to his rental car, placed the envelope in the glove compartment, and went directly to the spa.

"She's in the showers, Mr. Corbet," the attendant said uneasily as he walked up. She was another strikingly beautiful Hawaiian woman. "I... uh..."

"I know. Mr. McCracken has asked you to tell him if Mrs.

Rolston and I are seen together. That's all right, I completely understand. Do what you've been told to. We're prepared to deal with it."

"Yes, sir."

"Is she alone? Are there any other women in there with her?"

"No, sir, she's alone."

"Good. Don't let anyone come in for the next few minutes, okay? I won't be long."

"Yes, sir... She seems very tense... I don't think our massage did her much good at all."

Lee turned and walked into the women's dressing room. At the far end, there were five stall showers. The furthest from him, the shower against the wall, was the only one running. He walked up to it and opened the door. Grace had her back to him. From her body language—her bent figure, the palms of her hands pressed to her face, and her nearly gasping breath—it was clear she was weeping. The water ricocheted off of her shoulders and sprayed the front of his shirt and shorts. She hadn't heard the door open. He stepped forward and gently placed his hands on her upper arms. She flinched at first, but then relaxed and leaned her body into his.

"It's a good thing you're missing that damn finger. I'd recognize that touch anywhere. You're lopsided." She tried a laugh but it didn't come.

Grace twisted herself and latched onto him, pressing her wet breasts into his polo shirt, and rested her head on his shoulder.

"McCracken's going after Sally."

"I know. It's okay. I've taken care of it."

"I can't lose you, Lee, I can't. I don't know what to do. This is horrible."

"Don't worry." He pulled her in tighter. "We're going

to call McCracken's bluff. We're going to stay here at the club tonight. We're going to behave however we feel like behaving, and let the chips fall where they may."

"I can't... I can't do that to Sally, I really can't. She's been far too good to me."

"And to me... You know what? My Aunt Sally set this whole thing up, this meeting between you and me. You know her, you know she did. Think about it. She wanted me to meet you, she wanted you to meet me. I'm convinced of it. It's so... So Sally. Come on, you know this is exactly how she works. I hate to say this, but she adores me. She does. She has no kids of her own, and she thinks I'm a prince. And I'd venture to say she adores you, too. Why wouldn't she? She'd be tickled pink to see us together. You know that. McCracken won't fuck with Sally Fulton. He's not in her league, and he doesn't have the balls."

"I'd love to believe that."

"Believe it." He held her tight to his chest until her breathing matched his own, and then said, "Did you bring your passport with you?"

"Yes. Why?"

"I'm taking you to France tomorrow morning. I want you to meet my mother and father. I've already made the plane reservations."

She pulled her face away from his shoulder and smiled at him. Grace kissed him deeply. When they parted she said, "And everyone else can go to hell, is that it?"

"That's kind of the idea. We don't need any of them to survive."

12:15 p.m.

The upshot, Grace said, was that Lee believed he had beaten Tug McCracken at his own game, though he wasn't taking any chances with the envelope he'd addressed to Aunt Sally in the Palisades. McCracken might have been frightened enough to call off his dogs, but he certainly did not want that letter dropped into Sally Fulton's hands. He clearly had the means to intercept a piece of mail at any point along the way if Lee had been foolish enough to release it to the Pickering Club receptionist, no matter how sympathetic she may have been to the issues Lee and Grace were now facing. All it would take was a little more clandestine employee arm-twisting, which appears to have been McCracken's style. So Lee's intention had been to drive it straight to the main post office in downtown Waianae. He'd tried in earnest to convince Grace that McCracken wouldn't push the issue any further, suggesting she spend the time at the beach, but she was still shaken by the old guy's assault on her in the pathway. She was very pale, despite her ever-darkening suntan. She had no desire to remain at the club alone, within McCracken's reach, so she joined Lee and they drove into town together in the Mustang.

"You should have rented a convertible," she said with no real joy as they glided down Route 93.

"No such animal. Avis doesn't have any. Hardly anyone's making them anymore. Besides, no self-respecting New Yorker would drive a ragtop. There's no telling who you'd find sleeping in your car come morning."

Grace didn't so much as quiver at Lee's attempted humor. He reached over and placed his hand on her thigh, and when he did she flinched. Even though he could feel some of the anxiety drain from her body, she was clearly very much on edge. Her lips were slightly pursed and there seemed to be a half smile on her face that didn't make sense, or for that matter, belong there. He was unable to discern her thoughts, finding it impossible to determine what was going on within her mind far behind the dark glasses. They rode along quietly like that for five minutes or so.

"Do you think we'll have secrets?" she said, breaking the silence.

He didn't answer her. How could he? *Her husband's been cheating on her for years. With the same damn woman. How do I tell her that? Why do I tell her that? It's got to hurt her. What's the point?*

Grace let out a forced chuckle. "I'd like to think you didn't hear me. But that isn't the case, and we both know it."

He tapped his fingers on the steering wheel and said, "Yeah."

"Did you keep secrets from your wife?"

He considered this for a moment, and then said, "No, I actually didn't. I was an open book then. Hell, I was young. What could go wrong?"

"Oh no, you're not too bitter," she said with pointed facetiousness. "Did you ever tell her how you lost your finger?"

"It's kind of obvious, isn't it?"

"Not the details, no."

He removed his right hand from her thigh and placed it back on the steering wheel. "She never asked."

"Right. Of course she didn't. Good answer. She didn't like the looks of it. But did you offer to tell her? Did you ever try to share it with her?"

"No. She didn't ask. We only had five days."

"So you did have secrets, that's a perfect example. And if she was fooling around with your Best Man, your college buddy, screwing him silly while you were tromping around in the jungle popping off VC, she had a huge one of her own."

"What the hell brought all this on?"

Throughout the exchange, Grace had looked straight through the windshield, never once turning her head. "Nick has secrets, too. A lot. I just don't want *us* to have secrets, that's all. I want my life to be different. I don't want to run off to France with a man full of secrets. I want to know that if I ask you a question, you'll give me an honest answer, a straight answer. Otherwise, you can let me out of the car right here."

"Some things are better off kept to yourself," he said stonily. "If the truth is hurtful to someone you love, why tell them?"

"Like how you lost your finger? What you went through in Vietnam? What is it, classified government information? Do you think I'm going to laugh at you? What? Did you get it caught in a rat trap?"

"You know I didn't."

"Okay. Fine. So, I'm asking you for specifics. I want to know. You told me how some jerk stole it, fine, but you haven't said how you actually lost it. You said your sergeant found it in the weeds, your *Red Badge of Courage*, some physical pain. But what happened to your heart, your guts, your soul? Those are the wounds I need to know about. You had to have been dragged through an emotional horror show. What happened that day? I want you to share that with me. Right now. You said we're a product of our history. If I don't know what that history is, how can I buy the product? I don't want you to keep anything from me, Lee, I really don't."

His jaw tightened so that he could feel an ache in one of his molars. "I can't," he said.

She turned and faced him. "Ah, Jesus Christ... Can't or won't? That's such crap."

"It's ancient history, okay? It's over and done. I take that to my grave."

"Oh, well, there's a fucking enlightened attitude." Grace pointed to a small oceanfront park off to their left. "Could you pull in over there?"

"Why?"

"I want to get out of this car. I'm feeling trapped. My head's spinning. I'm in a cold sweat, and I think I'm going to puke."

"Are you serious?"

"Yes, damn it. Pull over."

He angled across traffic and parked under the shade of a date palm. Grace immediately stepped from the car, trotted over to a trash receptacle, and vomited into it. He was right behind her with three paper napkins that had been left in the glove compartment by the previous renter. She grabbed them and pushed him away.

"Please... Leave me alone," she said as she spit into the can.

"Are you alright?"

"Yes... Yes, I'm fine. I don't want you to see me like this. It's just something I ate, that's all."

He placed his hand on the small of her back. "What can I get you? There's a water fountain over there."

"Please, Lee." She pointed. "Go sit at that picnic table. I'll join you in a minute. Let me be. I don't want to be touched, alright?"

He did as she asked. He sat at the table keeping her in the corner of his eye as he watched the large breakers pound away at the rocky shoreline. The salty foam would spew high in the air with each new wave and crash down the jagged lava boulders, creating a loud roar and whoosh with each assault. He was surprised at how rugged the lava rocks remained. Despite centuries of pounding by the sea, none of the stones had smoothed off in the slightest. They all retained their hard, coarse edges.

Grace moved to join him a few minutes later. She stopped at the drinking fountain on her way and devoured large quantities of water. She sat on the picnic bench next to him, their thighs now touching, and said, "I'm sorry, it must have been those hot peppers I ate before going to the spa. I knew it was a bad idea."

He had his eyes fixed on the uneven rocks. He put his arm around her and held her firmly and began with, "Two kids died the day I lost my finger. Kids—they were both only nineteen-years-old. They died on my watch. All I did was lose one lousy finger."

"Lee... It's okay."

"It's actually not okay, it sucks. It's never been okay. Okay? It's about as far from okay as you can get." He chewed on the inside of his lip. "Jesus, what am I bitching for? I had it a hell of a lot better than most, a lot better. In my time I only lost eight of my guys." Again he bit his lip. "*Only*, there's a dumbass word. Some platoons ware hit a lot harder than mine. A good friend of mine who was with the Ninth Marines got absolutely creamed... a couple of times. But in the end it's all you remember. You remember who didn't come home and why. You wonder what you could have done differently to avoid what happened, to change the outcome. Go left here instead of right. You wonder what those kids would be doing now if they'd lived. It swamps you on a daily basis. They would have made great fathers, every one of them. The world has been cheated out of the children they would have raised, children with a sense of right and wrong, and that's the real tragedy, the tragedy of all wars. That's what the politicians never consider when they ask someone else to do their dirty work. These kids were honorable people, and they were all robbed of a chance to have honorable children of their own. The frauds and phonies don't get their hands dirty and then they pass their morals on to their offspring, who then become our new batch of leaders. It can keep you up at night. It never leaves you, but you keep your mouth shut about it because the only place to find your answers is in your own belly. No one else can make it straight for you, and to talk about it only brings it all back onto the focal plane, so you try to keep it buried as deep as you can. The reality is, there's no escape: there's no hole big enough... Shit, I'm sorry. I'm just blithering... How are you feeling?"

"Better."

"Good... I lost my finger in a firefight like I told you. I had my hand on my radio operator's helmet and an enemy bullet sheared it right off. When the dust settled, there it was on the ground. I don't know anything more than that, I really don't. Losing my finger was the easy part. What I do know is this: I know two really wonderful people died that day for absolutely no good reason. Their lives were pissed away by an uncaring administration and people out to make a buck. And I know I'm alive, and right now I'm glad. But I will miss those kids until the day I die. Every day I have is one more than those kids will ever see. Every time I see a little child on a swing in a park I think, *that could have been Carl*

Cokely's daughter." He turned toward her and kissed her lightly. "Why the hell did you eat hot peppers? Where'd you get them from?"

"I picked them up in the kitchen after I left your bungalow this morning. The short-order cook gave them to me. I think he's kinda new. They were out on the counter, and he couldn't seem to find anything else. He's a little spacey."

"Why?"

"Why? Why'd I eat them? I was hungry; why do you think? I didn't feel like waiting for you to drag yourself out of bed. You looked so peaceful, and I wanted to have something in my stomach before my massage. I was hungry. I didn't have time to wait for a waiter, so I walked into the kitchen and ate hot peppers."

"Filled you right up, did they?"

"Yes they did, thank you very much. I just ate too many, that's all. This guy put the whole jar in front of me, and I just didn't know when to stop. I think I was entertaining him."

He shrugged and said, "Makes sense to me." Then after a second added, "So, what are your big secrets?"

"I don't have any."

He laughed out loud and brought his arm up and laid it on her shoulder. He kissed her again more passionately. "I was going to say, 'you lie like a dog,' but I'll take you at your word for now," he said after their lips parted. But he was thinking, *What makes a family like Grace's scatter in all directions and never talk to one another again? There's an entire family built on secrets.*

Grace leaned forward, placed her forearms on the picnic table and then bent over and rested her head on the backs of her hands, almost as if she were planning to take a nap there. Lee stroked her stiff back muscles.

"It doesn't feel as if that massage did you much good. You're tighter than hell." He continued to work the rigid muscles of her shoulders.

She closed her eyes and said, "Penny Archer is Nick's New York agent."

Lee maintained his kneading and rubbing the length of Grace's back. He didn't speak. He knew who Penny was. *How many Pennys could there be in the world?* He knew this Penny—the woman Nick had been bringing into Saintes Maries de la Mer all these years, the one he'd assumed was Nick's wife, the sharply-dressed Wall Street woman with the sexy glasses.

"That's really why I'm here. I didn't want to leave Nick at first. So what if he had an affair with Carla Thompson in Morocco? So what if he's shacked up with another waitress? He'd get over it, just like he did with Carla... Just like he did four years ago with... And as we now see he has once more. Who didn't know it wouldn't last? Only Nick; he's the only one. Who didn't know he had no stomach for a messy divorce? *Variety* headlines, that's all he thinks of. And so what if I didn't love him? He saved me. He got me out of Long Beach. He took care of me. He gave me a nice house to live in. Got me some industry jobs. He's not an abusive person, really. I don't think. There's real generosity with Nick. He came from nothing himself. He's worked hard for everything he has, and he shares most of it."

A slow stream of tears left her eye and rolled across her nose and down onto her hands. She didn't move, or open her eyes any more than was necessary to let the fat tears escape.

"Sally told me about Penny on Friday and how long it's been going on. You're right: Sally had to set this up. She's trying to save us both. Anyway, that's when I realized I had to get out. I couldn't hold onto it any more. God, he was probably balling her on our wedding day. Freddy Keeley was right: I'm nothing more than a canary to Nick. His favorite canary, maybe, but a canary nonetheless. I don't have Penny's class, I never will. Vassar and all that crap. You've seen her, I'm sure." Grace was quiet for a minute, and then said, "You weren't going to tell me about Penny, were you? You were going to keep it a secret because I know damn well he must have walked into your restaurant with her at one point."

Lee bent forward at the waist and placed his arms on the table and dropped his head down so that he was facing her. He waited for her to open her eyes before he spoke. "I couldn't bring myself to tell you. It seemed too hurtful. Like I said, when you love—"

"But Sally thought it was the right thing to do. Sally believed I could handle it. Sally didn't keep it a secret."

"My Aunt Sally is a goddess. She's perfect. I can't compete with that. I'm only a human being."

Grace raised her head and placed her arm over his shoulders. She leaned over to kiss him, and her final tear dropped from the tip of her nose and landed on his upper lip. He smiled and licked it off.

"Kind of salty," he said.

"And I suppose you never cry, is that it?"

"Never."

"What a guy. Why is it that I'm always attracted to men who are so full of shit?"

2:00 p.m.

Tomas Pressten backed his lemon yellow Jaguar XKE roadster out of the Pickering Club garage a few minutes before two that afternoon. The vine-covered pink stucco structure was large enough to accommodate only five automobiles, however its primary function in 1979 had become to house the club's lawn mowers and gardening and pool equipment. Members' cars, many of which were rentals, were parked in an open-air lot adjoining the tennis courts. Tomas' Jaguar was the only car with a designated indoor parking space. The black canvas top was down as it almost always was. Tomas was known to wait out passing rain squalls in indoor pay parking structures and under overpasses for up to an hour rather than going through the trouble of putting up the canvas top. Because of his height, the crown of his head and his white-blond hair rose slightly higher than the upper edge of the windshield frame, forcing him to stoop and slouch whenever the weather demanded he drive with the top in place. It was uncomfortable in the extreme, and he saw no reason to put up with it. He very much enjoyed the image that he and his car presented and the fact that heads turned as this Norse God in his yellow car sped by.

Tomas pulled up to the club's kitchen service entrance precisely at two and lightly tapped his horn twice. Mitch was ready. He'd change into his own clothes—flowered shirt and cut-off jeans—and had removed the rubber band from his ponytail, allowing his hair to fall down over his shoulders, giving him a somewhat androgynous appearance. He trotted over to Tomas's car and slid into the leather passenger's seat.

"Man, this is one hell of a car, Mr. Pressten." He bounced lightly in the seat like a five-year-old. "See, that just shows you what life in the kitchen's like. I ain't never seen your kids, and I ain't never seen your wheels. Might as well be in a cave. But I like it. Don't get me wrong; I like the new job." He ran his hand over the burled walnut of the dashboard. "Who knew you had a Jag? This is some ride."

"Thank you." Tomas pushed the Jaguar into first gear and eased it slowly forward until he approached the service gate. He then reached across Mitch's exposed thighs, brushing them slightly with his forearm, and opened the glove box and removed an electronic garage door opener. He squeezed it, the gate slid to one side, and he pulled the Jaguar into the street.

"Bruno's shop is just up 93 in Waianae. It shouldn't take more than fifteen minutes. I called. He was able to give you a two-fifteen," Tomas said as he dropped the opener into the glove box and pushed it shut.

Mitch flipped his hair off to the side letting the breeze catch it. "Yeah, I ain't been to a barber in over a year now, but to be honest with you, I'm happy to get this stuff cut off. It'll be nice to be *groomed* for a change. Time for me to stop lookin' like a kid, or a girl for that matter. And I appreciate you gettin' the club to pick up the tab on this, too, Mr. Pressten. What's this guy Bruno charge, anyway?"

"Don't worry about it."

"I knew a guy named Bruno in San Diego, but he wasn't no barber though. He was a hustler."

Something made Tomas feel like speeding, so he did. Mitch seemed to enjoy it, and they arrived at Bruno's Hair Salon in twelve minutes. The salon was tucked away down a forty-foot, lushly landscaped wooden walkway. Bougainvillea and large hibiscus plants in shades of pink and red and orange decorated the path, as well as palms and ferns of all possible varieties. At the end of the walk, there was cluster of six small shops. Except for Bruno's, each sold upscale women's and men's clothing or jewelry.

"Ah, my newest victim," Bruno chortled as Tomas and Mitch entered his salon. "As they say," he winked at Tomas, "look what the cat dragged in. Fresh meat." He then walked up and behind Mitch, placed his hands on his shoulders, guided him toward one of his tailor-made leather and chrome barber's chairs, and forced him down into it. "Take no offense, junior; we just like to have fun here."

Bruno had been cutting hair for nearly forty years, fifteen of them at this location. He was getting on to sixty years of age. He was pure Portuguese, a direct descendant of the first laborers who had been brought to Hawaii to work the cane, banana, and pineapple fields, and he had never left the island of Oahu. His skin was dark and leathery from years in the sun and there was a constant cigarette burning in the ashtray next to his blow-dryer. But he never seemed to smoke these cigarettes—he would only light them, take one puff, set them in the ashtray, and then go to work on one of his clients as the cigarette would smolder away until the filter would drop onto the floor. At which point, Bruno would exclaim, "Oh, damn it," crouch down and retrieve the butt, stub it out in the ashtray, and light a fresh one. His hands were always in constant motion: either with scissors, comb, razor, hair dryer, or just plain gesticulating or fabricating some joke or impish prank. "If you can't make life fun, there's simply no point in breathing," was the credo by which Bruno lived.

The hair salon was set up with four chairs. The aged cedar walls were decorated with ancient black-and-white photographs of Hawaii set in ornate gilded Chinese bamboo frames. There was a receptionist, Fiona, and three haircutters: Bruno, Marla, and Keana. Marla and Keana were attending to clients of their own. As was their way, they paid little attention to Bruno's animated behavior or his smoldering cigarettes or the arrival of Mitch and Tomas for that matter.

Tomas and Bruno stood on either side of Mitch, and the three men studied their reflections in the mirror before them. After a moment, Bruno set his hand on the back of Mitch's head and forced his chin down onto his chest. He then began flipping Mitch's hair up in the air with both hands.

"Well, I certainly have plenty to work with, don't I?" He bent down and shouted into the back of Mitch's head, "No mice in here, are there?" He then sighed dramatically. "What are we looking at here, Tomas? Perhaps I should give him one of those butch Marine flattops? It would certainly make my job a lot easier. But then it would send both of you into cardiac arrest, I'm sure."

Mitch jerked his head to one side. "No. No crew-cuts for me. I don't want no crew-cut. Okay, Mr. Pressten?"

"I rest my case," Bruno said with a laugh. "Relax, relax. This is not the 1950s. And certainly not Alcatraz or Schofield Barracks, though I have to admit Burt Lancaster wore it well. Alas, that's the last thing I need is to have some doll like you walking around Honolulu looking like one of the Kingston Trio and telling people, 'Bruno did it. Bruno did it.'"

"I think just a clean razor cut, if you don't mind, Bruno," Tomas said in a rather serious tone. "Remember I have to present him to our all-too-stodgy club membership on buffet nights. I don't want to have to bring him back out here on Tuesday morning for you to 'Robert Redford' him. You might as well do it right first time."

"So be it. 'Robert Redford' it is—a little over the ears and a small flip in the back?"

"Not too fancy, alright? Something he can maintain on his own. It doesn't sound like his present roommate is into giving him a blow-dry."

Tomas gave Bruno a small wink and took a seat behind them under a photograph of Diamond Head taken at the turn of the century. He leafed through a copy of *Cosmopolitan* while Bruno shampooed Mitch's head and then went to work on his locks. Occasionally Tomas would look up from the magazine to see large wads of damp hair fall onto the salon's hardwood flooring. Fiona would walk by every now and then and sweep it up in an effort to keep Bruno from kicking it across the room or having one of his fallen cigarettes ignite it. All in all, it took Bruno a half an hour to finish the job. Mitch never opened his mouth throughout the entire ordeal. Bruno finally switched his hair dryer off, spun Mitch around to face Tomas, and said, "Presto, I give you the next Robert Redford."

Tomas stood. "As always, Bruno, you're magnificent." He then tipped him ten dollars and asked him to place the other charges on his personal account.

**

221

"So, what do you think?" Tomas said as he started up the Jaguar.

Mitch leaned out of the car and once more studied his cut in the side mirror. "It looks great, Mr. Pressten. Gotta be the best haircut I've ever had, that's for damn sure."

"Yes, it looks good. I'm glad you like it."

Mitch leaned forward in the seat, reached behind him, and shook the back of his shirt. "Course all this damn hair down my shirt and back is gonna drive me nuts behind that broiler tonight."

Tomas looked at his watch and ran his hands along the Jag's lacquered wooden steering wheel. "Well, let's see, it's getting on to three o'clock, but I suppose we have time to run up to my bungalow and you can take a quick shower, if you like? It's just up the hillside here." He pointed off to his left.

"Ah, jeez, that would be great, Mr. Pressten, if you don't mind. I'm goin' crazy already."

"It shouldn't be a problem."

Tomas swung the Jaguar off to the left and climbed a narrow, poorly-surfaced road for three-quarters of a mile where he pulled up in front of a single-level house that over-looked the ocean. He reached for the glove box once more and removed a second electronic opener and depressed it. The garage opened, and he eased the Jaguar in. The garage wasn't connected to the main structure, so the two men exited to the rear of the Jaguar and entered the house by way of the main entrance.

Tomas' home was a small three-bedroom ranch-style built in the late forties. He'd outfitted it completely in soft tan leather furniture, and the walls featured a series of small erotic prints from India and some local watercolors. The dining area table was inlaid teak with chairs that were fashioned out of beige suede and brushed aluminum. Bookshelves lined one wall of the living room, but they contained very few books, only colored glassware and stone carvings, again from India and erotic in nature. The three bedrooms were in a line off a short hallway—all had private bathrooms, TVs with VCRs, and decks that looked out to the west and the Pacific Ocean.

"We have wonderful sunsets up here," Tomas said. "Well." He gestured to his left. "Why don't you use the bathroom over there, in the first guest room to your right. It has the better view of the two. There are fresh towels on the rack."

"Great."

"Actually, maybe you should take your shirt off out on the deck and give it and your shorts a good shaking. That way you you'll get the hair out of them before you have to put them back on."

"Good idea."

"I'd offer you one of my shirts, but I'm afraid it would hang on you like a peach sack."

"Yeah, you're probably right there."

"I need to place a few phone calls, so just make yourself at home and let me know when you're ready to head back to the club. I'll use the kitchen phone. Just call out when you're done."

Mitch walked through the guest bedroom and out onto the deck. The sea was a dark, dark blue. Other than when he flew into Hawaii, he'd never seen the Pacific Ocean from this far up. He stared at the vista for five or six minutes and then removed his shirt and shorts and shook them vigorously until the hair had flown down the hillside. He returned to the bedroom and removed his underwear. He lay out all his clothing neatly on the red paisley spread that covered the king-size bed. Mitch then crossed over to the bathroom and ran the shower until it warmed. He stepped in and let the water roll over his head and shoulders. It felt softer, smoother, and gentler than the water in his brother's shower for some reason, and the tub was clean and squeaky under his feet and smelled of some sort of flowers. It all seemed very comforting. Mitch soaped himself up. He soaped his freshly-cut hair, his face, his arms, his legs, his shoulders. He then proceeded to soap his genitals. He stroked himself until he was hard as stone. He kept at it for a minute or two and then rinsed the lather from his body. He turned off the water, pushed the shower curtain open, and toweled himself off, his erection not softening in the least. He lowered the toilet lid and sat facing the door. And he then called out.

"Hey, Mr. Pressten. There ain't no towels in here."

Tomas frowned. He placed his hand over the receiver and called to Mitch, "Just a minute," and then into the telephone, "Let me call you back in a bit. I've got a slight problem here." He crossed the living room through the spare bedroom and approached the bathroom door.

"Are you sure?" he asked. "I thought the maid put some fresh ones in there just yesterday? Right on the rack. If not, there should be some others under the sink. Take a look."

Mitch continued to caress himself. "Yeah. I don't see any nowhere."

"Alright, hold on a sec." He pulled a flowered beach towel from a nearby linen closet and tapped on the bathroom door. "Are you decent?"

"Absolutely."

Tomas opened the door and was greeted by a full frontal view of his naked and completely aroused houseguest. He sucked in a huge breath of air. His heart quickly raced dramatically, and he was left speechless.

Mitch leaned against the cool toilet tank and slowly masturbated. "I'll bet you like what you see, don't you, Mr.

Pressten? I figured this was the only way I was going to be able to say thanks for all you've done for me—kinda pay you back, you know, give you something you'd want."

"I haven't fooled you one bit, have I, Mitch?"

"No. I knew you and me had something in common. But it wasn't 'til this week that I figured out what it was."

"Why don't we take this into the bedroom, then? Where we can both be more comfortable."

"I think I'd like that."

6:00 p.m.

They never mailed the letter to Sally Fulton. And they never noticed the blond men in the lemon yellow Jaguar as it passed them by on Route 93. They'd sat at the picnic table in the small roadside park until six when two Hawaiian clans, seventeen people in all, arrived to barbecue their dinners on the open-air public grills that had been constructed out of brown and black lava rock. The couple's sleepy patch of green grass and ocean foam and palm trees and never-changing rocks was immediately transformed into a playground, where a dozen children now laughed and giggled, tossed balls and Frisbees, and chased one another to the accompaniment of jubilant screams, shouts and the lilt of a slack-key guitar coming from a boom box. It seemed the perfect familial spot to feast and watch the sunset.

Lee and Grace hadn't done much talking for the time they'd been there alone, but enough to learn the ups and downs of their lives. Mostly they'd just sat, holding onto one another's limbs, watching the surf pound the jagged rocks while the sun dropped methodically in the sky and the day cooled off. The fact that they held two plane tickets for Nice by way of Chicago and Paris had relegated the subject of Nick Rolston to nothing more than a trivial piece of ancient history.

"I'll bet the post office closed at five," she said as they ambled toward the Mustang hand in hand, leaving the locals and the happy sounds of their voices and music in their wake.

"There's probably an outside box, but I'm not going to mail it."

"I didn't think you would. In fact, I would've bet on it."

"What's the point? McCracken'll back off, so why put him at odds with Aunt Sally? Same old story: why hurt someone you love? We'll be in Paris the day after tomorrow. Why stress her out with this mess? And if McCracken's position at the club ever became tenuous, it would kill him. He's got too much invested there. It's his life. He's just an old guy with false teeth and a comb-over. I don't need to prove anything. I don't need to do battle with him."

"He's a mean and spiteful person, Lee, and I don't think he can be trusted. I've seen his type before. I know him."

Lee shrugged.

"But you will keep the letter?" she asked.

"Until we get to France, anyway. After that, who knows?"

"What if he decides to have Sally tossed out of the club later on down the road? After we've left? I don't give a crap about McCracken one way or the other, but I don't want to see Sally hurt in any way."

"I'll talk to him before we fly out, how's that? I'd like to leave the Pickering Club just as it was when I arrived, and after all is said and done, McCracken doesn't want to lock horns with Sally. I have nothing against these people. I have no need to change their way of life."

"No, but they'd sure as hell like to change ours, there's the difference. I'd be just as happy to burn the place down on the way out the driveway."

He laughed and opened the car door for her.

"We have one more dinner left in Hawaii," he said after he crossed in front of the Mustang and dropped in behind the wheel, "but there's nothing that says we have to eat it at the Pickering Club. I say we mosey on into Honolulu tonight and see what we can find. Something with a little nightlife, with people under the age of ninety. Do you like to dance?"

"I love to dance."

"How did I know that?"

Her face lit up brighter than any of the kids playing out on the grass, as if everything that had transpired in the last nine hours had been washed out to sea. "It's been a while, though. I don't know about hopping up and down to, 'I Will Survive' and 'YMCA.' I'm more of a C.C.R. girl."

"I'm sure we can find a place."

An orange Ford Pinto pulled into a parking space twenty yards off to their left and idled. After a moment, the driver turned off the car and stepped out. She was young and blonde, wearing shorts and a halter top and smoking a cigarette. A small purse dangled from her shoulder. She walked over and behind Lee's car and looked at his license plate. She then approached the driver's side window. "This is a rental, right?"

"Yes."

"I thought so." She puffed on her cigarette. "I take it that means you're not a cop?"

"No... Do you need a cop for some reason?" Lee opened the door and stepped out of the Mustang thinking she was in some form of trouble. "There's a payphone over by the trash can." Grace also got out on the other side. A concerned look covered her face as well.

"Hell, no. I don't need no cop. Relax. I figured because you was sittin' here with a lady and driving a rental car you were tourists and you weren't no cops, but I wanted to make sure, that's all. Sometimes the undercover jerks will hang out in this park, trying to bust the hippies for smokin' weed. A cop is exactly what I don't want."

She returned to her Pinto, slid up, and reclined on the hood, using her brand-new windshield as a back support. She then removed a marijuana stick from her purse and lit it from the remaining ember of her short cigarette. She dropped the butt onto the gravel and inhaled deeply from the joint.

"I wish I could be that free and easy," Grace said with a slight sigh. "Look at her. I'll bet she doesn't have a care in the world."

Lee laughed quietly and leaned against the Mustang and folded his arms over his chest. "I'll refrain from saying, 'That's the dumbest thing I've heard all week' because I'm so fond of you."

"Why's it dumb?"

"What's the difference between what she's doing and some guy drifting into a bar all by himself and throwing down a couple shots of Jim Beam? He's just not breaking the law, that's all. She's not out here for a little social repartee like those families over there or us for that matter. She's out here to escape. She's out here to get stoned. If she was with other people, I might be inclined to agree with you, but she's here alone. She wants to be alone, and I'll bet she's not in the least bit happy about where her life's heading."

"Thank you, Doctor Freud." Grace leaned on the car next to him. He wrapped his arm around her once more and kept his eyes fixed on the woman as he spoke.

"I see these people all the time, Grace. The bar at Saintes Maries de la Mer is tiny—it only has four chairs. There's no bartender. The waiters mix the customers' drinks, or I do. It's not a social bar, it's not an Irish pub. The few people that actually sit at my bar come there by themselves to be by themselves. Ninety percent of them are businessmen from out of town. They don't want bartender chat, they don't want to meet anyone, they seldom return a second time. They only want to drink at a spot where nobody knows them, where they can forget about how miserable their lives are and not be bothered by chatty bartenders or people shouting at the Knicks game." He nodded his head toward the woman. "Just like our friend over there. The only difference is that the people who come into my place are wearing coats and ties."

"I can't believe that. She looks very happy to me."

"She is now that she's getting stoned. That's the whole idea. Reality's been put off for another day. She has a wonderful view of the present, and her past and future have just become completely nonexistent."

They stood and watched her. She seemed oblivious to their staring.

"I've never smoked any pot," Grace admitted. "Have you?"

"In college, yeah. Ellen was a fairly big pothead. And in Vietnam a few times, but only back at base camp. I got paranoid about taking care of my guys. I wouldn't have been able to live with myself if the shit had hit the fan and I was stoned, so I swore off that kind of stuff early on in my tour. Besides, the Marine Corps really frowns upon their officers being dopers."

She leaned her body into his and put a fairly devious smile on her face. "Would you get annoyed if I tried it? Would that bug you?"

"Now? You're not going to go ask her for some weed, are you?"

"I was thinking about it, yeah. But you have to smoke it with me. I don't want to do it alone. I'm afraid to."

"If I was a nice guy, I'd say no."

She laughed. "That's exactly how this whole mess got started. And if I remember correctly, I said, 'You're not a nice guy. Nice guys don't lose their fingers,' and truer word were never spoken."

Grace then took hold of his hand and dragged him off toward the woman on the Pinto, Tracy Tillis.

6:30 p.m.

"**S**ure I got some more, tons more."

Tracy opened her small, red leather purse. She nearly rolled off the hood of the Pinto with the move. Lee placed his hand on her shoulder to steady her as she pitched her upper body weight into him, seeming to have already forgotten what he'd asked for. He straightened her gently and leaned her back against the Pinto's new windshield.

"Right, the weed," she said with a giggle.

She then removed a hard-pack of Kools from her purse and flipped open the top, displaying eight neatly rolled marijuana sticks mixed in with the filter cigarettes. She handed the box to Lee.

"Help yourself. And don't insult me by offering to pay for it. They ain't mine anyway. I threw my boyfriend out last week, and he left his stash behind. Somebody's gotta smoke it, right? I've been working on it, but there's too much." She took a hit off her joint and added, "I'm Tracy," as the smoke departed her mouth in a quick gush of air.

"My name's Lee, and my drug-addicted friend here is Grace."

Lee removed one of the hand-rolled sticks and dropped the package of Kools into Tracy's purse. She tapped the slight ash off of her joint, handed it to Lee, and he lit up from the fiery red ember. He inhaled deeply and passed it to Grace. She followed his lead, mimicking his moves, trying to duplicate the way he'd pulled the smoke deep into his lungs. She held it there for as long as she could, patiently waiting for Lee to exhale. When he did, she let hers escape as well. She coughed three times and handed the joint back to him.

"I don't feel anything," she said, forcing Tracy to burst into a high-pitched laugh.

"What is this? The first time you smoked any dope?" she asked through her amusement.

Grace nodded.

"Some drug addict. It'll take a few hits," Tracy said. "But don't worry—this is kick-ass stuff. First shot or not. Local, from right up in those hills back there. You'll be flyin' in no time. I'm completely wigged already."

Lee and Grace passed the joint back and forth until it was down to burning the tips of their fingers.

"Just flick the roach," Tracy said. "I got plenty. I got more at home. No point..." She coughed. "Ya wanna fire up another one?"

Lee raised his hands in the air. "Whoa, let's slow down. I'm coasting already." He looked at Grace. "Feeling anything yet?"

"Uh-huh... Uh-huh... Uh-huh."

Tracy and Lee started to guffaw, and Grace asked, "Why'd you throw your boyfriend out?"

"Why? I saw him sucking on some guy's dick, that's why."

This forced all three of them to erupt in laughter, and it seemed to go on forever. After they settled down a bit, Tracy said, "Hey, it ain't funny," which brought on yet another extended period of hilarity.

"I mean it, it ain't funny." The third time around it was

only followed by a light chuckle. "It's crazy. Two guys goin'
at it? Goin' down on each other? Rollin' around on the bed
like stray dogs lickin' each other? Wantin' us girls to sit
there and watch them? Then us to do the same thing? I just
can't get into that stuff. I got nothin' against other people
doin' it, really. Live and let live. Some of my *colleagues* are
gay, who cares. I just don't want to watch. It don't interest
me." She pulled another joint from her purse and lit it. "Let
me know if you want a pull. I'm goin' to outer space and ain't
comin' back."

"What do you do?" Grace asked.

"What'd I do? What do you think I did, I walked the hell
out. Told him I never wanted to see him again."

"No. No. What do you *do*? For work?"

"Oh, I'm a dancer."

"You mean as in *A Chorus Line*? That kind of dancer?
Broadway stuff? He's from New York. Maybe he's seen you
in something? He's big on dancers. He used to date a dancer.
Elizabeth Egan, maybe you know her." Grace's jaw went
slack. She was ready to be impressed.

"No. I never been to New York. Dancer, as in Cookie's
Joint. I'm an exotic dancer."

"A stripper?"

"Exotic dancer."

"Ahh," Grace drew out at length. "Maybe I will try some
more of that." She crawled up onto the Pinto and sat next to
Tracy. Tracy handed her the joint. She took a hit and offered
it to Lee, who waved it off.

"Not just yet," he said, leaning both hands on the fender
next to her for support while studying the pebbles at his
feet. "So, Tracy, I guess you've got to find yourself a new
boyfriend, don't you?"

Tracy looked from Lee to Grace and back to Lee. She rolled

her head slowly, up and down, and then side to side. "Hold on, are you two into threesomes? Is that what's goin' on here? You're swingers? Ya wanna pick me up? I just told you—"

"No, no, I'm just trying to talk. Make conversation. I'm attempting to see if my lips still work, while at the same time keeping my tongue from falling out of my mouth and onto the gravel."

The three again indulged themselves in a round of stupid laughter.

"Oh man, I am so fucked up," Tracy said in a long drawn-out sentence. "And socially, I'm screwed, too. I got one guy's gone gay on me, and then I'm stuck on another one who thinks I'm a friggin' punching bag. And now both of them are sharing the same apartment because they're brothers, as in they have the same parents supposedly. But I'm not so sure about that. What a damn mess."

"You're dating both of them? Both brothers? How's that working out?" Lee wondered aloud.

Grace had focused more on the "punching bag" comment. "You mean he hits you?" she asked. Her head dropped back against the Pinto's windshield with a small thud. "That's no good, Tracy. You can't let someone do that. You can't let a guy hit you. You can't let anyone hit you." She sucked in more of the thick smoke and handed the marijuana stick off to Tracy, who did likewise and shoved it toward Lee.

"Take this fucking thing, will ya? My brain's melting." She pointed to her still reddened lip where Ray had punched her. "He did that... But it's okay; it's healing pretty quickly. Ain't gonna leave a mark."

"He gave you a fat lip, and you're stuck on this guy?" Grace attempted to sound incensed, but the weed wouldn't let her pull it off.

"I don't know. Maybe not. But there's something about

him that gets my juices movin'. He reeks of sex. You know the type; real... I don't know... manly, I guess, a man's man. Not like your guy here." Tracy tried to focus on Lee. "Sorry, but you're kinda too *Esquire* for me. Too squeaky-clean."

"I don't hit women, if that's what you mean?"

"Yeah, I know, but I can't stay away from him. He's hot. He's just got some problems, that's all. So then he starts to scare me, and I run away. I'm tryin' to figure it all out. He just needs someone to take care of him, is all. I don't think he's ever had anyone who really loved him, that's his main problem."

Grace lifted her head to focus on Tracy. "And that's a rational motive for you to love him? You're going to love someone just because no one else does? Sounds to me like there's a reason no one loves him."

"He's just in a bad space now. I mean his brother loves him, I know that, and I'm sure he's had a string of girls. I mean, he is a looker. He'll come around... Jus' needs a body to take care of him, that's all." She laughed unconvincingly and pointed to the marijuana Lee was holding. "I don't know if that helps or not, but I could take on the fuckin' Navy right now. See, that's *my* problem and I know it: I get horny sometimes and there's nothin' I can do about it. I just melt. I need someone to show me which end's up, I think."

Lee squeezed the ember off the end of the joint, opened Tracy's purse, and put it into the Kool box.

"Walk away from it, Tracy," he said. "You don't need to be pushed around."

"Do I look like Carly Simon to either one of you," Grace almost shouted, making an attempt to sit up straight, but failing miserably. A pinched brow and overly serious look had swept across her face.

"No."

"No."

"Well, that's who I am. Who are you people? You're not in the band are you? You need instruments to be in a band. No one plays in my band without an instrument." She began singing "Anticipation," much to the amusement of Lee and Tracy.

"She's trippin'," Tracy said. "This stuff'll do it for you, if you let it. Ya gotta be open. If you are, you can go anywhere. But if you got too many gremlins chasin' after you, you'll never forget who the hell you are, or where you came from. Or who's done what to you."

"She has her gremlins, don't fool yourself," Lee said with a hint of sadness, knowing that Grace was in no condition to hear him, or even realize she was being talked about for that matter.

"Yeah...? Everything's relative, ain't it?" Tracy lamented, giving Grace an envious glance. "Or... she coulda figured out a way to chase them away. Some people can do that. I'm not so good at it."

"Bury them is more like it."

"I guess. But she's sure buried them deep... It's like that old Pandora's Box thing—ya really want to know what's inside, but findin' out ain't no treat neither. Whatever it is, I wish she'd teach me her trick because it's workin' like a charm for her."

They then joined Grace in the singing of "Anticipation," but since none of them remembered any of the lyrics, they were left with crooning only the song's title over and over again. Their boisterous performance attracted the attention of the picnicking families, who found the show to be thoroughly entertaining: stopping their games and feasting to turn and watch the stoned Haoles. Once the trio had finished with the lengthy rendition of their one-word mini-opera, the oldest of the men strolled over to the Pinto. His skin was a deep and dark shade but as smooth as a child's, as if the sun's damaging rays had blessed him with eternal youth. He was rail thin, most likely in his seventies, but Grace told me it was impossible for her to tell for sure.

"After you three come down from wherever the hell you are," the man said softly, "you're going to have a serious case of the munchies. We've got baskets of food over there, so why don't you join us? No singing, though, okay?"

"You want some weed?" Tracy asked.

He stood still for a moment, and then said, "Sure, I'll take some for later, but I really don't like anyone smoking it next to my grandchildren, okay? If you're planning to fire-up again, I'd appreciate it if you'd keep it over here in the parking lot."

Tracy handed him two joints. "I don't think neither one of us girls can stand right now, so we're just gonna ride the Pinto into the sunset. Okay if we come over in a little while?"

He lifted his left hand, keeping the three middle fingers pressed to his palm, while his thumb and pinky remained extended. He then twisted his wrist two or three times and returned to his party. "Ohana."

"What's that mean?" Grace asked.

"Technically, I guess—We are family," Tracy answered. "In this case, I'm kinda reading it as, 'be cool, see ya later.' I don't know, but I'll bet their food is damn good."

Lee lifted his left hand toward Tracy and duplicated the Hawaiian's gesture, but since his pinky was missing, it appeared as if he was hitchhiking, and brought on yet another wave of uncontrolled laughter.

Finally Grace said, "I don't think I'm Carly Simon anymore. That was weird. I really believed it."

"Got them gremlins all locked up safe and sound," Tracy voiced plaintively.

It took forty-five minutes, but they finally believed that certain amount of coordination had returned to their limbs, enough to allow them to place one foot in front of the other and venture across the grass to where the Hawaiian's were still working on their feast. The families had pulled three picnic tables together end to end and spread out a luau as fine as any Waikiki hotel would have presented. The old man hadn't been lying; there was enough food to feed a small army, from large pork spare ribs, to barbecued chickens, to fruits of every color, shape, and size. Tiki torches had been placed in the ground around the table. The sun was just meeting the Pacific Ocean, and one of the younger men was lighting the torches with a rolled-up newspaper. Clearly, these people were planning to make an evening of it. The children had all found seats at either end of the long table and seemed to have already eaten their fill and were waiting for the word from the elderly man in the middle to tell them that it was okay to leave and get to their games. All the adults had grouped themselves in the center, next to the old man, where they took leisurely samples of food and spoke in subdued voices. When they saw the Haoles approaching, they ended their conversation. The old man stood, shooed away the three children sitting closest to the adults, and opened his arms to the late arrivals.

"Welcome. Welcome," he said. "We're just getting started. Help us finish this food and kiss this day goodbye."

9:00 p.m.

After an hour and a half of local food and jovial, but oddly intimate, banter, Grace pushed her plastic plate aside and said, "That's it. I've had it. I can't eat another thing."

"Old Hawaiian saying: don't eat until you're full, eat until you're tired," the grandfather said to her with a warm smile. "You don't look at all tired to me. You look as if you just woke up. Like you're prepared to start another day. You have a glow to match the sunset. You must be a very lucky person."

His name was Loke, and he was clearly the paternal head of both families. When he spoke, everyone fell silent and listened. "You haven't had any ahi yet. No one grills ahi like Malika," he said with a sly smile.

Without another word, Malika, his eldest daughter, reached behind her, removed a piece of the tuna from a large blue-and-white cooler, and walked over to one of the barbecue pits. Grace raised her hands in friendly protest. "No, please don't make me eat any more. I'm going to burst."

"But then you insult your host," Loke replied. He seemed to be teasing her, possibly letting her off the hook, but the fish went on the grill without hesitation.

"I really can't, Loke. I haven't been feeling well. Really. It's the truth. In fact that's the only reason we stopped here.

I was going to be sick. In fact, I was sick. I got sick. Over there." She pointed to the trashcan.

Loke's, other daughter, Kieki, smiled and said, "Don't worry, that passes with time. Usually after the third month. But then you will be happy and round and without a care in the world. You'll get fat like me, just you watch. With all four of my children it was the same. With some women it lingers longer, the sickness, but I don't think so with you. You're very much like me, I think. You're good for making children. And good for loving children, I can see that in your face. Don't worry, you'll be fine in three months."

"No. No," Grace said, raising her hands once more and laughing, "I'm not pregnant. Is that what you thought? That I was going to have a baby?"

Kieki laughed softly. "You're pregnant. Obviously you just don't know it yet. Well..." She smiled and shrugged. "Now you do. I'm happy to be the one to tell you."

"But I can't be. I take birth... control... pills. Well, I did."

Loke stood and looked down at Grace. "Kieki is never wrong about these things. Medical science has yet to challenge her or catch up with her. Your pills are not working. It's that simple. Which warms your husband's heart. I can see in his face that he has no use for those pills. I'll bet he switched them on you. He looks like a crafty one to me." He crossed over to Lee and grabbed his hand. "Congratulations. The proud father-to-be. It pleases me to know that you have learned of this great news at my table. Your child will be welcome at my table always. Your child will be my child whenever he... or she returns to Hawaii. It's early, but Kieki will be able to determine if it will be a boy or girl in a month... If you care to know. At any rate, from this day forward you have family on Oahu."

Lee stood. He was speechless. Loke wrapped his arms

around him and pulled him tightly to his chest. He laughed once more. "The new father is in a state of shock. You see? Maybe I am wrong and he is like me. Maybe he has no idea how babies are made. He thinks they roll in on the ocean's waves or drop from the clouds. Or better yet: the Haole stork brings them."

All the men laughed.

"I..." was all Lee could get out. He sat down and pulled Grace close. "Is this possible?"

"I'm on the pill, Lee. I mean... I was taking the pill. When do they stop working? No, it's not possible. How could it be possible?"

"Kieki is never wrong."

"I'm never wrong. Your face has the color. There is no mistaking it. Your cheeks tell the truth, and your unpredictable stomach confirms it."

Malika returned to the table with the freshly grilled ahi and set it down in front of Grace. "This is very good for babies. Look at my children." She waved her hand over the end of the table. "Enjoy your food. It will make your child strong and healthy. If it's a girl she will be as beautiful as you, and if it's a boy, he will live to be a very old man... Like my father here."

The women's husbands and all the children laughed at this, as if it was one of the funniest things they'd heard in months.

"I think Kieki is right," Malika said, "you have that blush. The look of a very contented pig. A skinny pig, but a pig nonetheless. This is a good omen for everyone at this table."

Tracy joined the children laughing, and then said, "Man-o-man, better you than me, that's all I can say. I ain't nobody's lucky charm."

"I'm not pregnant, okay?" She looked down at her flat

stomach. "How could I be?" She then reached for a plastic cup filled with a spicy pineapple and papaya relish, ladled a healthy portion onto the ahi, and picked up her fork and began eating it, seeming to have no memory that she had maintained that she was stuffed to the gills only a few minutes earlier. Everyone again erupted in laughter, including Lee.

"This is a good man," Loke said waving the palm of his hand toward Lee. "He is why I asked you to join us. He has the eyes of an old man. He has a gift. He is a man who can laugh with women. You could have no better father for your child. A woman can have no better friend than man who can laugh with women. Eat, you make us all happy."

"What?" Grace said between forkfuls of tuna, letting Loke's comment glide through her and into the evening. "So I'm still a little hungry? I'm doing my best not to insult you, Loke. And I hate seeing good food go to waste." She slid the plate a few inches to her left. "Here, Lee, you can help me with this. It's fabulous."

Lee loosened a piece of the ahi with his fork. He leaned into Grace and kissed her on the cheek, and then slipped the fish into his mouth. The papaya-pineapple sauce was so outrageously spicy that he reacted as if someone had run a saber through the back of his head. He coughed, reached out for a glass of fruit juice, and finished it off in three large swallows. Once more, the entire table howled.

"What a wimp," Grace said after she was able to stop laughing. She looked at Loke. "Don't mind him. He's French. He only eats French food. I was weaned on tacos, burritos, and Mexican salsa. This sauce is unbelievable, Malika." She pulled the plate away from Lee. "His loss, my gain... What a wimp."

**

Tracy had left. The families were packing up their baskets. The sleepy kids were scouring the area for lost shoes and Frisbees and collecting pieces of trash whenever they found some. When everything had been assembled on the long table, Grace and Lee helped Loke and Malika and Kieki and their husbands ferry it all to their cars. By a quarter to midnight, they found themselves once again alone in the park.

"I wouldn't trade this evening for anything," Grace said as they strolled hand in hand along the grassy edge of the jagged rocks. The three-quarter moon highlighted the ocean spray as each new wave sent the salty water flying through the night air.

"Could you really be pregnant?" he said softly.

"I've been thinking about that... I haven't taken a pill since I found out about Nick and his damn waitress. I was pissed. I threw them in the trash and forgot all about them. I wasn't going to let him touch me, so why not?" She counted on her fingers. "Well, it has been over a month, I know that much. Closer to six weeks. They're probably out of my system by now, right?" She stopped and faced him. "Huh. Pregnant. Wouldn't that be something?" She shrugged. "Be careful what you wish for."

12:20 a.m.

Mitch Slack dragged himself back to Ray's apartment shortly after midnight. As with the previous night, he was beyond weary. His afternoon adventure with the Pickering Club manager hadn't served as any kind of rest period. It was fast, furious, and exhausting; they were both left drenched in more sweat than if they'd been toiling behind the flaming broilers for hours on end. Tomas and Mitch had then been forced to scramble out of the house in a flurry in order to make it back to the club by five o'clock to prepare for the early diners.

Throughout the evening, whenever there'd been a lull in kitchen activity, Mitch said he tried to step out back for a smoke, but Kami or Chef would take the opportunity to teach him something new: how to make a brown gravy, a cream sauce, how to French-cut beans, bind a chicken the Pickering way, filet and stuff a pork chop. The instructions had been endless and taken their toll on him mentally as well as physically. So understandably, he again dropped onto Ray's couch with a thud and groaned loudly the moment he'd reached a prone position. He was pleased that his brother wasn't there to greet him or engage him in conversation. The peaceful interlude lasted less than thirty seconds as

Ray stepped from his bedroom wearing only a pair of olive drab boxer shorts. The leather thong that once dangled from his truck's rearview mirror now hung about his neck. He was clearly high on something.

"What the hell happened to your hair, Mitchie?"

Mitch sat up and rubbed at his spine. "Had to get it cut for work." He followed the words with another slight groan. He lit a fresh cigarette and then tossed the match into the over-full ashtray. "Ya can't have it that long and work behind the range, it ain't healthy," he said, not looking at Ray, but watching the smoke leave his mouth as he spoke. It drifted to the ceiling without disbursing, trapped in a single cloud, bound by the dense night air. "Man, I'm glad I don't hafta be in 'til noon tomorrow. These hours are kickin' my ass."

Ray crossed over to the refrigerator and grabbed the handle, more for support than anything. The door fell open, so he removed a beer. "You want one?"

"Nah."

He stared at his younger brother for almost three minutes, debating what to say to him. Mitch methodically smoked his cigarette, unaware that he was being studied, happy all was quiet, thinking Ray might just decide to leave him be and return to his bedroom if only he would remain silent and kept his movements to a minimum.

"You didn't hear nothin' from Tracy, did ya?" Ray finally said.

Mitch wanted to scream and pull out what hair he had left, but instead he simply said, "Like what?"

Ray turned on him instantly, raising his voice aggressively, snapping like a caged cat. "Like, did she fucking call you? That's, 'like what.' Did she stop by the club at all? Like where the fuck is she?"

Mitch leaned back and put his feet up on the wooden

spice crate, somewhat oblivious to Ray's hostility. "I can't go through this anymore, Ray, I really can't." He shook his head slowly. "I don't give a damn about Tracy; she don't give a damn about me. You know I can't get phone calls at the club. I ain't talked to her. I gotta see her once more when I move my crap outta her place. That's it." He then added, "What is it with you and this fixation on Tracy?" and immediately regretted having said it.

Ray opened his beer and sat on the couch next to Mitch. His moves were slow, deliberate, and menacing, much like a cougar moving in on a wounded rabbit.

"Well, see, Tracy's been sniffin' after me, Mitchie. Givin' me the come-on, like she wants to take me to town... Again, that is. Like she did last Tuesday, know what I mean? She tells me she's gonna give me a ride tonight, and then she don't show up at her place. She's the one's got the 'fixation,' it ain't me... But see, she leaves me sitting out there in my truck in the parkin' lot with my dick in my hands and then don't never come home. So I'm tryin' to figure out if the two of you's jerkin' me off. If you got some game goin' on. Is this fuck-over-big-brother week? Is that it, Mitchie?" He dropped his hand on Mitch's thigh and squeezed hard just above the kneecap. Mitch shoved his hand away and stood, moving alongside the darkened TV set.

"Cut it out, will you? That hurt like hell." He rubbed his leg. "I've got nothing to do with whatever she's up to. That's between you and her. I don't care if you fuck her into next week. She's yours, okay? Take her. Leave me out of it."

"Cut it out, will you? That hurt," Ray repeated in a whine, using a high-pitched voice. He laughed and patted the couch next to him. "Come on, Mitchie, have a seat. I ain't gonna hurt ya." He lit one of Mitch's Kools. "Yeah, Tracy told me all about why she tossed you out, all about how you and

this guy, Eddie, were havin' a little sucky-sucky the other night on Lainie's bed." He laughed again, stretched out on the couch, and placed his hand under the elastic of his boxer shorts.

"What do ya mean? What?" Mitch said as he pushed his cigarette into his mouth and drew in more blue-gray smoke than he intended, which all brought on a small coughing fit. "What'd she tell you?" he choked out, hands now shaking slightly. "Don't listen to her, Ray, she don't know what she's sayin'. Tracy's just tryin' to make trouble, that's all. She loves to make trouble. You know that. She's just tryin' to stir things up between you and me. She's just steamed because I slapped her on the ass, that's it. She'll make up anything."

"Hey, so you're a faggot, who cares? The world's full of them. I got an open mind about these things. As a matter of fact," he slid his shorts down to expose himself, "I could do with a little servicing right about now myself, since I got stood up by your girlfriend. One mouth's as good as the next, that's what I always say. You know how it's done, don't ya, Mitchie? You been here before."

"Don't, Ray... I... Pull your pants up."

"Come on, just like when we was kids. You were good at it then, Mitchie. Sounds to me like you ain't lost your touch. That's what I hear-tell: once ya got a taste for it, ya never let it go. End up spendin' your life on your knees, ain't that right?"

"Look, Ray, Tracy gave you some bad information. I'm straight as a damn arrow. You know that. I don't know what the hell she's up to, but I don't do that shit. I never have... 'cept them times to you, but that was twenty years ago and you made me do it, Ray. You know that. We were kids, and you made me do it. I never wanted to. Them days are over, right?" Sweat now began to ooze from Mitch's brow and the side of his face. He could feel his hair becoming wet and matted with the perspiration. His hands were sweating. Fear had consumed him.

"Come here, you little fag. It's time for Daddy to collect the rent."

Mitch stood frozen and trembling.

"What?" Ray said with another calculated laugh. "I gotta get my baseball bat? We gotta play some Little League Baseball? Some hardball? Is that it? Remember how we played Little League Baseball when we was kids? You need some persuading? Like back then? You like it rough like Tracy, I bet. Is that the way it is?"

Ray rose and smashed his cigarette into the ashtray. He kicked his shorts across the room. They flew into Mitch's chest, where they dropped at his feet. He was fully aroused.

"I'll do it, man, don't push me. I'll get that bat of mine and bash your goddamn brains it, I swear to Christ I will. So you'd better get down on those fucking knees of yours, fag-boy."

Mitch began backing up uneasily as Ray stepped toward him.

"Tracy's makin' all that up, Ray." He put his cigarette in his mouth, pulled his wallet from his back pocket and tossed his last twenty dollars onto the end of the couch. "There. That's all the cash I got. I'll get you the rest when I get paid. Or I'll get some from the bank tomorrow morning. I don't need to stay here tonight neither. But I ain't no faggot, okay?"

"Yeah? Where you gonna spend the night this late? Back in the damn park? On a bench?"

"The club manager, Mr. Pressten, said he could help me out. He's got a big house."

"What, at midnight?" Ray cackled. "You're gonna call your boss at fucking midnight and tell him you wanna bunk in? And, 'he's got a big house,' does he? How the hell do you know that?"

"He's a... rich guy," Mitch stuttered. "He's gotta have a big house, right? He's the manager. I seen his car. He has a Jag. I'll work something out. Just... don't come after me, Ray, please. I don't wanna do this. Not with you no more."

"Yeah, right. I know damn well Tracy wasn't lying about you and Eddie. I know she was tellin' the truth about that, I could see it in her face. And I knew it weren't no first time for you, neither... It don't take no genius to figure out what you were up to all that time in San Diego. All them damn sailors? You think word wouldn't get back to me? You think people wouldn't tell me about my fag bother if I asked around? Hustlin' bucks on University Avenue, probably too, ain't that right? And look at this little sissy haircut you got your self, walkin' around' like one of the damn Partridge Family, all pretty and whatnot. You're lookin' as sweet as they come, Mitchie-Mitchie. Don't tell me you don't still like to suck cock. I ain't stupid."

Mitch continued to back up. "Tracy's lying," he almost screamed.

"No. No. No. It's time for you to pay the rent, my friend. Get your ass over here. Now."

"Yeah, well if I go down on you, that makes us both queer." Mitch blurted as tears began to roll from his eyes across his cheeks.

The comment stopped Ray in his tracks. "Where'd you get that from?" he said, as a look of befuddlement mixed with anger settled into his face. "You don't see me goin' down on nobody, do ya?" His eyes squinted and his jaw tightened.

"Don't make no difference. You want some guy to have sex with you, to give you a blowjob, that makes you queer, too. It doesn't matter who's on their knees," Mitch whimpered.

"That's the way it works. It takes two, and everyone's a part of it."

"You callin' me a faggot, Mitch? Just 'cause I let you suck my dick when we was kids? That what you're sayin'?" Ray remained frozen, still weighing the logic of Mitch's statement. Finally he reached down and retrieved his shorts and stepped into them. "You callin' me a fag? Is that what you're sayin', Mitch?"

Ray walked into his bedroom and returned a minute later wearing his jeans and carrying one of his baseball bats. His jaw was still tense and his words were enraged and came from behind tightly-clenched teeth. "Nobody calls me a fucking faggot, nobody. Brother or no brother."

Mitch was still sobbing softly. "Don't, Ray. Don't hit me. Please don't. I didn't mean it." He raised his hands in front of him. "Nothing happened, okay? We didn't do nothin', okay? That stuff when we was kids don't mean nothin'. Just kid stuff. So, nobody here's a fag, okay? Just let me leave. Please. I won't bother you anymore. I swear I won't."

"You ain't goin' nowhere, Mitch," he shouted. "Nobody calls me a fag and gets away with it."

Ray advanced with the bat grasped in his right hand. The muscles in his forearm were tightly knotted, the skin covering his knuckles was stretched and red. Mitch circled, placing the couch between them, tripping over his own feet as he did.

"I want to hear you say it, you little crybaby. I want to hear you admit to me that you're a big-time cocksucker."

"Tracy was lying," Mitch pleaded, convinced the truth would only anger Ray further.

"So, this Mr. Pressten, is he a fag, too? Is that how you got your big-ass promotion? That's why you know how big his house is? 'Cause you two are sweet on each other? Ya probably know how big his dick is too."

"No. Jesus, Ray, just let me get out of here, okay?"

Mitch tried to edge his way to the door, but Ray jumped at him and swung the bat low at his chest. Mitch stepped back. The tip of the bat scraped against his ribs as it flew past. Ray stumbled, lost his balance, and fell to the floor. Mitch made a move to run for the door, but Ray reached out for him and grabbed his foot. Mitch stepped out of his flip-flop and retreated to behind the couch again, holding his right side. His shirt had been ripped, and a small drop of blood had formed where his skin had been abraded by the baseball bat.

"Just let me outta here, okay?"

Ray struggled to his feet. "Where the hell is Tracy?"

"I don't know, I swear," Mitch whimpered.

Ray leapt up onto the couch and vaulted over, swinging the bat furiously. Mitch backed up against the far wall. He then crouched in fear as Ray hurled the bat at him with all the strength he could pull up. The bat spun around twice, and the fat end slammed into Mitch's head just above his left ear. He dropped to his knees and then fell flat on the floor, face-first, feigning unconsciousness. A light stream of fresh blood drifted down from his hairline and rolled across his nose, forming a small pool on the carpet. Ray crossed over to him.

"Ah, shit, Mitch. Ya shoulda ducked, ya stupid bastard."

He crouched down and checked Mitch's pulse. He then slapped him twice in the face. He got no response. He pushed Mitch's hair back and studied the wound.

"Ah, Christ, you'll live, you fuckin' pussy. A stitch or two will clean that right up, assumin' nothin's busted inside. Hell, who knows, maybe it'll straighten you the fuck out."

Ray stumbled to the kitchen and retrieved his beer. He chugged it down and threw the empty can at the wall above where his brother had fallen. It dropped to the floor between Mitch's legs.

"This is all Tracy's fault, you know that, Mitch? She set you up for this, I swear to Christ she did. That type of broad— yeah, she's the one turned you into a fag. Likes to make out she was shocked, but that's all she was aimin' for. Another goddamn notch in her belt."

He pulled a bottle of Jack Daniels from the kitchen cabinet and took a large swallow straight from the neck. He then opened another beer and sat on the couch, his back to Mitch's prone body.

"Fucking bitch," he mumbled. "Where's she get off treatin' us like this? Probably try and do the same thing to me, if I let her. Make the whole family fruitcakes before she's done with us..." He took a long drink from the beer and sat stonily for a moment. When he continued, the anger in his voice had subsided. "You know the old man was into that shit?" He took another drink from his beer can and belched. "I never told you that... Yeah, you were next in line, my friend. Sweet little ten-year-old, you were. I saw how he was lookin' at you. I knew what he had in mind. I knew what was comin'. You're lucky he croaked when he did. Weren't no fun, I can tell you that. He was a class-A bastard. I kept him away from you... Don't you ever forget that, Mitch, I kept that piece of shit away from you."

Ray sat on the couch quietly and sipped slowly at his beer. After a moment, he twisted his torso and looked down at his brother stretched out on the floor. He lit another one of Mitch's Kools and said, "Ya feel like takin' a drive, Mitch? Jus' you an' me?"

No answer came. Mitch remained still.

"This place is closin' in on me. I gotta get some air. What do ya say? I don't give a shit you're the way you are, I really

255

don't. You're my brother, for Christ's sake... We'll go down to the beach. Watch the ocean for a while, what do ya say? Just like when we was kids, talkin' about the things we were gonna do. We had some times, didn't we? Remember that Rambler I fixed up for ya when you turned sixteen? A piece of shit, but she ran like a jackrabbit, didn't she? Yeah... We had some times."

He stood, turned away from Mitch, and fell face down over the back of the couch. His beer slipped from his hand, spilling onto the floor. Mitch remained motionless except for his small, shallow breaths. He believed playing dead was his only safe option.

"You're worthless, ya know that, Mitch?" Ray said as he struggled to his feet, "Ya got no spice for life. Ya don't do nothin'. Ya got no sense of adventure, that's your problem. Ya just wanna play it safe. Well, there ain't no safety in this world, buddy boy. Everywhere ya been, everything ya done is locked up in your brain, and there ain't nothin' ya can do about it. It ain't like a damn toilet, ya can't just flush it down. The world can catch up to ya in a blink of an eye if you're not careful. Ya could die tonight and then where the hell would ya be? Just dead and nothin' under your belt. Nothin' good to show for it, leavin' no legacy at all. People are gonna remember me, I'll tell you that right now."

Ray crossed to the refrigerator and removed another beer. He opened it, took a long swallow, and stumbled over to Mitch where he proceeded to pour what was left of the beer onto his brother's head. Mitch slowly rolled over and blinked his eyes three or four times before focusing on the situation. Playing dead wasn't going to work.

"I ain't no faggot, Ray," he said weakly. "I ain't. I mean it."

"Yeah, yeah, that's what they all say... I'm gonna get me some air."

Ray returned to the refrigerator, grabbed two more beers, and headed for the front door, stopping to grab Mitch's pack of cigarettes along the way. Before exiting, he turned back to his younger brother. Tears had formed in his eyes. "All I wanted, Mitch, all I ever fuckin' wanted outta my life was for you to be somebody. For you to get the hell outta the shit and be somebody. And you had a chance, I never did. The fuckin' war and all the bullshit caught up to me. I just wanted to be able to look at my little brother and point and say, 'Fuckin'-A, that's my brother, damn it.' And look at you. You're a bigger fuck-up than... than..." Ray's aggressive stance at once had lost its edge and the tension in his shoulders slackened off. "What the hell happened, Mitch? Why the hell couldn't you at least been somebody...? Answer me that, answer that one question... Christ, you're a bigger fuck-up than me. What happened to us, Mitch? What'd we do wrong? All them other people? They got the world and we got nothin'. We got nothin' at all. Look at this fuckin' dump." He opened the door and turned to his brother one last time. His anger had returned as quickly as it had dissipated. "Well, you do what you want with your life, Mitchie, and I'll do what I want with mine. Careful you don't die of boredom. And when I come back, I don't wanna see your ass here. I don't want to see your sorry ass ever again. Go spend your life on a bench. Turn into a fuckin' bench for all I care, ya piss-ant."

Wearing only his jeans and the leather thong—no shoes, no shirt—Ray walked out to his pickup truck, draped the thong back over the rearview mirror, started the engine, and went for a drive.

1:17 a.m.

In his ten or so years of living on the island of Oahu, Ray Slack had most likely passed through the intersection over a thousand times. On more than one occasion, Sami said Ray'd opted to travel to work by this particular path in an effort to beat the Friday and Monday traffic slowdowns on Route 93. He knew there was a toy store on the southwest corner, Kim's Korean Restaurant across the street, and an empty lot and a drugstore on the other two corners. There used to be a Mission-style house on the empty lot but it burned down in the winter of 1977. Mitch and Tracy had watched it crumble into ash one Monday night. It was quite a sight: all wood, Mitch said it went up like a matchstick. Nothing had been built in its place. Some people said a gas station was coming in, others said Pizza Hut, but at that point in time nothing had been set in stone.

Ray was well aware that the intersection was controlled by a stoplight. He knew it was a twenty-five-mile-an-hour zone. He was traveling at thirty-seven—not really speeding, everyone went forty on this stretch and they still do. Possibly Ray noticed that the light had turned red and chose to ignore it, thinking it was late at night, and as was usual, no one seemed to be on the roads. He may have seen the light turn yellow from thirty yards off and thought he could make it; his sense of time and distance having been severely altered by the substances he'd added to his bloodstream. No doubt his brain was not working at full capacity. Maybe he didn't see the red light at all that night, or possibly he had already blacked out. And then maybe, just maybe, he did it all on purpose. Maybe Raymond G. Slack was trying to kill himself. Maybe he was trying to destroy the demons that had eaten away at his soul. Whatever the case, when the other car entered the intersection in front of his pickup Ray never got his foot anywhere near the brake pedal. The police report noted that there were no skid marks whatsoever. His truck slammed into the car at the hinges on the driver's side door. The force of the impact carried both vehicles through the intersection, across the sidewalk and into the toy store's display window. The street sign, traffic signal, and lamp-post were sheared off at the base, and all three toppled into the intersection in the wake of the two vehicles. Four news-paper vending boxes were flattened as well, the loose change eventually rolling along the asphalt toward the storm drain, the few remaining day-old newspapers flying through the dark sky like lost and frightened angels. Neither Ray Slack nor the couple in the other car were wearing their seat belts. Viewing the black-and-white police photographs of the scene, it seems impossible that anyone could have been pulled from the wreckage alive.

It was very quick for Ray. His body lurched forward at impact. His forehead collided with the top of the windshield frame, his face pushing the glass out and onto the shiny red hood of the car he'd broadsided. His skull was nearly sheared in half at the eyebrows, and his neck snapped like a dried twig under a hiker's boot. In the same instant the Chevy's steering column rose up from the front axle and impaled Ray at the groin, driving his abdomen straight into the back of the driver's seat and compressing his torso down to a thickness of less than five inches. I suppose Ray Slack never knew what hit him. But I would also guess that was the way he'd always hoped he would go out. He was, after all, a coward.

My mother, Grace Rolston, had been sitting in the passenger's seat of the Mustang. Like Ray, she never knew what hit her. His pickup pushed the Mustang's transmission almost through to the fender on Grace's side of the car, breaking her left leg in two places just above the ankle and ripping tendons in both her knee joints. Her head collided with the side window with enough force to shatter the glass into thousands of flecks that cascaded to the street and sidewalk like a bushel of diamonds. She lost consciousness instantaneously. As the car came to a stop in the middle of the toy shop's display, a dangling piece of plate-glass served to punctuate the end of the event by dropping down onto the Mustang's metal roof and sliding off to the right side of the car. Before it came to rest on the store's carpeted children's play area, the shard of glass opened a five-and-a-half-inch gash in Grace's scalp as her head hung out of the side window. It would later take the emergency room doctors twenty-seven stitches to close this gash. Two of her ribs were broken on the right side, and her right hand was pinned between the seat and door panel. Her collarbone was also broken on the right side. For the rest of her life, Grace would walk with a very slight, almost undetectable, limp, but internally she had survived in fairly good shape—she would not lose her child. She had always told me the limp came from the time she fell off her bicycle when she was eleven-years-old.

Sitting in the Mustang's driver's seat, Lee Corbet, my father, was virtually at the epicenter of the impact. The radiator of the pickup now sat where Lee's thighs had once been, and Ray's battered and bloodied head rested on the truck's steering column five feet off to Lee's left. The entire lower half of Lee's body had been pulverized, crushed between the Chevy's engine and the Mustang's transmission. His spine had been completely severed at the third lumbar vertebrae which, when all was said and done, must have been a minor blessing because Lee Corbet did not immediately lose consciousness, and I would assume he could feel nothing from his waist down.

The noise from the accident woke people four blocks away, but the only individuals brave enough to venture to the crash site were Mr. and Mrs. Kim, the owners of the Korean restaurant. The eatery had been closed for the evening since eleven o'clock. Mrs. Kim had been asleep in their apartment above, but instantly leapt from their bed. Mr. Kim had been toying with the lock on the front door and he witnessed the entire grizzly event. As the couple tenuously approached the scene, they wore only their bathrobes and flip-flops.

The pickup truck was so fused to the left side of the Mustang that the couple couldn't see Lee or Grace until they decided to approach the car from the other direction. They did this by climbing through the toy store window. Tiny pieces of glass dug into the foamy soles of their sandals but failed to cut through to their skin. Upon surveying the scene, Mrs. Kim sat on a child's stool crafted out of unpainted pine and began to sob. However her husband wasted little time. He quickly removed a tee shirt from a large green stuffed dragon and pressed it firmly against the gash on the side of Grace's head. He then looked through to Lee whose eyes were open and oddly very much alert.

"I called the police the moment I heard the crash. I was awake," Kim said. "An ambulance is on the way. The fire station is not far from here. It won't take the medics long to arrive."

"Thanks. Is she still alive?" Lee asked, blindly placing his right hand on Grace's thigh.

"Yes. Her pulse is strong. I can see the vein on her neck moving evenly. Her heart working well. She may be okay, I think... She will live. But I can't get this door open without some help. Her hand is trapped at the wrist, and her head is still bleeding badly. This tee shirt is already soaked through. Can you turn the ignition off? It may start a fire."

"Yes. I've got it."

Lee tried to square his shoulders and turn his upper body toward Mr. Kim and Grace, but the move was impossible. He was barely able to rotate his head in their direction. He groped around until he located her limp left arm. He took her hand in his and squeezed it gently. He could feel her pulse as well. "Don't let her die on me," he said in a voice even he didn't recognize.

"She won't die. How are you doing?"

"I've felt better."

"The other driver is dead. There's nothing left of his face."

"I can see that." Lee looked at Ray's slouched-over body. Where the skin was not blanketed in blood, it had turned a pale white-blue. Lee's jaw tightened at the sight. Anger and frustration forced his burning eyes to expand in their sockets as his brow stiffened and cast long dark shadows down to his cheekbones. He set Grace's hand in her lap and pushed his palms forcefully into the Mustang's steering wheel until it bent down to meet the instrument panel. Lee could see the writing on the wall very clearly; the life he had envisioned with Grace all but evaporating before his eyes. "I could kill this bastard," he said, making no attempt to disguise the hostility he felt. He pulled the steering wheel towards him. The upper half snapped off in his hands, and he hurled it through the Mustang's windshield at Ray.

"Did you run the light? I didn't notice the color." Kim asked.

Lee sat like a stone statue, his eyes glued to Ray with abject loathing. The Korean was forced to repeat his question. "Who ran the light?"

Lee took another moment, and then said, "I don't think I ran it... I don't think any of this is my fault... But I could be wrong. Fuck, I don't know. I'm not feeling anything in my goddamn legs. My spine must be broken... Jesus, I could tear this bastard's throat out. What gives him the right to take her away from me?"

"Don't worry. An ambulance will be here soon. Don't let yourself get angry. That won't help you. He's dead. He will pay for what he's done. He will have to answer for this; it's not over for him. You must hold onto your energy."

"Hold on... There's a laugh." He coughed, and a pocket of blood formed at the corner of his mouth and rolled down his chin. "I'm sorry. Thank you for coming to help... God I love this woman," he said, licking the blood from his lip. "I'd give anything, anything, if she'd just open her eyes and look at me right now. If she'd just say my name one more time— just once. Send me out with a smile." Lee looked beyond the man, trying to focus on the flickering orange-and-red neon lights of the Korean restaurant. "Is that your place on the corner?"

"Yes."

"Thanks again for coming out. Thanks for calling the police."

Lee continued to dab at the blood with his tongue as the crimson liquid emerged from his mouth. He tried in vain to sharpen the images his eyes were sending to his brain. He reached across the Mustang's center console and took hold of Grace's hand once more. "How's business?" he said.

Kim smiled. "It's been a good summer so far."

"Yeah, for me, too. But I'm closed in August. This is my vacation. Hell of a way to amuse yourself, right?"

"You have a restaurant?"

"In New York City. It's French."

"I like French food."

"I like Korean food. Not likely to be having it any time soon, I'd guess... I can't tell you how much this pisses me off."

"Have you tried *Bonne Nuit* on Aloha Drive?" Kim said in an effort to keep Lee calmed. "It's very good. They only opened last November, but they've been given some very good write-ups."

"No. I haven't been to Hawaii in years." Lee closed his eyes for fifteen seconds, seeming to get his thoughts together. He now felt chilled despite the warm night air. When he opened his eyes again, he said, "What do you pay your waiters?"

"A buck an hour plus tips. You?"

"Same."

"And they make out with that? In New York City?"

"They make out just fine. Hell, they make out better than I do."

Kim smiled again. "Mine piss and moan every chance they get... And they're all my nephews."

Lee laughed and then winced as a sharp pain shot up through his chest making his heart rate stumble. He waited for the pain to lessen, and then said, "Listen... Do me a favor, will you? I never told her I loved her. I thought I had. I tried, but I now realize I never got it out... How could I be that stupid? Why didn't I do that? Then I wanted to save it all for the airplane. It seemed like such a grand idea two hours ago. Champagne, thirty-thousand feet in the air, no one but us two. Fuck. I don't know what I was thinking of. I guess I thought we had forever..." He cocked his head toward Ray. "Then this fucker comes... I hope he rots in hell... It's amazing, isn't it? When you're happy, you see nothing going wrong. You've got your whole life ahead of you. You're lulled into thinking the end is a million miles away..." Another pain came and went. "Would you do that for me? Would you tell her I love her? When she comes to? It's important. She has to know it."

"Don't worry; you'll be able to do that yourself. And I have a strong feeling she already knows it. Women have a way... I can hear the sirens. It should be less than a minute now."

"I can't hear them at all. And now... I can't see... I can't see a blessed thing; my eyes have shut down." Lee breathed in deeply and let the air slowly fall from his lungs. "No. No... I'm not... telling her anything... ever again. You know, I always thought that when my time came I'd easily say, 'I'm ready'... But I'm not ready. I'm not even close. I don't want to leave her."

Lee closed his eyes once more. It was totally involuntary. He would not open them from that moment on. As the ambulance neared the scene, his missing finger continued to sway lazily back and forth on the leather strap suspended from the pickup's rear view mirror, only few feet from the hand from which it came.

Mr. Kim dropped his head, genuflected, and said, "Bonne Nuit."

Grace

After the collision, it took my mother a little over a year to muster up the courage to turn the tables on Nick and ask him for a divorce—seventeen months to be exact. He was in Detroit when she filed the papers, scouting locations for his film about disenfranchised autoworkers and, yes, having another affair. In the end, Grace held onto the house in the Palisades, which is where I grew up. She even held onto a good portion of Nick's artwork. Whenever she was strapped for cash, she would put one of the paintings or lithographs on the auction block. It would inevitably sell to an anonymous buyer, and then within a few weeks it would miraculously resurface, hanging on one of the walls in Nick's beach bungalow in Malibu. As a child I called these paintings "the swallows" because it seemed as though they most often made this migration northward along the Pacific Coast Highway in the early spring. "Guess what, Frances? Another swallow has landed in Malibu," I've said more than once. As a teenager I was thrilled to see a piece of art make that seven mile trip up the highway to the bungalow; in most instances it meant that my mother would soon be looking at a new car. And in reality, some of the oils weren't bad and I was secretly happy they hadn't disappeared from my life altogether.

Lee's restaurant, Saintes Maries de la Mer, never reopened. In its place is a boutique specializing in fragrant imported soaps and nonessential bathroom products.

As the years progressed, Grace would never once return to Hawaii. Often I would beg her to take me there on school vacations. "Come on, Grace, it's close. There's nothing between us and the islands except the Pacific Ocean." And her reply was always the same, "I don't want to ever pass over deep water again. It scares the hell out of me just to think about it."

Nonetheless, one of her last requests had been for me to take her ashes to Oahu and place them in the ocean off of the Pickering Club beach. I found this wish of hers a difficult one to fulfill. I've made three trips to Hawaii in the last year, but each time I've purposely left Grace's ashes behind, not wanting to lose her in a way that made it impossible for me to ever retain that tangible vestige. But at last I realized I had a duty to see her desire met. And Frances wouldn't let it drop.

"Just get off your ass and go back to Hawaii. What are you waiting for? It's what she wanted. You owe it to her, you owe it to Sally, and you owe it to me, too. You're not the only one who loved her."

So I went back. I had asked Sally and Frances to make the journey with me, simply because I didn't think I had the courage handle it alone. They balked, insisting I make the trip to Honolulu by myself. It is amazing to me that Aunt Sally was able to keep Grace's secret over so many years, never telling a soul—not me, not Nick, not Frances, not Jesse, no one. Never once revealing to me that we were related—that she was, in fact, my great aunt. Never once revealing what Grace had gone through. I now understand why my mother loved her so.

I walk into the Pacific Ocean on a warm Tuesday evening. The air, the water, and the sky seem the landscape of a dream, of a painting I could never hope to produce. I wade out until I'm in up to above my waist, fearing that the long rolling waves will only toss Grace back on to the thin strip of dark sand if I fail to take her into deeper water. I move further away from shore, seawater now surrounding my chest. Am I standing at the exact spot Grace and Lee stood in 1979? It's low tide. Could it have been high tide then? I dutifully open the bronze cask and release her. I suppose the tide must be still going out because the gray-brown cloud that her ashes create in the sapphire water quickly swims away from me and out to sea, toward the horizon and a sunset that is unmatched by any I've seen in my lifetime. I stand in the ocean until there is no longer any discernible sign of my mother, knowing full well that this time she will not come back; she is free to do whatever she chooses. I have a very distinct feeling that Lee is out there, just on the other side of that horizon, waiting for her. I want to be a much taller person so that I can look beyond the horizon, over its edge, and see Lee's face just once. And I think Grace's many years of feeling cheated are over.

Acknowledgements

Careless Love would not have been possible without the great support of Vine Leaves Press: in particular Jessica Bell, Melissa Slayton, and Amie McCracken. Many thanks to my wife, Cordelia Biddle, and her unwavering belief in this book, and dealing with my seemingly endless struggles with it. Thanks to Chris Dietrich for giving me a peaceful retreat in which to write. Special thanks to the Marines who saved my life in ways they are unaware of: Tim Traister, Jack Meighan, Bob Schilling, and Ken Anderson. Great appreciation goes to the Soldiers who helped me maintain my sanity during a rough patch: Eugene Lee, Steve Jones, Cotter Smith, Charlie Brown, Sam Jackson, and Denzel Washington. And a big shout out to Madeleine Peyroux, whose recording of "Careless Love" in its sly way inspired this book.

Vine Leaves Press

Enjoyed this book?
Go to *vineleavespress.com* to find more.

CPSIA information can be obtained
at www.ICGtesting.com
Printed in the USA
LVHW031642200621
690709LV00012B/1753

9 781925 965582